19 ONE-ACTS, MONOLOGS, SHORT PLAYS

by
Edward Crosby **Wells**

Cover by MK M Riddell

Copyright © Edward Crosby Wells 2020.

All rights reserved. Except for brief passages quoted in newspaper, magazine, radio or television reviews, no part of this book may be reproduced in any form or by any means, electronics or mechanical, including photocopying or recording, or by an information storage and retrieval system, without permission in writing from the author.

This material is fully protected under the Copyright Laws of the United States of America and all other countries of the Berne and Universal Copyright Conventions and is subject to royalty. All rights including, but not limited to professional, amateur, recording, motion picture, recitation, lecturing, public reading, radio and television broadcasting, and the right of translation into foreign languages are expressly reserved.

No one shall commit or authorize any act or omission by which the copyright of, or the right to copyright, this play may be impaired.

No one shall make any changes in this play for the purpose of production.

Publication of this play does not imply availability for performance. Both amateurs and professionals considering a production are strongly advised in their own interests to apply to the author or the author's agent for written permission before starting rehearsals, advertising, or booking a theatre.

All producers of any play contained in *ONE-ACTS, MONOLOGS, SHORT PLAYS* must give credit to the Author of the Play in all programs distributed in connection with performances of the Play, and in all instances in which the title of the Play appears for the purposes of advertising, publicizing or otherwise exploiting the Play and/or a production. The name of the Author *must* appear on a separate line on which no other name appears, immediately following the title and *must* appear in size of type not less than fifty percent of the size of the title type.

COMEDIES

20th Century Sketches
Civil Unionized
Dick and Jane Meet Barry Manilow
Harry the Chair
Missing Baggage
Next
Pedaling to Paradise
Sisters of Little Mercy
Tough Cookies
Vampyre Holiday
Whiskers

DRAMATIC MONOLOGS

21 Today
Pink Gin For the Blues

DRAMAS

Cornered
Empire
Leaving Tampa
Road Kill
Samson and Delilah
Slow Boat to China
Tough Cookies

COMEDIES

20th CENTURY SKETCHES

20th CENTURY SKETCHES (2W/2M Minimum, No Set, Each Skit approx. 3 to 5 Minutes Each) Comic highlights from each decade of the Twentieth Century are captured in this series. These work best when produced along with song and dance from each decade. Included are:

1903: HOORAY FOR NEW JERSEY
1912: A REALLY BIG BOAT
1929: THE BIG CRASH
1933: THE REPEAL
1945: THE MANHATTAN PROJECT
1959: HONK (BEATNIK SPOOF)
1969: A WOMAN ON THE MOON
1974: A LEAK AT THE WATERGATE
1981: NANCY & RONNIE GO SHOPPING
1999: HOORAY FOR THE NEW MILLENNIUM

HOORAY FOR NEW JERSEY (Circa 1903)

MOTHER, FATHER, DAUGHTER and SON are seated in theatre seats facing the audience waiting for the very first movie ever to be shown. They are sharing a bucket of hard-boiled eggs and are obviously excited about this historical event.

DAUGHTER: Well, what exactly is it? What are we waiting for?

SON: I hear it's like looking at a huge photograph that moves on that big sheet up there. They call it moving pictures. It gives some people motion picture sickness.

DAUGHTER: Gee Whiz, I hope it doesn't make me sick. How does the picture get up there?

SON: Yeah, and what makes it move?

FATHER: Well, it's all done with mirrors, children. It's very complicated. When you're older maybe I'll explain it to you.

SON: Explain it to us now.

DAUGHTER: Yes, father. Explain it to us now

FATHER: Not now, children.

SON: Why not now?

FATHER: Because.

DAUGHTER: Because why?

FATHER: Just because!

MOTHER: Listen to your father, children. Father knows best.

DAUGHTER: Well, I wish it would hurry up and start. What's it called again?

SON: "The Great Train Robbery." Pass the eggs, please.

MOTHER: Now, don't eat too many, son . . . just in case you get motion picture sickness. *(Passing the bucket.)* The nerve of those people! Charging five cents for one little bucket of hard-boiled eggs . . . highway robbery.

SON: No. "The Great Train Robbery."

FATHER: Now, mother . . . it is called a concession stand, isn't it?

MOTHER: Why is that, I wonder?

FATHER: Because you have to stand and concede that they make more money selling eggs than they do from the price of admission. This moving picture thing will never be a moneymaker. Tom Edison can sit over there in Jersey and pump them out till the cows come home, but he won't see a penny on the dollar. Yep, there's much more money to be had in the egg business.

MOTHER: Oh, I don't know. There's been a lot of hoopla in the papers about the moving picture business. They say it's the future. Might be a good thing to invest in, dear. Pass the eggs, please

FATHER: It will never catch on.

MOTHER: Why is that, dear?

FATHER: Because.

MOTHER: Because why?

SON: Because father knows best.

FATHER: *(Slapping SON on the head.)* Don't you get smart with me! *(The LIGHTS dim.)* Oh, it's starting. Quick! Pass the eggs!

ALL: *Shhhhh...*

The LIGHTS flicker and ALL react with exaggerated animation at what is being projected on the screen. They cover their eyes and scream until the LIGHTING returns to normal signifying the end of the movie.

FATHER: *(Suddenly, the "critic!")* On a scale of one to four stars I would give this first effort by Mr. Edison three, possibly three and one half stars. Although the approaching train did seem realistic, the camera photographing the steaming locomotive never moved causing the audience to fear for its life. One must be careful about thrilling an audience unnecessarily with oncoming trains, chases, too much action, and robbers rushing towards you. It will never be accepted by the masses and will lead to untimely deaths from moving picture fright. If this new entertainment form is to survive, a more sedate route must be taken. *(They ALL begin to move toward exit.)* Furthermore, the New Jersey scenery was both recognizable and adequate. I wish I could say more for the actors who were stiff and wooden. The eggs, however, get a big thumb's up! Perhaps, the next time I will sample the pickled pigs' feet... *(Exit.)*

END

A REALLY BIG BOAT (Circa 1912)

BASIL and NIGEL, two men of flamboyant character, are leaning over the railing of the Titanic and sipping champagne. It is night.
BASIL: *(Raises glass to make a toast.)* April 14, 1912 – our first anniversary.

NIGEL: Chin-chin, darling. *(They drink.)* I say, who would ever have imagined we'd be celebrating our first anniversary on this really big boat, the Titanic? I feel like the queen of the word.

BASIL: Careful, love. Somebody will hear you.

NIGEL: Oh, bother! As a member of the Oscar Wilde Society, I am coming out of the armoire! Hear me, world! Hear me roar! *Grrrr . . .*

BASIL: Oh, dear! That champagne is going directly to your head, Nigel.

NIGEL: I feel like the queen of the world! Out of the armoire, boys, and into the streets!

BASIL: *(Spots something off in the distance.)* Oh, I say, what is that, dear chap?

NIGEL: What is what, Basil?

BASIL: *(Pointing.)* That. Out there, darling. It looks like . . . Oh, Zeus on Olympus! It looks like a giant penis!

NIGEL: Oh, I say! It is a giant penis, what? Pray tell, however do you suppose a giant penis floated out into the middle of the north Atlantic?

BASIL: And whose penis do you suppose it is? I mean, that ought to be the really big question.

NIGEL: No one I know, darling. It must be fifty feet tall. Quick, Basil! Get those really big oars out of that really big lifeboat over there.

BASIL: *(Retrieving oars.)* Whatever do you plan to do with these?

NIGEL: We're going to row, darling. We're going to row this really big boat over to where we can get a really good look at that really big penis.

BOTH put the oars in water and row.

BASIL: Oh, Mary Queen of Scots, this is exhausting!

NIGEL: We're almost there. Row, darling, row! Row your little, round, firm tushy off! Look at that! *(They stop rowing.)* It . . . it's . . . it's an iceberg.

BASIL: Still . . . it looks like a penis.

NIGEL: Kind of . . . I mean, if you squint.

BASIL: Big.

NIGEL: Really big.

BASIL: Nigel.

NIGEL: Basil?

BASIL: I think it is going to hit this boat, what?

NIGEL: I think you're right.

The SOUND of the iceberg hitting the Titanic. BASIL and NIGEL hold on to the railing for dear life.

BOTH: OOPS . . .

NIGEL: Quick! Get rid of the evidence. Throw the oars overboard.

BASIL: NO. We'll need them for the lifeboat. *(Spots someone he recognizes on the deck.)* I say, there's that busybody American woman over there.

NIGEL: Who?

BASIL: Molly somebody. Ah yes! Brown . . . Molly Brown from Denver, Colorado. Very rich. Loves the royals.

NIGEL: Then she'll love us! BASIL: *(Calling out to her.)* Hello, Molly! Over here! Care to share a lifeboat?

NIGEL: We'll save you, Miss Brown! You'll be safe with us!

BASIL: What's that, dear? *Queer?* The nerve of that woman!

NIGEL: We are not queer, dear. We're British! Ah, you mean the accident. Ah yes, very queer . . . a very queer accident indeed. Inexplicably queer, what?

END

THE BIG CRASH (Circa 1929)

HE is out on the ledge of a building. SHE is in the window and is wearing several long strands of pearls.

HE: I've nothing to live for. Don't try and talk me out of it. I'm a loser. I've lost everything. I'm going to jump. There's nothing you could say that could change my mind.

SHE: *(Fingering her pearls.)* All right.

HE: My entire life's savings are wiped out. All my stocks and bonds, worthless. I'm destroyed. I'm nothing. I'm useless. I'm going to jump.

SHE: All right.

HE: There are no more tomorrows. There is no light at the end of the tunnel. There is only . . . what do you mean *"all right?"*

SHE: You're making a spectacle of yourself, dear. If you're going to jump . . . jump. I'm sick to death of your whining. You get hysterical over every little thing.

HE: We're poor! We're destitute! The stock market has crashed! Stocks are worthless. Or, haven't you heard?

SHE: So? What has that got to do with us?

HE: All our money was tied up in the stock market. Every last penny! Today my company closed its doors. I've been let go. I don't have a job to go to anymore. Next thing you know, we'll be on the bread line, eating our meals in soup kitchens, living in cardboard boxes under a bridge somewhere. No, not me! I'd rather be dead. Boy, am I depressed! I'm going to jump.

SHE: All right.

HE: All right, all right? Would you stop saying all right!

SHE: Okay.

HE: Okay?

SHE: Okay, all right?

HE: All right, okay! Aren't you at least going to try and stop me?

SHE: Okay.

HE: Is that okay yes or okay go ahead and jump?

SHE: All right.

HE: All right?

SHE: Okay.

HE: You're not going to try to stop me, are you?

SHE: Nope.

HE: Nope?

SHE: Nope. I know you. Once you make up your mind there's no changing it. Besides, we live on the second floor. The awning over the window below would break your fall.

HE: Well . . . I could jump headfirst. Maybe, I'll break my neck.

SHE: *(Fingering her pearls.)* All right. But first you ought to know that you didn't lose anything in the stock market crash.

HE: Of course I did. The stocks in all the companies we invested in are worthless. Not only that, there was a run on the bank last Tuesday and now we can't even get to our savings.

SHE: Well . . . that's true. But, I sold all those stocks nearly a month ago . . . just after I withdrew all our savings.

HE: What?

SHE: That's right. I had a hunch something terrible was about to happen so I got all the cash I could get my hands on and invested in something that will never lose its value.

HE: Really? What did you do with it?

SHE: *(Showing-off her pearls.)* Pearls.

HE: Pearls?

SHE: *Faux* pearls . . . better than the real thing.

HE: You spent all our money on pearls?

SHE: *Faux* pearls. *(After a pause.)* And beans.

HE: *Beans?*

SHE: *Magic* beans. For the cow.

HE: *(Yelling to those who may be on the sidewalk below.)* Heads up! *(Takes a diving position.)* Here I come!

END

THE REPEAL (Circa 1933)

GEORGE is seated in his comfy chair reading the newspaper while GRACIE is busy with her feather duster.

GEORGE: Gracie, it says here that Prohibition is being repealed.

GRACIE: Thank goodness! I never thought I'd live to see the day.

GEORGE: But you don't drink.

GRACIE: Well, that's right, George . . . but poor old Aunt Pansy does.

GEORGE: I didn't know you had an Aunt Pansy.

GRACIE: We don't like to talk about her. For thirteen years she's been a tippler . . . ever since Prohibition began. Before that she wouldn't touch a drop. Well, maybe now she'll be able to get back on the apple cart.

GEORGE: You mean, get back on the wagon?

GRACIE: Nope. I mean get back on the apple cart. Her drinking almost ruined
Uncle Arnold's cider business. She went astray with quite a few of Uncle Arnold's apple pickers, if you know what I mean. Well, you get boozified and you get loose.

GEORGE: She was a bad apple, huh?

GRACIE: George, you shouldn't make jokes about people's weaknesses. Besides, if she hadn't been such a good church-going Christian, she may never have fallen by the wayside.

GEORGE: Off the apple cart?

GRACIE: And right into the gutter.

GEORGE: But what has the church got to do with her falling by the wayside?

GRACIE: She fell in with the preacher's wife – another tea-total-Tess until Prohibition began.

GEORGE: One would think that falling in with a preacher's wife would be a good thing.

GRACIE: Oh no, George. There's nothing more tempting to a good Christian soul than prohibiting something. You can be sure it's going to make that something that's prohibited very popular. About the time poor Aunt Pansy fell off the apple cart, Tess – the preacher's wife – ran off to Chicago, bobbed her hair, and started hanging out in speakeasies. The last time Aunt Pansy heard from her she had gotten a tattoo and was doing the striptease.

GEORGE: In a Burlesque house?

GRACIE: In a parking lot!

GEORGE: Poor Tess.

GRACIE: And all because of Prohibition.

GEORGE: Well, maybe things will change now that it's being repealed.

GRACIE: Won't do Cousin Herbie any good.

GEORGE: It won't?

GRACIE: Nope. Dead as a doornail.

GEORGE: Too much alcohol killed him, huh?

GRACIE: Prohibition is what killed him. He never touched a drop of alcohol.

GEORGE: How's that, Gracie?

GRACIE: Well, George, Cousin Herbie was murdered in Chicago during the St. Valentine's Day Massacre.

GEORGE: He was a gangster?

GRACIE: A mechanic. He was working on a faulty distributor when Capone and his boys came in and gunned down the Bugs Moran gang. Prohibition was a terrible thing, George. I say, thank goodness it's finally being repealed!

GEORGE: I see your point, Gracie. But I'm sure those people who pushed for Prohibition were good, upstanding, and righteous in their beliefs.

GRACIE: You may be right, George, but sometimes the righteous are more dangerous than the sinners.

GEORGE: Out of the mouth of babes . . . Say goodnight, Gracie.

GRACIE: Goodnight, Gracie.

END

THE MANHATTAN PROJECT
(A monolog, Circa 1945)

SENATOR FOGHORN: *(Speaking into telephone.)* Hello, hello! Ah say, ah say this is Senator Foghorn here. Put me through to the President. Ah say the President of these here United States of America!

Harry, ah say Harry, is that you, Harry? I just got a bill for two billion dollars from General Blowhard to pay for somethin' called The Manhattan Project. As Chairman of the Appropriations Committee, Harry, I'm required, ah say I'm *required* by law to investigate all requests for taxpayer funds. Unless, of course, it's money for the great state of South Carolina.

What do you mean it's a WPA project to develop musical plays? I hear that Al Einstein and Dr. Oppenheimer are workin' on it. Somethin' to do with, ah say somethin' to do with a bomb. *What?* You say you plan on sendin' a bomb to Broadway? Are you crazy, Harry? Haven't they had enough already? Well, yes. That's a big one and I'm sure the great state of Oklahoma is very proud of it, but that don't put tobacco in your pouch in South Carolina . . . if you know what I mean. I want to know why in Sam Hill do we need taxpayer money to send a bomb to Broadway? Hitler? What are you talkin' 'bout, Harry? Ain't nobody gonna pay a dollar fifty to see a Broadway musical about Adolph, ah say Adolph Hitler!

I think somebody's tryin' to hoodwink somebody, Mr. President. I heard somethin' 'bout radium and rockettes. Now, what in tarnation are you talkin' 'bout? *Rockettes?* What do Einstein and Oppenheimer have to do with the Radio City Rockettes?

I think, ah say I think you're trying to pull the whole sheep over my eyes, Mr. President. The whole, ah say the whole stinky sheep, sir. I heard it had somethin' to do with atomic fission. *Atomic,* Harry, *Atomic.* Who? *Tom*

Mix? Course I remember Tom Mix. What's he got to do with any of this? Starring in it? Now, let me see if I got this right. Stop me, ah say stop me when you think I've gone astray. The Manhattan Project is a musical play on its way to Broadway about Adolph Hitler and starring Tom Mix and the Radio City Rockettes. And written by, ah say written by Einstein and Oppenheimer. And it is designed to be a bomb. Why is that, Harry? Why is it designed to be a bomb? I see. A tax write-off for who, Harry? We're talkin' two billion smackers, Mr. President. War cost overruns? Top secret?

Well, I'll tell you, Harry. If, ah say *if* I'm gonna sign over a check for two billion dollars to General Blowhard, then I want, ah say I want a front row seat on opening night. Better yet, if, ah say *if* it's as big a bomb as all that ah want, ah says ah want to see it during the out-of-town tryouts just in case it never makes it to Broadway. Can you promise me that, Mr. President? Where? New Mexico? Isn't that a bit out of the way for a Broadway musical? You'll actually have a special seat for me right on the stage? Really? That close, huh? Thank you, ah say thank you, Mr. President. I'm sure the wife and kids will get a big bang out of it. All that what F.D.R. said about you just ain't true, sir. You are a gentleman, sir. The check, ah say the check is in the mail!

END

HONK (Circa: 1959)

HONK is a spoof of the beatnik poetry of the 1950s and should incorporate finger snapping, bongo drums, black berets and smoking cigarettes in long cigarette holders. The ACTORS sit on stools in individual spotlights. Each actor should have some kind of horn, each distinctive from the other, to accompany the word "honk" with. This is written for four actors but can be done by any number, including one as a monolog.

ONE: I saw the best minds of my generation destroyed by plastic sticking to their buttocks, by Playboy, by runaway slinkies, TV dinners & Howdy Doody. *Honk.*

TWO: I saw the best and brightest of my generation go dim from Colliers, Look & the Saturday Evening Post. *Honk.*

THREE: I saw them up there on the screen: Marilyn Monroe, Marlon Brando and James Dean *Honk.*

FOUR: I read sharp like razor-blade minds till I nearly went blind: Kerouac, Ferlinghetti, Ginsberg and Genet. *Honk.*

ONE: *Honk* on Eisenhower & honk on Nixon. *Honk* on the Mickey Mouse Club & Donner & Blitzen.

TWO: *Honk* on my hairy palms from reading Peyton Place & Lady Chatterly's Lover. *Unexpurgated!*

THREE: *Honk* on the bomb & the underground shelter where I first showed Betty Lou Solomon from Sheepshead Bay to duck & cover.

FOUR: *Honk* on the Cold War & the Bamboo & Iron Curtains.

ONE: *Honk* on. *Honk* on. *Honk* me baby till the cows come home. *Yeah.*

TWO: Listen to the McCarthy Hearings sizzling like pig rump on a hot 21 inch black & white Dumont or Emerson TV. *Honk.*

THREE: Watch the latest episode of I Love Lucy. Honk.

FOUR: Get hip. Get slick. Get bent. Buy an Edsel. *Honk, honk.* Get on the road and get off the road.

ONE: See the USA in your Chevrolet. See all the tacky little houses all in a row. *Honk.*

TWO: Tail fins & T-Birds & Dyna-Flo transmissions. *Honk.*

THREE: Blackboard Jungle. Poodle skirts. Duck Tails. Flat tops. *Honk,* Daddy-O*, Honk.*

FOUR: *Honk* if you are now or if you have ever been.

ONE: *Honk* on Rock & Roll & all that jazz.

TWO: *Honk* on switchblades, zip guns, gravity-knives & exactly how much is that doggy in the window?

THREE: I saw the best minds of my generation end up on the floor of the Café Wha, the Café Bizarre & and the Café Chino. *Honk.*

FOUR: Wow, man. Lay another espresso on me daddy-o. *Honk.*

ONE: I saw the best & the brightest minds of my generation dancing in lemon sky hula hoops and black leather jackets. *Honk.*

TWO: I saw you out there on the couch where you bring the hookers to watch Ed Sullivan, Steve Allen, Arthur Godfrey & Jack Parr. *Honk.*

THREE: It's real cool to be beat. *Honk.*

FOUR: Real cool. Honk.

ALL: *Honk. Honk. Honk* yourself to pieces.

END

A WOMAN ON THE MOON (Circa July, 1969

Two women, GLORIA and BETTY, are seated at a table tallying the check from their luncheon.

GLORIA: Did you watch the moon landing the other day, Betty?

BETTY: No, Gloria. I didn't care to see a man lay claim to yet one more piece of real estate. You had the fruit salad. Men already think they own the world . . . and now they've got to have the moon, too. I had the three-bean soup. "One small step for man; one giant leap for Mankind." Give me a break! I wonder who wrote that bit of misogyny? Sixty cents for the soup. That's mine. Do you know why they didn't send a woman to the moon? Seventy-five cents for the fruit salad. That's yours.

GLORIA: No, why is that?

BETTY: Imagine how those men in Washington would react to hearing, "One small step for woman.

GLORIA: They'd freak.

BETTY: You bet they'd freak. Egg salad sandwich, ninety-cents. That's mine. One day it will be our turn. Fried bologna on rye, seventy-five cents. That's yours. One day there will be a woman on the moon. That will be a day to celebrate!

GLORIA: I'd be happy to get to Las Vegas one day. Too many seeds in the rye and he never did bring the horseradish. My bra is killing me. I think I'm going to buy one of those living bras.

BETTY: *What?*

GLORIA: Yeah, it's called a living bra and it's supposed to hold your breasts gently but firmly – like it had a mind of its own.

BETTY: Now, isn't that just what I need – something with a mind of its own holding up my . . . *euphemisms*. The side order of slaw was forty cents. That's yours.

GLORIA: But you ate it.

BETTY: Okay, we'll split it. Twenty cents you owe and twenty cents I owe. One hot tea with lemon, a quarter. That's mine. One day I'd like to burn mine.

GLORIA: Burn your what, your tea?

BETTY: My bra, Betty. One day I'd like to burn my bra.

GLORIA: Why?

BETTY: Gloria, do men wear bras?

GLORIA: No, not even when they obviously need them.

BETTY: Well, that's my point! One coffee, black. That's yours. Twenty-five cents. So, what's in Las Vegas?

GLORIA: *Huh?*

BETTY: You said you wanted to go to Las Vegas. You do know that women are enslaved in Las Vegas, don't you? The fruit cup was mine – forty cents. Haven't you ever heard of showgirls?

GLORIA: Sure. I wanted to be a showgirl when I was a little girl.

BETTY: That's like wanting to be a performing dog!

GLORIA: It's not the same thing!

BETTY: It certainly is! Miss Gloria Steinem, the show dog!

GLORIA: Don't call me that! I hate it! Miss implies that there is a man missing in my life. How much was the rice pudding, Miss Friedan?

BETTY: Sixty cents! Don't change the subject!

GLORIA: How about Mizz? Not Miss or Missus. That way you're not being defined as being manned or manless. You ate some of my rice pudding.

BETTY: Ten cents! I didn't eat more than ten cents worth! Mizz: M-I-Z-Z. I like the sound of that. All right. Rice pudding – you – sixty cents. Rice pudding – me – ten cents. Let's see. That comes to one dollar and fifty-five cents each.

GLORIA: That's not right! You charged me more somewhere. Give me that check. *(Grabbing check.)* Now, let's see. You had the three-bean soup – sixty cents. We split the slaw fifty-fifty, which means you owe twenty cents and I owe me twenty cents, right?

BETTY: *Right.*

END

LEAK AT THE WATERGATE (Circa 1974)

Two plumbers, BUD and LOU, complete with tool belts and plungers, are fixing a leak in the basement of The Watergate.

BUD: *(Tossing duct tape to AL.)* Hey, LOU! Heads up! Here's your duct tape. That basement door won't be locking up behind us no more.

LOU: Aren't you worried that somebody who don't belong here will get in?

BUD: *Naah.* I do it all the time. I've been doing the night shift here at The Watergate since it opened.

LOU: What about that lady?

BUD: What lady?

LOU: The short dumpy one with the funny accent and the ugly wig lurking around Party Headquarters.

BUD: That was no lady . . . that was Henry Kissinger. The regulars around here call him Deep Throat.

LOU: *Oh. (Working on plumbing.).* Does this place have a lot of leaks, or what?

BUD: You bet your bippy! And it ain't all H2O!

LOU: *(Pulling out tape recorder from behind pipes.)* Hey, Lou! Look what we've got here.

BUD: What is it? A big leak?

LOU: Nope. It's a tape recorder and it's recording everything we're saying.

BUD: *Shhhh!* Put it back! It belongs to Tricky Dick. They're all over Washington. I bet he'd bug his own brother. Did you find that leak yet?

LOU: *Yeah.* It's on this here pipe tagged. *(He leans in to read tag on pipe.)* Nat Demo Head, head, head something.

BUD: Headquarters. National Democratic Headquarters.

LOU: That's it. It's a little leak coming from the National Democratic Headquarters.

BUD: Fix it and let's get out of here.

LOU: It just needs a few good turns of the wrench. *(Takes and wrench.)* There. Done. *(Obviously speaking into tape recorder.)* I have fixed the leak to the Nat Demo Headquarters. Wow, was that hard work. But I never complain. I enjoy being a plumber. Plumbers love their work. *(Holds out recorder for BUD to speak into.)* Ain't that right, Bud?

BUD: *(Speaking into recorder.)* Yup, that's right, Lou. And I vote republican in every election. *(Hand signals to LOU that he's lying for the sake of the tape recorder.)*

LOU: And so do I. *(Sticking a "gag me" finger in his mouth.)*

BUD: And there ain't no commies in the plumbers' union.

LOU: And that wasn't Henry Kissinger lurking about.

BUD: That's right. That was somebody else.

LOU: Definitely not Henry Kissinger! It was some other short, fat man with a funny accent, wearing a dress and a bad wig..

BUD: Okay, Lou, put the recorder back where you found it. Be careful you don't delete anything.

LOU: I'm putting it back. Watch me. I'm putting it back. *(For the benefit of the recorder.)* It's good to be a plumber in America. *(Puts recorder back in place.)* And it wasn't Henry Kissinger. It was a Democratic hooker named Deep Throat.

They BOTH tip-toe toward exit.

BUD: And I never saw her before in my life.

END

NANCY & RONNIE GO SHOPPING
(Circa January, 1981)

NANCY and RONNIE are at a department store counter. A SALESMAN (or WOMAN) is behind the counter.

NANCY: *(Pointing.)* I'll take that scarf.

SALESMAN: Which one, madam?

RONNIE: Nancy, tell him you're not a madam.

NANCY: The red one, of course. And, I'm not a madam. I'm the soon to be Queen.

RONNIE: *(Correcting her.)* The First Lady. You're the soon to be First Lady, Nancy.

NANCY: I like Queen better. Oh, well . . . whatever! *(To SALESMAN.)* And gift-wrap it, please. It's a coronation present to myself.

RONNIE: You mean inauguration.

NANCY: Right. Whatever, Ronnie.

SALESMAN: Will that be all, Mrs. Reagan?

NANCY: Call me "Your Highness" and, yes, that will be all.

SALESMAN: That will be one hundred and sixty dollars plus tax.

NANCY: We don't pay tax. Do we, Ronnie?

RONNIE: Whatever you say, Nancy.

NANCY: No. I say just say no to taxes. Give me some money, dear.

RONNIE: *(Removes a twenty-dollar bill from his wallet.)* Here's a two hundred-dollar bill, Nancy. Make sure he gives you the proper change.

NANCY: *(Handing twenty-dollar bill to SALESMAN.)* Here you go. And, mind you, we don't pay taxes. It's only a big waste of paperwork anyway, isn't it? It only comes right back to us in the end anyway, doesn't it?

SALESMAN: *(Very nervous.)* But, madam . . . I mean, Your Highness, this is only a twenty-dollar bill.

NANCY: My dear young person, when the President-elect of these United States tells you that you have a two-hundred dollar bill in your hand – you had better believe it.

SALESMAN: Yes . . . Your Holiness.

NANCY: Now, kindly give me my change of forty dollars. I will take one twenty, one ten, one five, and five singles.

SALESMAN: *(Counts out the change.)* Thank you for shopping with us, Your Ladyship.

NANCY: You are quite welcome. *(Handing SALESMAN a dollar bill.)* And this, my dear boy, is a one-dollar bill for your efforts. It is, after all, the moral thing to do. Morality—it kind of filters down from the top somehow."

SALESMAN: Oh, Thank you, Your Grace.

RONNIE: Spend that wisely, son. You've just had your first lesson in trickle-down-Reaganomics. And remember: *(The following is an actual and often used quote by the former President.)* There is nothing so good for the inside of a man as the outside of a horse.

END

HOORAY FOR THE NEW MILLENNIUM
(Circa Dec. 31, 1999)

MOTHER, FATHER, DAUGHTER and SON are seated in front of the television. They are wearing New Year's Eve party hats and have an assortment of noisemakers that they use from time to time.

DAUGHTER: Well, what exactly is it? What are we waiting for?

SON: Don't you know anything, dweeb? The world is going to end.

DAUGHTER: Chill out, butt wipe! It's not going to end.

SON: It could if all the computers in the world shut down.

FATHER: If you ask me, this Y2K thing has been grossly over-exaggerated. I remember when they said computers were going to take over the world. But did they?

SON: No, but Bill Gates did.

DAUGHTER: Bill Gates didn't take over the world.

MOTHER: Andrew Lloyd Weber did.

SON: Well ... we'll find out in two minutes.

FATHER: I'm telling you the world isn't going to end. Did it end when Elvis died?

MOTHER: Oh, Father . . . Elvis never died. He was seen at a Las Vegas gas station just last week.

FATHER: Listen to your mother. Mother knows best.

DAUGHTER: Elvis wasn't seen at any gas station. That was an impersonator.

SON: You mean imposter.

DAUGHTER: No, dick head, I mean impersonator.

SON: Vagina fingers!

DAUGHTER: Ball-sack stench!

MOTHER: Children, behave yourselves.

FATHER: Listen to your mother, children. Mother knows best.

MOTHER: All I've got to say is that if the world is going to end I've done my last load of laundry. Pass me the tofu, please.

SON: *(Passing the tofu.)* Well, when there's no power, no food, no water, no nothing – you'll all wish you'd paid attention to me.

MOTHER: That would be too much of a departure from custom, son.

DAUGHTER: *(To SON.)* Get a life, bozo! Nobody's ever gonna pay attention to you. You're a geek!

SON: And you're twat mold! I am not a geek. Mother, please you tell her that I am not a geek.

MOTHER: Well . . . Son . . . it's like this . . . sometimes . . . not all the time . . . but once in a very great while . . .

FATHER: Listen to your mother, son. Mother knows best.

DAUGHTER: There it goes! There goes the ball! It's coming down!

SON: The world is coming to an end!

MOTHER: Isn't this exciting? I'm about to pee my pants.

SON: Could you wait till after the world ends, Mother?

FATHER: Stop frightening your mother, Son.

ALL stare in suspense at the Television.

SON: Five . . . four . . . three . . . *(The TV screen goes black.)* What happened?

MOTHER: The television went out.

FATHER: Did you pay the cable company, Mother?

MOTHER: I think I did. Well . . . maybe . . . .

SON: That's just great, isn't it?

DAUGHTER: Shut up, scrambled scrotum for brains.

SON: You shut up, bean pods for tits.

MOTHER: Now, children . . .

SON: The world could have come to an end and we don't even know it.

MOTHER: Oh, I'm sure somebody will tell us in due time, dear.

FATHER: Listen to your mother, Son. Mother knows best. Mother, did you take your Prozac?

MOTHER: Oh, yes. I couldn't face the end of the world without them. Did you take your Viagra, dear?

FATHER: I certainly did. Just in case the world doesn't end.

MOTHER: Oh, goody. It doesn't look like the world's going to end tonight, dear. *(Extending the plate of tofu.)* Tofu, anyone?

END—*20th Century Sketches*

CIVIL UNIONIZED

(1W/1M/1E, No Set, A Post Office Service Window. This short play takes a tongue-in-cheek look at the debate over gay marriage and civil unions. A counter in a U.S. Post Office. Behind the counter is the CLERK and in front of the counter is the MAN.

CLERK: Married or single?

MAN: Excuse me?

CLERK: Married or single?

MAN: Why? Why do you need to know?

CLERK: *(Shuffling paperwork.)* Do you want a passport or not?

MAN: I want to go to France.

CLERK: You'll need a passport for that, sir.

MAN: Yes, I know.

CLERK: Then, are you married or single?

MAN: Married.

CLERK: And your wife's name is?

MAN: Harold.

CLERK: Sir, your wife's name is Harold?

MAN: Well, he's not exactly my wife.

CLERK: He?

MAN: Harold.

CLERK: Then you are not married!

MAN: Of course I am. We had a civil union.

CLERK: Where are you going with this?

MAN: France. I want to go to France.

CLERK: No. Where are you going with this nonsense?

MAN: We had a civil union. We're married.

CLERK: No, you're civil unionized.

MAN: Well, it's the same, isn't it?

CLERK: Is it? How do you get from civil union to marriage?

MAN: Well, it is when two things—in this case, two human beings—merge into one, a kind of galvanization.

CLERK: You and another man are galvanized—together? Was it painful?

MAN: You're being flippant at my expense. Harold and I are legally married. We had a legal civil ceremony and that is all there is to it.

CLERK: Do you know how many marriages end in divorce?

MAN: Probably fifty percent.

CLERK: Well, what are you going to do when you want a divorce?

MAN: I don't plan on having a divorce. We don't plan—

CLERK: Consider yourself lucky. You can't get divorced 'cause you're not married. That gives you some kind of special right, doesn't it?

MAN: I don't want special rights. I just want equal rights.

CLERK: What about the children?

MAN: What children?

CLERK: The children you are going to confuse and dumbfound.

MAN: I don't know what you're talking about.

CLERK: If you're not married you can't get divorced. If you can't get divorced you'll slip into polygamy and there you have it!

MAN: Have what?

CLERK: Special rights!

MAN: I don't plan on getting a divorce.

CLERK: Then, are you going to get de-unified—de-galvanized?

MAN: We just got married.

CLERK: Sir! You are not married! Only a man and a woman can be married! You've been civil unionized!

MAN: Call it what you will, we're married! And by the way, is there a wife in your life?

CLERK: There certainly is. I'm what you legally call married in the eyes of Man and God. No special rights for us.

MAN: I see, big church wedding, the Bishop was in attendance, aye?

CLERK: Nope. The Bishop went to prison for diddling little boys. It was a quiet civil ceremony down at City Hall.

MAN: I see. Then you are not married. You're civil unionized, too!

CLERK: I am no such thing, sir! I am a man and she is a woman. *(Or, if played by a woman, the other way around.)* We are married. You and Rudolph....

MAN: Harold.

CLERK: You and what's-his-name, on the other hand, will never be married. You are civil unionized and that is all there is to it.

MAN: Well, it's the same thing.

CLERK: No it isn't!

MAN: What about the marriage of two elements of Nature blending to make one union in the eyes of God?

CLERK: Nonsense! You're a fruitcake! So, let's see...married or single— *(Checks box on application.)* Single!

MAN: I want to go to France.

CLERK: Then you will have to change your marital status.

MAN: What are you talking about?

CLERK: Sir, there is a line behind you.

MAN: I'm not leaving here until you accept my application for a passport.

CLERK: And you are not going anywhere until you marry a woman or get de-unionized from Raymond.

MAN: Harold.

CLERK: Whatever.

WOMAN: *(Entering.)* Hey, buster! I've been waiting in this line for twenty minutes and my lunch half-hour is almost up. Are you going to get on with it or what?

MAN: I'm trying to get my passport.

CLERK: Are you married, lady?

WOMAN: What's it to you?

CLERK: It's this box, madam. It says, "married" and it says "single." And we have to fill out every box on this application.

WOMAN: Married.

CLERK: Your husband's name?

WOMAN: Martha.

MAN: Excuse me, but I believe this gentleman *(Or "lady.")* was waiting on me.

WOMAN: Think so, do you?

CLERK: Stand aside, sir!

MAN: I want my passport! I want to go to France.

WOMAN: Hey, buddy! Did you hear the man *(Or "lady.")*?

MAN: I heard, but he *(Or "she.")* isn't done with me yet. I'm not leaving till he *(Or "she.")* accepts my application.

CLERK : Please stand aside, sir. The Postmaster will have to examine your case.

MAN: What case? I only want to go to France.

WOMAN: *(Pointing.)* And I want you to go over there and shut up!

MAN: I want to see the Postmaster.

CLERK: He'll be here a week from Thursday.

MAN: I can't wait that long!

CLERK: Stand aside! *(MAN stands aside and mumbles.)* Okay, lady. Now, let's see. Married or single?

WOMAN: Married.

CLERK: And your husband's name?

WOMAN: Martha.

MAN: What kind of a name is that?

WOMAN: It's a perfectly good name. She was named after her Grandmother on her father's side.

CLERK: Her grandmother?

MAN: On her father's side?

CLERK: Are you saying that your husband is a woman?

WOMAN: No. My significant other is a woman.

CLERK: So, you are single.

WOMAN: No. We had a civil union—has all the benefits of marriage.

CLERK: Except for the fact that you're not married, and if you're not married you're single! And if you are single you are living in a state of sin! There is no box on this application for your current arrangement! Either you are married or you are not married! What is it with you people and your special privileges?

MAN: Sounds to me like you and Martha have been civil unionized, lady.

CLERK: Yeah, like this guy and his wife Herman.

MAN: Harold.

WOMAN: Just cut the crap and approve my application. We've got to get to Spain!

CLERK: I'm afraid you've just missed the running of the bulls.

WOMAN: Look, Martha and I are going on our honeymoon whether you like it or not—in Spain!

CLERK: Without a passport they won't let you in Spain, lady. And, sir, they won't be letting you in France either.

MAN: I've got to get to France!

WOMAN: I've got to get to Spain!

CLERK: How do we know you're not terrorists?

MAN: What has being married or not being married have to do with terrorism?

CLERK: Everything! You people multiply and multiply and push and push and pretty soon there is nothing left that is sacred anymore. When nothing is sacred, you people are capable of anything.

WOMAN: And a passport is sacred?

CLERK: *(Holding up application.)* The box says, "married" or "single." You are one or you are the other! Look, why don't the two of you marry each other and let Harold marry Mary?

WOMAN: Martha.

MAN: This is ridiculous! I want my passport and I want it now!

WOMAN: So do I!

CLERK: I'm trying to help you here. It's all about paperwork! It's all about preserving our institutions! It has nothing to do with your absurd plans for special privileges! One last time! Married or single?

MAN & WOMAN: Married!

CLERK: And your husband's name?

WOMAN: Harold.

CLERK: And your wife's name, sir?

MAN: Martha.

CLERK: See? That wasn't so hard, was it? *(Rubberstamping the applications.)* One last question—was this a civil union or a marriage?

MAN & WOMAN: *Marriage!*

BLACK OUT.

END—*Civil Unionized*

DICK AND JANE MEET BARRY MANILOW

SYNOPSIS: It is Labor Day. DICK and JANE—most any age—are in their backyard grilling hotdogs. They discover that a large hole has appeared overnight. They cannot see its bottom, but occasionally they hear, from deep within it, Barry Manilow singing Copacabana (At the Copa).

SETTING: 1M/1W, no set necessary other than a couple lawn chairs, a charcoal grill, maybe a small folding table, and a black hole about 3 feet in diameter.

DICK and JANE sit in lawn chairs, staring at a large black hole (A cardboard cut-out, perhaps). Hotdogs are cooking on the grill. At the moment, they are listening for something to hit the bottom of the hole.

DICK: *Shh!*

JANE: Do y'hear anything?

DICK: Shh! Tryin' to listen.

JANE: Well, if you haven't heard anything by now…

DICK: Nothing. Probably bottomless.

JANE: Nothing's bottomless.

DICK: I didn't hear it hit, that's all I know…I didn't hear it hit.

JANE: Doesn't mean it's bottomless.

DICK: Excuse me, I must have had a brain fart.

JANE: Don't be a smart ass. *(Throwing up her arms.)* I guess we just didn't hear it, and that's all there is to it.

DICK: I guessed that, too. That's all there is to it. Poor old Harry Moody's chair.

JANE: It could have been Irene's.

DICK: Nope. Definitely a man's dining room chair.

JANE: Why? It could be a woman's. It could have been hers.

DICK: Nope. It had arms. Had to have been his.

JANE: Why's that?

DICK: That's what I was taught. The one with arms is the man's chair. Head of the household. Head of the table.

JANE: *Wow.* There ain't nothin' to say to that, Dick. In any case, the chair with the arms—for the head of the table—sure made a soft landing.

DICK: *Yup.* Like the Mars rover.

JANE: Yeah. You know, if the old man hadn't taken a powder, his wife might never have had that breakdown.

DICK: *Huh?*

JANE: His wife. I said, she might never have gone mental, if old Harry hadn't gone and taken that powder.

DICK: That ol' gal went way beyond mental.

JANE: *Yeah.* Kind o'.

DICK: Up and down the aisles in Walmart screaming, "...the landlord loves Barry Manilow...the landlord loves Barry Manilow..." over and over until the cops came and hauled her off. (A sudden realization.) Poor ol' Harry.

JANE: Poor ol' Irene.

DICK: Hey, maybe, she murdered the ol' man...you know...went real psycho.

JANE: Don't be silly. He took a powder. Men do that, you know. That's a man thing. They just up and take a powder.

DICK: Some men do that, Jane. Just some men.

JANE: Okay. Some. So, until there's a body, I choose to think the best. . .if you don't mind. No murder...he just took off...like some men do.

DICK: Why should I mind?

JANE: You shouldn't. *(She pauses to ponder.)* Dick?

DICK: Yeah?

JANE: It's not right...throwing all their stuff into the alley like that.

DICK: No respect in this world, Jane. Not like there used to be.

JANE: Landlords!

DICK: Landlords!

JANE: There used to be? How do you know? You can remember that far back?

DICK: Ha, ha. Chuckle, chuckle.

JANE: You do know, it starts at the top.

DICK: Huh?

JANE: Examples. Take 'respect.' You said that there ain't no more respect in the world.

DICK: Not in our world.

JANE: Nope. Not in our world.

DICK: *(Gets on his knees at the edge of the hole, listening.)* You'd think we would have heard something by now.

JANE: You'd think. *(Gets on her knees and leans over the hole. A pause to listen.)* Wait! I hear....oh my gawd, it's Barry Manilow. *(She sings what she hears.)* "*At the Copa/Copacabana/The hottest spot north of....*

DICK: *(Cutting her off.)* What's Barry Manilow doing down our hole?

JANE: How would I know, Dick? But I know Barry Manilow and that's Barry Manilow.

DICK: *(Leaning farther over the hole to listen. He too hears Barry Manilow and sings what he is hearing.)* "*...Music and passion were always the fashion/At the...*" Fuck a duck! It's him. It's Barry Manilow.

JANE: Singing in our hole.

DICK: *(Still listening.)* He stopped.

JANE: Guess he got tired.

DICK: *Wow.*

JANE: *Yeah.*

DICK: *Yeah.*

JANE: *Wow.*

DICK: *Yup.* What do you s'pose it was that made this hole?

JANE: And how did Barry Manilow get down there?

DICK: Not a clue. A mystery, isn't it?

JANE: It sure is. Bam! Our lives are filled with mysteries.

DICK: Yup. That's life. Mysteries.

JANE: *(After a pause to think.)* Dick, I've been giving this hole some thought. It wasn't here when we went to bed last night, right?

DICK: Right. I can vouch for that.
JANE: Then, it must have been a meteor.

DICK: You think?

JANE: Something from space. Space junk! Lots 'o junk up there. What goes up. . .

BOTH: *(Together.)* ...Must come down.

DICK: Crash! You'd think it would've woke us.

JANE: Us...and the whole neighborhood, for that matter.

DICK: But, Barry Manilow?

JANE: Clueless, Dick. Clueless. Listen!

DICK: What?

JANE: I heard a thump. It hit. It finally hit.

DICK: You don't know it was the chair's thump.

JANE: I can assume. I'm allowed. *(Rises. Goes to grill.)* I'm having a hotdog. What about you?

DICK: Sure. Why not. Happy Labor Day. *(He raises a bottle of beer.)* Cheers! Let's hear it for the workers!

JANE: *Shh!* Keep your voice down. . .the neighbors.

DICK: *(A loud whisper.)* Here's to the neighbors.

JANE: Had to come from space.

DICK: Yup. Unless…

JANE: Unless what?

DICK: Did you ever hear of a sinkhole.

JANE: Of course.

DICK: There you have it. A sinkhole.

JANE: *Hmm.* What about Barry Manilow? What's he doin' in our sinkhole?

DICK: *(A pause to ponder.)* Beats me. Hey…I got it. A meteor…size of a cinder block…came crashing down on top of Barry Manilow just as he was taking a shortcut through our backyard.

JANE: Very funny. One hotdog, or two?

DICK: Two. With everything. Maybe it was just an act of God.

JANE: What was?

DICK: The hole. Maybe it was an act of God.

JANE: What's God got to do with it? What's God got to do with anything?

DICK: That kind o' talk could get you in trouble, Jane. Real trouble.

JANE: What kind o' talk, Dick?

DICK: Questioning God.

JANE: Sometimes you're really stupid, Dick! God's just an excuse for not taking responsibility.

DICK: Keep your voice down. Neighbors could hear you. That's dangerous talk, Jane.

JANE: Bull poop.

DICK: How do you explain Barry Manilow. What's he doin' down that hole.

JANE: I'm sure I don't know. *(After a thoughtful pause.)* It's a sinkhole. It's definitely a sink hole. Sink holes happen all the time.

DICK: And Barry Manilow.

JANE: I don't know. Maybe we should call the landlord.

DICK: Yeah. We don't wanna get blamed for the hole.

JANE: Tell 'im we just woke up and there it was. Call 'im.

DICK: *(He takes his cellphone from out his pocket and calls and waits, and waits.)* Ain't no answer.

JANE: Let it ring. He's hard of hearing. *(After a pause to listen.)* I hear Barry Manilow.

DICK: So do I.

JANE: *(Sings.)* "At the Copa/Copacabana/The hottest spot north of. . .

DICK: He ain't gonna answer. *(He disconnects the call.)*

JANE: He stopped. Barry Manilow stopped singing. *(A quick realization.)* Call the landlord again.

DICK: He didn't answer, Jane.

JANE: Call 'im! Call 'im again!

DICK: He ain't gonna answer, Jane. *(He calls him again.)*

JANE: *(Sings.)* "At the Copa/Copacabana/The hottest spot north of…Oh my God! It's the landlord. He's down our sink hole!

END—*Dick and Jane Meet Barry Manilow*

HARRY THE CHAIR

SYNOPSIS: (2W) Poor Gladys. She left the room for less than a minute, and when she returned her husband was gone. Well, not exactly gone—Harry turned into a chair. Can a marriage survive when one of the partners is an overstuffed recliner?

CHARACTERS: GLADYS (the chair's wife) and BLANCHE (her friend and neighbor). They are both ordinary middle-aged women of modest means.

The SETTING: GLADYS' living room. There is a comfy overstuffed recliner with a TV table next to it covered with an open pizza box and empty beer cans or bottles. Somewhere there are two occasional chairs separated by an end table with tea things on it—little else.

AT RISE: A conversation is in progress. GLADYS and BLANCHE are pondering the comfy chair.

GLADYS: I swear on my . . . *(Trying to think of something.)* . . . whatever is most precious to me. I can't think of anything at the moment.

BLANCHE: Your teapot collection?

GLADYS: *Yes.* My teapot collection. I can't believe how I almost lost one of them to Margie's temper tantrum. The mess she made. Had to throw out the tablecloth. Can't never get the stains out—*Orange Pekoe.* Almost lost the teapot. As it is, there's a chip on it now.

BLANCHE: Still, I can't believe it.

GLADYS: What? That Harry turned into a chair or that Margie's a destructive bitch who shouldn't wear maternity clothes just because she's fat? All poor Sharon Weeks wanted to do was to see if the baby was kicking.

Well, there wasn't any baby. Just a big ol' tub of blubber. It all goes to show you should never wear deceptive clothing.

BLANCHE: Sharon Weeks shouldn't go around touching and feeling people.

GLADYS: I think that may have broken her of the habit.

BLANCHE: One can only hope. *(After a thoughtful pause.)* Did Harry . . . you know . . . leave you? You needn't be ashamed to tell me.

GLADYS: For Pete's sake, Blanche! I'm not ashamed. Harry metamorphosed.

BLANCHE: *Excuse me?*

GLADYS: He metamorphosed into a chair—like that man who turned into a cockroach.

BLANCHE: *(Incredulous.) What man?* Nobody turned into a cockroach.

GLADYS: It's in a book.

BLANCHE: That doesn't make it so. *(A pause to scrutinize.)* Gladys, you're not taking those diet pills again, are you?

GLADYS: Of course not!

BLANCHE: This is all too inexplicable.

GLADYS: That's why I'm trying to explain it to you. Harry wanted a beer, so I got up and went into the kitchen to get him one and when I came back . . . *(Wipes a tear from the corner of her eye.)* . . . he was gone.

BLANCHE: That doesn't explain anything.

GLADYS: Certainly does. The chair was a chair one minute and the next minute . . . *(Wipes another tear.)* . . . it was Harry.

BLANCHE: How can you tell?

GLADYS: *(Caresses chair.)* I can tell. I know my Harry. I know his smile, his chins, his hairy chest . . . *(Sniffing chair.)* . . . his smell.

BLANCHE: Gladys, he lives, eats and sleeps in that chair. Of course it smells like him; cigarettes, beer, Old Spice and stale farts.

GLADYS: Blanche, that's enough! Either you believe me or you don't. *(Glances at end table.)*

BLANCHE: Well, I don't!

GLADYS: Suit yourself. *Tea—Orange Pekoe?* *(Crosses to the occasional chairs and sits.)*

BLANCHE: Sure. *(Following her, sits.)* I love this tea pot. Isn't this the one that Margie almost broke?

GLADYS: It sure is. *(Holding it up and showing.)* See the chip?

BLANCHE: *(Looking.)* No . . . *ah, yes.* There it is. 'Though it's hardly noticeable. No one would ever know.

GLADYS: *I* know.

BLANCHE: Of course *you* know. I meant anyone else.

GLADYS: I can't look at it without seeing it.

BLANCHE: Try not to look and don't let Margie near it . . . What's happened to her, by the way? I haven't seen her since the tea pot fiasco.

GLADYS: I'm sure she's around. She'll turn up . . . *(A pause to pick up the tea pot.)* . . . sooner or later. *(Filling both cups with tea.)*

BLANCHE: They always do—her kind.

GLADYS: Yes, they always do—her kind—sooner or later. *(Sips tea.)* Nice.

BLANCHE: *(Sips tea.)* Very nice. *(After a pause to sip more tea.)* So . . . Gladys, tell me the truth. Where's Harry?

GLADYS: I told you. *(Pointing to chair.)* How many times do I have to tell you, Blanche? There . . . there's Harry.

BLANCHE: Just doesn't seem—

GLADYS: I don't care how it seems. Nothing ever is as it seems. He turned into a chair and that's it, plain and simple.

BLANCHE: Not so plain and not so simple.

GLADYS: Look at Harry. *(To chair.)* What's it like being a chair, Harry?

BLANCHE: You've lost your mind.

GLADYS: I'm talking to Harry.

BLANCHE: *You're talking to a chair!*

GLADYS: He only looks like a chair! *(Rises and crosses to Harry.)* But, he's the man I love. When I came back with the beer, Harry was gone and the chair smiled at me.

BLANCHE: The chair smiled? *(Following her.)*

GLADYS: That's how I knew it was Harry.

BLANCHE: Come to think of it, that chair is the only place I've ever seen him—only in that chair, *always*.

GLADYS: Precisely. He practically lived in it. I brought him his meals while he sat all weekend watching his shows. As soon as he came home from work, there he'd be until it was time to go to bed. And now ... *(Wiping tears.)* ... Harry *is* the chair.

BLANCHE: Figuratively speaking, I can see it. I mean, we do become the things we are attached to.

GLADYS: What's that supposed to mean?

BLANCHE: You know—like you are the things you eat.

GLADYS: Blanche, I eat kumquats! Does that make me a kumquat?

BLANCHE: *(Coyly.)* Maybe. *(Staring at the chair.)* He does look comfortable, doesn't he? *(She is about to sit in the chair.)*

GLADYS: NO! Don't sit on Harry!

BLANCHE: I just thought—

GLADYS: What? That you could sit on my husband without me giving a wit . . . like we were one of those . . . those . . . swinger couples. We don't *swing*, Blanche. The nerve! Trying to have your way with my husband? And right under my nose. *Shameless*.

BLANCHE: What on Earth are you talking about?

GLADYS: Harry. You always had your eyes on—

BLANCHE: Harry?

GLADYS: Just because he vibrates.

BLANCHE: *What?*

GLADYS: He vibrates.

BLANCHE: Harry vibrates?

GLADYS: The chair did. I assume that Harry—

BLANCHE: Vibrates, too?

GLADYS: Well, yes. He's kind of a massage chair.

BLANCHE: Have you checked to see if he does vibrate?

GLADYS: Not yet. When I'm alone I'll slip into his lap, sniff his arms . . . his back . . . his seat.

BLANCHE: Good, God, Gladys! It's a chair. It's a big, old, smelly La-Z-Boy—that vibrates.

GLADYS: That's my husband you're talking about, Blanche!

BLANCHE: It's a chair, Gladys. It's a goddamn chair and that's all there is to it.

GLADYS: It's Harry! The goddamn chair is Harry.

BLANCHE: Would you like me to call a doctor?

GLADYS: You think I need a doctor?

BLANCHE: Nobody turns into a chair, Gladys. Now what's going on here?

GLADYS: I've lost my husband!

BLANCHE: Maybe he just went out to pick up something.

GLADYS: I lost him the day before yesterday. He'd be back by now.

BLANCHE: Well . . . I'm sure there's a perfectly good explanation.

GLADYS: There is. He became a chair. One day you, too, might become something.

BLANCHE: It won't be a chair.

GLADYS: I'm only saying— *(Addresses the chair.)* Harry, say something. Do you love me, Harry?

BLANCHE: Gladys, you need . . . God! I don't know what you need. How about we have some more tea? *(Puts her arm around GLADYS and walks her to the chairs by the tea things.)* Now you sit down, Sweetie, and have another nice cup of tea.

GLADYS: Are you patronizing me?

BLANCHE: I believe so, yes. *(Picks up tea pot and pours.)* I really like this teapot, Gladys. It's my second favorite.

GLADYS: *Second?*

BLANCHE: The hand-painted Russian one is my favorite.

GLADYS: Really? Then the next time we'll have to use the Russian one and I'll keep Margie on the shelf.

BLANCHE: *(Drinking tea – stops abruptly.)* What!?

GLADYS: Didn't you notice? It's Margie. She turned into that teapot shortly after ruining my tablecloth. Orange Pekoe—can't never get the stains out. *(Drinks tea.)* Blanche, why don't you take these tea things into the kitchen and as soon as I have a talk with Harry, I'll make us a nice pot of tea in the Russian teapot?

BLANCHE: *(Rises.)* I don't know what game you're playing, but I think you need professional help. *(Picks up the tray of tea things.)* You need help. We need to do something about these hallucinations.

GLADYS: Yes, we do, indeed. Take this stuff to the kitchen and I'll be right in.

(BLANCHE exits into the kitchen while GLADYS heads towards Harry the chair.)

GLADYS: *(To the chair.)* Harry, why did you do it? *(Listens a bit.)* I miss you. I love you, Harry. I don't care if you are a chair.

BLANCHE: *(Calling from kitchen.)* I can't find the Russian teapot. Where is it, Gladys?

GLADYS: *(Calling back.)* For Pete's sake! It's on the shelf over—

BLANCHE: *Help! (Then silence.)*

GLADYS: *(To kitchen.)* I'll be right there! *(To Harry the chair.)* I'll be right back. Don't go anywhere. *(Disappears into kitchen.)* Okay, Blanche. What's your problem? Where are you? Where'd you go? Blanche? Oh no. Oh, Blanche. What did you do? *(Enters carrying the Russian teapot. To teapot.)* Blanche, Blanche, Blanche. What did you do? *(Quickly turns towards Harry the chair.)* What's that, Harry? *(After a pause to listen to Harry.)* Yes, it's Blanche—a teapot. This was her most favorite. Well, things happen. *(To the teapot.)* I hope you're happy, Blanche. See, I'm not crazy now, am I? *(Looking around.)* Where should I put you? *(Goes to table and sets the teapot down.)* Sit here for a while, Blanche, until I figure out what to do with you. I don't think you'd like sitting next to Margie. Stay here while I think about it. *(Crosses to Harry the chair.)* Hello, Harry. Finally alone. Wait a minute. *(Crosses back to the Russian teapot and turns it around so the spout is in the back.)* There. I need a private moment with my husband, Blanche. We'll talk later. You just sit there and face the wall for awhile. *(Shouts to kitchen.)*

Margie, relax. I'll wash you later. You don't want to go into the dishwasher, do you? *(Returns to Harry the chair.)* Where were we? Well, of course. I'd love to Harry. *(She caresses the chair lovingly, sniffs the arms and then a quick sniff of the seat cushion before she sits. She then moves in the chair, swaying with pleasure. She flips the vibrator switch and begins to vibrate as the LIGHTING FADES.)* Oh, Harry! Oh, oh, Harry. Yes . . . yes..

BLACK OUT.

END—*Harry the Chair*

MISSING BAGGAGE

SYNOPSIS: 1 M/1 either, Customer service counter, 10-minutes. An irate traveler is missing his luggage. A customer service representative tries inventive ways to pacify him. The man's weapons are demands and threats, however the clerk remains imperviously invincible.

MAN and CLERK (M or F) are at an airline service counter, conversation in progress.

CLERK: I told you, sir. It's almost here. You'll only have to wait until the plane from Dallas arrives.

MAN: *(Shouting.)* Why is my baggage in Dallas?

CLERK: Please, sir. Shouting will get you nowhere. Besides, it is not *in Dallas. (Looking at watch.)* It's *in* the air.

MAN: I'm going to sue you!

CLERK: That will be nice, sir.

MAN: Did you hear what I said?

CLERK: With both ears, sir. You're going to sue me, wasn't it?

MAN: Are you retarded or something . . . *backwards?*

CLERK: My life is so backwards that I find myself standing on my head when I least expect it. In the service industry it is often required.

MAN: Standing on your head?

CLERK: I'm very good at it, sir. I find myself in that position one or two times a day. Shall I show you? *(Begins bending to show him.)*

MAN: Stop it. *(Looking around.)* You'll embarrass me.

CLERK: I cannot imagine that, sir. You can only embarrass yourself, sir.

MAN: I've never embarrassed myself.

CLERK: As you say, sir. Most people do, you know. I see it every day.
MAN: I am not most people. I'm a person who is missing his baggage.

CLERK: Most people would find that a distinct advantage. It lightens their load . . . makes them more agreeable.

MAN: All I want is my baggage. I'm not here to be agreeable.

CLERK: Indeed, you're not.

MAN: You're taking a tone with me, aren't you?

CLERK: I certainly am not, but if I were taking a tone I wouldn't know where to put it.

MAN: I can tell you where to put it!

CLERK: And I would gladly, sir. Then you shouldn't mind if I bend over backwards for you. *(Starts to bend backwards.)*

MAN: Stop it! Are you insane?

CLERK: It's this job, sir. It's required of me.

MAN: What am I supposed to do without my baggage, huh?

CLERK: It's almost here, sir. It will be here within two hours.

MAN: I have a meeting in one.

CLERK: Will it be a short meeting?

MAN: Relatively.

CLERK: Relative to what?

MAN: To how long I've been waiting for my baggage.

CLERK: The plane will arrive in almost no time—barring incident.

MAN: Incident? What kind of incident?

CLERK: The usual. One never knows. Chances are everything is honky-dory, or is it hunky-dory?

MAN: I don't know.

CLERK: That's too bad. I'd hate to be the purveyor of ill-used words.

MAN: Honky and hunky mean two entirely different things.

CLERK: Yes they do. Anyway, barring *"incident,"* your baggage should be on the plane.

MAN: *Should? Aren't you certain?*

CLERK: Unless there is an incident, as I said, or there was a mix-up, sir.

MAN: *(Shouts.) Mix-up!*

CLERK: Please keep your voice down, sir. It could be an act of God.

MAN: What could be an act of God?

CLERK: Just about anything, sir.

MAN: What has God got to do with my baggage?

CLERK: Well . . . maybe the time is up for everybody on the flight and . . . *oops* . . . the plane goes boom. Are you a God-fearing man, sir?

MAN: Maybe.

CLERK: Well then, maybe you weren't meant to have that baggage. You certainly won't need it when you meet the man upstairs.

MAN: I have no intention of meeting any man upstairs.

CLERK: Almost everyone does, but I can see how you might be an exception . . . *Now.* Should I stand on my head?

MAN: Go ahead. Stand on your head. What do I care? I'd rather talk to your
feet anyway.

CLERK: Too late. Maybe you would like to watch me bite my tongue, instead?

MAN: Do you actually work here?

CLERK: Where's that, sir?

MAN: *Here, here.* Are you really a customer service clerk?

CLERK: Indeed I am. I have a badge to prove it. *(Proudly showing badge.)* See?

MAN: *(Spotting something some distance away.)* What the . . . What is going on over there?

CLERK: Over where, sir.

MAN: Down there? *(Indicating.)*

CLERK: *(Turns to look.)* Oh, that's nothing, sir.

MAN: *Nothing?* He's beating him with a piece of baggage.

CLERK: They do that sometimes.

MAN: You're crazy!

CLERK: I certainly am, sir. Crazy for Italian food and hot dogs from a cart.

MAN: Look. There's a man being beaten with his baggage by a Sky Cap.

CLERK: They do it all the time. At least once or twice a day. Death by baggage.

MAN: *What are you talking about?*

CLERK: D-B-B. Comes with the territory. Sometimes those Sky Caps just get overwhelmed by all that—

MAN: *Baggage.* You're kidding.

CLERK: I never kid, sir. Sometimes Sky Caps forget to turn the other cheek. Would you like to see me turn the other cheek?

MAN: I'd like you to call security.

CLERK: Is that man being beaten your brother, sir?

MAN: No.

CLERK: You're uncle, your father or your grandmother?

MAN: What is wrong with you?

CLERK: I'm trying to establish a relationship between you and the victim . . . some sort of connection.

MAN: There isn't any.

CLERK: Please excuse my impertinence, sir—but if there is no connection between you and the victim, why is it any business of yours?

MAN: That man is a human being and he's being abused.

CLERK: You care about human beings?

MAN: I course I do!

CLERK: That comes as quite a shocker, sir.

MAN: It shouldn't.

CLERK: Can't argue that.

MAN: You don't know what it's like to be abused in a public place.

CLERK: Is that different from being abused in a private place?

MAN: You know what I mean.

CLERK: Presumption has never been my strong suit, sir. *(Repeatedly turns head, showing his/her profile first one way and then the other.)*

MAN: *What are you doing?*

CLERK: I'm turning the other cheek, sir.

MAN: Why?

CLERK: That's what I am paid to do.

MAN: You're paid to make yourself look like an idiot?

CLERK: I don't think I make myself look like an idiot. Do you see me that way?

MAN: *Almost, if not totally.* And stop turning your head. You're drawing attention.

CLERK: I don't think so, sir. That man down the concourse appears to be dead. *Ah, yes.* The medic is zipping up the bag as we speak. *Death by baggage.*

MAN: He was murdered by a Sky Cap.

CLERK: It wasn't his fault, sir.

MAN: Of course it was! He beat the man to death with his own baggage!

CLERK: Sky Caps do not receive the same training as customer service representatives. It's the fault of the system, sir. Bad training. That's why they didn't arrest him. *See?* He's walking away and the police are leaving. Look at all that stuff that was in his baggage. People have no consideration. They leave all their stuff behind for someone else to clean up.

MAN: This is insane. People getting away with murder.

CLERK: Only the Sky Caps, sir.

MAN: What do you mean?

CLERK: It's common place, sir. It's all a matter of training. Would you like me to apologize profusely? I'm sorry. I'm so sorry, sir. I understand your predicament and I am truly very sorry. Have you had enough?

MAN: I want to get out of this insane asylum!

CLERK: I am so very, very sorry you see it that way, sir. How can I ever make it up to you? How about a free ticket to down under? I hear it's very pleasant this time of year.

MAN: *I don't want a ticket to down under. I don't want a ticket to anywhere. I want my baggage. Where is my baggage?*

CLERK: It isn't here, sir. I told you, it's almost here. It went to Dallas. Shall I call a Sky Cap to assist you?

MAN: NO! No Sky Cap!

CLERK: He can assist you when the plane from Dallas arrives.

MAN: I don't want any assistance. I just want my baggage! Can you tell me why it went to Dallas? I was not even going in that direction.

CLERK: Why indeed. I've never thought Dallas an agreeable destination. But then one man's paradise is another man's hell.

MAN: Or the other way around.

CLERK: If you look at it backwards. Did I tell you that you look very smart? Nice shirt. Great shoes. Quite the fashion plate, aren't you?

MAN: I try to be.

CLERK: And you succeed splendidly. I admire you, sir. I am required to wear this same uniform day after day. But then that is why it is called a *uniform*, isn't it?

MAN: Look! I just want—

CLERK: *(Removing can of brown shoe wax from under the counter.)* Yes, yes, yes. I know what you want, sir. And you deserve to have it all. *(Applies a bit of the brown shoe wax to the tip of his nose.)*

MAN: *What are you doing?*

CLERK: Brown-nosing, sir. It's one of the things we are taught. In fact, it is the first thing we are taught. I think I'm going to bite my tongue now. Stand back.

MAN: Stand back?

CLERK: I don't want to get blood on you, sir.

MAN: I certainly don't want your blood on me either.

CLERK: Did I mention *mine?*

MAN: I want my baggage and I want it now!

CLERK: *(Glances at watch.)* It's quite close, sir. It's almost here. If you can wait just—

MAN: *Almost ain't quite! Never was and never will be!*

CLERK: About your baggage, sir— *(Retrieving MAN'S baggage from under the counter.)* Would you look at this! It was here all the time. I can't imagine what I could have been thinking.

BLACK OUT.

END—*Missing Baggage*

NEXT

SYNOPSIS: 4 Actors (male and/or female), Minimal Set. A humorous existential exercise where four characters in a waiting room are unaware of what it is they are waiting for. They argue, threaten, manipulate and vie for superiority. It is about how many of us remain in a kind of limbo where we wait to live and we wait to die – experiencing neither, experiencing nothing.

AT RISE – NEXT, 12, 13 and 14 are in a waiting room. There are chairs and there is a door. After a long SILENCE.

12: Seems like we've been here forever.

14: How long has it been since anyone's been called?

NEXT: I fell asleep and lost track of the time.

14: Did everybody take a number?

12: I did. *(Examines ticket. To NEXT.)* Twelve. I'm number twelve. You must be eleven.

NEXT: Must I?

12: Well, yes. You were the only one here when I came in and I'm number twelve. So, you must be eleven.

NEXT: If you say so.

12: Look at your ticket.

NEXT: I'll take your word for it.

14: Fourteen.

12: Excuse me?

14: My ticket says fourteen.

12: Then we all know who unlucky thirteen is.

13: Why? Why unlucky?

12: It's just a saying.

13: Twelve could be unlucky too, you know?

12: I suppose. It's just a saying.

13: Some things are better left unsaid.

12: All right. I got your point.

NEXT: I could be ten. Maybe, nine. Seven. I bet I'm seven.

12: You're eleven.

NEXT: How do you know that?

12: I told you. You were the only one here when I came in.

NEXT: That doesn't mean anything. I could be seven as well as next. I could have let eight, nine, ten and eleven go ahead of me.

12: Why would you do a thing like that?

NEXT: For altruistic reasons.

13: Really?

NEXT: I fell asleep. I could have been taken advantage of in my sleep. Strange things happen to people while they're sleeping. It's an opportune time for negative forces.

14: Like what?

NEXT: Like dreams and nightmares and spirits from the other side.

13: What other side?

NEXT: Of the door. Slipping in while you are least aware. Making yourself their home. Living in your body. Dictating your every move. Your life is no longer your own. Stranger things have happened. These and ideas, yet more horrifying, are the foundations for countless systems followed by millions.

14: Jesus Christ!

NEXT: Exactly.

14: Stop pointing fingers.

12: Give us a break! Look at your ticket.

NEXT: I don't want to look at my ticket. I'm next and that's all anybody needs to know.

12: Suit yourself. We all do.

14: We all do what?

12: We all suit ourselves. In the end, we always suit ourselves, don't we?

13: Sounds selfish, if your asking me.

12: After all, it's all about self-love, isn't it?

14: That's the trouble with people nowadays – no room at the inn for others.

13: What about the rest of humanity?

12: The best kind of self-love embraces all of humanity.

NEXT: Still, everything starts and ends with me, doesn't it? I'm next and there's no question about that.

14: Did anyone knock on the door?

13: From this side or from the other side?

14: From either side.

12: One of us would have answered had it come from the other side. Did anyone on this side think to knock on the door?

NEXT: Other than yourself?

13: Who would be there to answer?

14: They could have forgotten that we're here.

12: Or, never really knew.

13: You only just got here. What's your hurry?

14: What are we all waiting for anyway?

NEXT: Me. I'm next. So relax. Don't try to get ahead. Everybody here knows I'm next.

12: No they don't.

13: The two of you were here when I came in. Either one of you could be next for all I know.

14: You were all here when I got here. Any one of you could be next. Besides, sooner or later, we all get to be.

NEXT: To be?

14: Next. Eventually, we all get to be.

13: That makes you last, doesn't it?

14: For the moment.

NEXT: Don't try any funny stuff! I'm next and that's all there is to it!

12: All right. You're next. I was just pointing out that everybody doesn't know unless you show us your ticket.

NEXT: I know. I know I'm next and that's all that matters.

13: What you know is all that matters, is it?

NEXT: There is nothing else. It's everything. There is you and there is me and I'm next and that's all there is to it.

14: I haven't got all day.

12: Why? Better things to do?

14: Maybe.

12: *Umm.* Have you cancer to cure? The world to save?

14: No.

12: Then why haven't you got all day?

14: Don't be a smart-ass.

12: It's my nature – spots and all that.

14: Then change them.

NEXT: Can't change spots. I don't know who said that, but somebody did and it's true enough for me.

12: Just curious to know what's so pressing.

14: It's my time and I don't care to waste it.

13: Our time is shared by all of us. Maybe we don't have time so much as it has us. What do you think?

14: I don't have time to think about those things.

13: That's a point well taken.

NEXT: What about me? I've been here forever! You don't hear me complaining, do you?

14: Why should you? You're next.

NEXT: I could sell it to you.

14: What? *Next?*

NEXT: That's right. I could sell it to you.

14: How much?

NEXT: I need time to think about it.

13: You'd be last. You'd go from next to last.

12: *(Ibid.)* That's right. You're not going ahead of me.

14: Well? What's the price? Everybody's got a price.

NEXT: I said, I need time to think about it.

13: Everybody doesn't have a price.

12: I think they do.

14: There must be something better.

NEXT: Better than what?

13: Better than this? This time? This awareness? It's the best of all possible worlds, isn't it.

14: Waiting. There must be something better than waiting.

12: Don't you threaten us!

14: I'm not threatening anybody. All I said was that there must be something better.

NEXT: Well, there isn't. There's nothing! There's nothing better. If you came in here looking for trouble you're sure as hell going to find it!

14: I came in here because this is where I'm supposed to be. This is where I found myself. And now I see that I am last and, yet, there must be something better.

NEXT: Then wait. Wait like the rest of us. And you can forget about me selling you my place. I've made up my mind and my mind is made up! You can't have it and that's final!

12: Careful, he's a malcontent.

NEXT: Then he'd better start a riot 'cause the deal's off!

14: I might. I just might be forced to riot.

12: One alone cannot riot.

14: Why not?

12: It's just not done. It's *unseemly,* but it's certainly not a riot.

13: It'll look like St. Vitas Dance. I knew a man who blew himself up once.

12: What?

14: He said "once." You only get to blow yourself up once.

13: Explosives. He had explosives strapped around his waist and he blew himself up without so much as a wink to warn anybody. Pre-meditated spontaneous combustion. Took at least a dozen people with him. Blood and shit all over the place.

NEXT: Why?

13: Because that's what happens when people blow themselves up. It's something they can do all by themselves – when they're completely alone.

NEXT: No. Why did he blow himself up?

13: He was trying to make a point.

12: I don't understand people like that.

14: I know why.

NEXT: You would.

14: What is that supposed to mean?

NEXT: You're a malcontent. You deal in chaos. You undermine the *status quo*. That's your stock and that's your trade.

14: When you've nothing left to lose only your death has meaning.

12: Ah, the platitude of the malcontent.

13: *Umm.* My life would never become so meaningless that I'd blow myself up!

NEXT: My son died in the service of his country.

14: And what country was that?

NEXT: This country. What country did you think?

14: I wasn't sure. You do look a bit foreign to me.

NEXT: He died at the hands of the enemy.

12: What enemy?

NEXT: Does it matter?

13: It should, shouldn't it?

NEXT: The enemy – the enemy *du jour.*

12: Of course, they're always in a state of flux; friends and enemies are funny that way.

NEXT: I'm George, or Mary. Or, maybe I'm God.

14: What?

NEXT: You heard me.

14: Don't you get personal! Don't you dare get personal! You're next and that's all anybody needs to know!

12: That's right, you're next. Everything else is irrelevant.

NEXT: That I am God is irrelevant?

12: As irrelevant as excuses for yourself.

NEXT: I can be anything I damn well please! None of you have any history of me. I am whoever I say I am.

13: People can't just be who they say they are, can they? Especially not God! People can't be God!

NEXT: They can, if it doesn't change who it is they really are.

14: Certainly not. He's next and that's all there is to it.

NEXT: Says who?

14: You. You told us you were next.

NEXT: That's right. And, now I am telling you that I am something altogether different. Can't I be both?

13: You can't be two things at once. It isn't polite.

12: You can't be something else because you say so. Nobody can be anybody just because they say so. It doesn't work that way!

NEXT: Of course it does.

13: It isn't done.

14: Show us your ticket.

NEXT: I ate it.

13: What kind of person eats their ticket?

NEXT: Altogether something else. We do whatever we damn well please.

13: That's not acceptable!

14: People can't do whatever they damn well please.

NEXT: Why not?

14: I don't know why not. But, there must be a reason.

12: There is no reason, is there?

NEXT: Isn't there?

(NEXT crosses to door and knocks. As the LIGHTING FADES we hear the voice from the other side of the door:)

VOICE: *Next!*

(*SILENCE.*)

FADE to BLACK OUT.

END—*Next*

PEDALING TO PARADISE

SYNOPSIS: 2W, No Set, 10 Minutes. Sally and Teddy have reached a point in their lives where their insecurities and lessening sense of worth have begun to affect their good judgment. They pedal and pedal on their exercise bikes and get nowhere while trying to "get fit." It's all about cosmetics and getting your man in order to feel complete, or is it? Is "getting fit" worth it? Are men all that necessary? Is Paradise all it's cracked up to be? What exactly is "fit?" Pedal, girls, pedal!

CHARACTERS: SALLY and TEDDY, two women of indeterminate age.

AT RISE – TEDDY and SALLY are seated on exercise bicycles pedaling like mad. BOTH wear colorful exercise outfits.

TEDDY: *(Stops pedaling. Exhausted.)* That's it! I've had enough.

SALLY: Pedal, Teddy. *Pedal.*

TEDDY: For God's sake, Sally, haven't you had enough?

SALLY: I'm going to get fit if it's the last thing I do. If it kills me, I'm going to get fit. You're not pedaling.

TEDDY: *(Resumes pedaling.)* I'm pedaling, Sally. I'm pedaling.

SALLY: *(After a pause.)* I'm going to leave that sonofabitch!

TEDDY: Who? What sonofabitch? Harry?

SALLY: *Yeah.* Harry.

TEDDY: You wouldn't, really.

SALLY: I might. I'll give him something to think about, that's for sure. I won't be taken for granted anymore – something less than I am – I'll tell you that. Not after I'm fit. Then, I'll have options.

TEDDY: *Yeah.* I know what you mean. Norm's got another think coming, too. After I'm fit, I'm going to get out more. Take some classes, maybe. Flirt with my yoga instructor.

SALLY: When did you start taking yoga?

TEDDY: Well, I haven't, yet. But, when I'm fit, I will. And, then, I'll flirt with my yoga instructor. I'll be the best little lotus position you ever saw. Pedal, Sally. *Pedal.*

SALLY: *(After a pause.)* You know that new bank going up downtown? Yesterday I had to go past all those construction workers. *Terrible.*

TEDDY: I know what you mean.

SALLY: I took my time. Nearly loitered my way past the construction site. I may even have unbuttoned another button on my blouse . . . I can't be sure. And, do you know what those sonsofbitches did?

TEDDY: Nope. What did they do?

SALLY: Nothing.

TEDDY: You're kidding!

SALLY: Nope. Nothing. Not a thing. No catcalls. No whistles. Not a peep! *Nothing.* They just went on about their business like I was their mother or something.

TEDDY: What a bunch of assholes! Pedal, Sally. Pedal.

SALLY: I mean, who did they think they were? I have feelings, you know.

TEDDY: Maybe, they were just being polite. Maybe, inside, they were all hot and bothered but, outside, they were showing you respect.

SALLY: Teddy, who in hell wants respect from a goddamn construction worker? Times sure have changed, I'll tell you that.

TEDDY: Maybe, when we're fit, things will be a whole lot different.

SALLY: You bet they will!

TEDDY: *(After a pause to pedal.)* I noticed the waiter in The Happy Sprout giving you the once-over when he brought us our salad.

SALLY: He was gay.

TEDDY: Oh, I don't think so.

SALLY: He was gay, Teddy. Not that I have anything against gays. . . but what kind of a man wants to know where I bought my turquoise turtle, huh? You tell me that.

TEDDY: Maybe, he wanted to buy one for his mother.

SALLY: Maybe, it was the way he asked.

TEDDY: Well, then, maybe you're right. Still, he did take an interest . . . and he sure was cute, I'll tell you that.

SALLY: A lot of good that does! That's like having your cake and not being able to get your hands on it. Much less, your mouth.

TEDDY: I see what you mean . . . I think. *(After a pause to pedal.)* Where did you get your turquoise turtle?

SALLY: K-Mart? I don't think it's real turquoise.

TEDDY: Oh. I wouldn't tell anybody that if I were you. You could really give the wrong impression, if you know what I mean.

SALLY: That's why I told him it was a present.

TEDDY: That's good. That's a good answer, Sally.

SALLY: That's what I thought.

TEDDY: *(After a pause to pedal.)* Maybe I'll leave Norm, too.

SALLY: What?

TEDDY: Maybe, I'll leave Norm.

SALLY: You wouldn't.

TEDDY: Well, if you're going to leave Harry, I could leave Norm and then we could move in together . . . be roommates. Wouldn't that be fun?

SALLY: Fun? We're not schoolgirls, Teddy.

TEDDY: No, but when we're fit, we could give them a run for their money.

SALLY: Who?

TEDDY: Schoolgirls. I mean, we're not old. We're just . . . well, you know—

SALLY: Not fit?

TEDDY: Not completely. No, but not bad, either.

SALLY: Pedal, Teddy. *Pedal.*

TEDDY: *(After a pause to pedal.)* It'll be wonderful, won't it?

SALLY: What? What will be wonderful?

TEDDY: Life. When we're fit. Life will be wonderful again. I'll be able to wear clothes. Not just any clothes, but clothes. Slinky, sexy, clingy clothes. Sporty clothes. And tweeds! Oh, God! I love tweeds.

SALLY: And go dancing.

TEDDY: Yes!

SALLY: Go to cocktail parties without sitting in a corner, hugging a pillow in your lap.

TEDDY: Or, hiding out in the kitchen.

SALLY: Or the bathroom.

TEDDY: Oh, God! Don't remind me.

SALLY: Dinner parties. Elegant, little dinner parties.

TEDDY: Oh, yes. But, not too many.

SALLY: And tennis!

TEDDY: You play tennis?

SALLY: I could learn. And sex!

TEDDY: I could give lessons.

SALLY: Hot, wild sex . . . with strangers.

TEDDY: Oh, my! Pedal, Sally. *Pedal. (After a pause to pedal.)* Would you really have sex with strangers?

SALLY: Sure. Why not?

TEDDY: What about Harry?

SALLY: Well, he was a stranger the first time we did it.

TEDDY: But, that's not the same thing. Harry's your husband.

SALLY: He wasn't then. Husband or not, Teddy, everybody's a stranger until you do it.

TEDDY: Not always. I knew Norm six, seven months before we did it.

SALLY: Did you really?

TEDDY: I did. And that's the truth.

SALLY: Norm always did strike me as kind of funny that way.

TEDDY: He's old-fashioned, that's all.

SALLY: Then, why won't he marry you? I mean, you've lived together all these years.

TEDDY: He's waiting for his mother to die. He doesn't want to hurt her feelings.

SALLY: Hurt her feelings?

TEDDY: She doesn't want to share him with another woman.

SALLY: That's sick! He told you that?

TEDDY: Well . . . yes.

SALLY: Pedal, Teddy. *Pedal.*

TEDDY: Besides, he doesn't really feel that he's ready for marriage, yet.

SALLY: Honestly, Teddy, if a man's not ready by *his* age, when will he be ready?

TEDDY: I don't know. Soon, maybe.

SALLY: I think you're being had. We both are. I think if we were . . . well, you know.

TEDDY: Fit?

SALLY: Fit . . . men would treat us a whole lot different.

TEDDY: *Yeah.* Life would be fun. Something to write home about, wouldn't it?

SALLY: You bet it would! Those sonsofbitches would treat us with respect.

TEDDY: Not too much respect, I hope.

SALLY: You know what I mean. They can't see but skin level. Or rather, they don't bother to take the time to look . . . to see us for ourselves. But just wait a few months. We'll pedal our way back to how we looked in high school – physically, that is. Then Harry and Norm can both go and eat dirt!

TEDDY: That would be awful. I mean, Harry and Norm can go and eat dirt all right. But, I don't want to get back to the way I was in high school. I was really fat in high school. I mean, really fat. Double what I am now.

SALLY: That's disgusting! I mean, poor baby. I mean pedal, Teddy. *Pedal. (After a pause to pedal. Sotto voce.)* Harry farts.

TEDDY: What?

SALLY: Harry farts.

TEDDY: Sally, everybody farts.

SALLY: Not in front of me they don't. Harry farts in front of me. I mean, he doesn't even try to hide it. Now, you tell me: If a man were in a room with a beautiful woman, would he fart?

TEDDY: One wouldn't think so. Not with a beautiful woman. No.

SALLY: Right. He'd make an excuse to leave the room or he'd hold it in. My marriage is down the tubes, Teddy. Right in the sewer, that's where it is. In more ways than one, it stinks!

TEDDY: It sure sounds that way. *(After a pause.)* Betty Staub had her face chemically removed. Her tits, too.

SALLY: Had her what?

TEDDY: They put implants in her tits and took a layer off her face.

SALLY: You're kidding.

TEDDY: No. She couldn't get the ones with silicone. So, she got the ones filled with water. I guess if she doesn't jog or bounce around a lot no one will ever know the difference. But, getting a layer of skin burned off her face really made a difference.

SALLY: I bet it did.

TEDDY: You should see her. Maybe, I'll have my face removed.

SALLY: That . . . well, it . . . *uhh* . . . sounds painful.

TEDDY: Still, you should see the results. She's gorgeous!

SALLY: She always was.

TEDDY: That's true, but not like now. . . . You think they can make feet smaller?

SALLY: I don't see how.

TEDDY: I'd sure love small feet. What do you think of my tits?

SALLY: Not bad. Not bad at all. They're perky. I've always liked a pair of perky tits.

TEDDY: Really? What about my ass? Do you like my ass? Do you think it's too big?

SALLY: I think it's just fine. What about mine?

TEDDY: Oh, I've always liked your ass, Sally. I mean. . . .

SALLY: Pedal, Teddy. *Pedal.*

TEDDY: *(After a pause to pedal.)* God! It's so painful.

SALLY: Well, we're almost finished. Just a few more minutes and we'll grab a bite at The Happy Sprout.

TEDDY: No, not the pedaling. The way they make you feel.

SALLY: Men?

TEDDY: Yes, men. I don't think men like women. You know, as people.

SALLY: You don't?

TEDDY: No, not like they do other men. They only lust after women. They don't really like us.

SALLY: I've thought that too, Teddy.

TEDDY: They make you feel unwanted. Like an object. A used condom. Deflated. A thing without feelings. Without . . . oh, I don't know. Dignity, maybe. You know, like I should feel guilty . . . like I did something really bad. . . .

SALLY: A used condom?

TEDDY: Once, when I was fifteen, I tried to kill myself. I took a whole bottle aspirin. God! I was sick for days!

SALLY: I can imagine.

TEDDY: Why, Sally? Why must it always hurt so much? It's just not fair! *(On the verge of tears.)* It just isn't fair. I'm a good person, aren't I? I don't want to hurt anybody. I've never hurt anything, except for cockroaches. I hate cockroaches.

SALLY: Who doesn't?

TEDDY: But, other than cockroaches, I've never hurt anything . . . or anybody. I just want to love and be loved. That's all.

SALLY: Oh, honey . . . even skinny girls feel that way sometimes.

TEDDY: Oh no they don't! They have no idea how it feels! *(Angry.)* A skinny girl finishes everything on her plate and she's got a healthy appetite. A fat girl finishes everything on her plate and she's a pig. I'm a person, Sally. A person. I'm not a goddamn pig! *(Jumps off bicycle.)* I quit!

SALLY: Teddy, get back on that bicycle.

TEDDY: No! I quite!

SALLY: Come on now. We agreed.

TEDDY: It's all cosmetic, anyway. Isn't it?

SALLY: What? What is?

TEDDY: Life, goddamn it! Life.

SALLY: Teddy, I don't know what you're talking about.

TEDDY: It's not who you are, or what you do, or why you do what you do. It's how you look doing it. When you're beautiful, life can be heaven. And we all know that everybody is beautiful in heaven.

SALLY: I've heard you've got to feel beautiful to be beautiful. Come on and get back on the bike.

TEDDY: What a crock! You can't feel a thing unless it's there to be felt in the first place. And, I feel like shit!

SALLY: Does that mean that you are shit – or that you've just got your hands in it?

TEDDY: I don't know what it means, Sally! Honestly, for God's sake!

SALLY: Then, will you get back on that bicycle?

TEDDY: *(Mounting bicycle, reluctantly.)* I just get so mad sometimes.

SALLY: I know. So do I. Pedal, Teddy. Pedal.

TEDDY: I'm pedaling, I'm pedaling!

SALLY: *(After a pause to pedal.)* My first husband, good old George, didn't care how fat I got . . . because he loved me. Only, I didn't love him. I wanted something like in the movies – in Technicolor with an orchestra. So, I proceeded to lose forty-seven and a half pounds without even trying.

TEDDY: And a half?

SALLY: Depending on what I was wearing.

TEDDY: I see.

SALLY: I was svelte. I divorced George to marry Harry. Only Harry didn't know that after a year I'd put every single pound back on and then some. And I didn't know that he'd grow to hate me for it. No, it's not like in the movies. No one's running slow-motion towards the other and the forest isn't wired for sound.

TEDDY: Surely, he doesn't hate you.

SALLY: Whatever it is, it's not love. It doesn't feel like anything even closely related to love. I know that.

TEDDY: Maybe, you should've stayed with George . . . worked it out.

SALLY: Teddy, I don't like men who like fat women.

TEDDY: I never met one. So, I can't really say for sure. *(After a pause.)* Do you think this is all going to work out? I mean, all this exercise, the salads, the sprouts, all that stuff? It seems like it'll never end.

SALLY: It'll end. Before you know it, it'll end and we'll be different people.

TEDDY: Different people. *(A sigh of sadness, of loss.)* And happy. I can't wait to be happy. You think it'll happen all at once? Or, little by little?

SALLY: What?

TEDDY: The change. Getting happy. The sense of worth. A new life.

SALLY: Oh . . . little by little, I expect.

TEDDY: But, it'll click. I mean, one day all of a sudden, it'll click. Won't it?

SALLY: It'll click. One day we'll wake up and everything will click. We'll be different people. We won't even remember who it was we were.

TEDDY: If you were a man would you love me the way I am?

SALLY: I've always loved you, Teddy.

TEDDY: Really?

SALLY: Really.

TEDDY: Men! Who needs them? Ain't nothing but a bunch of pricks! *(A sigh of relief before—)* Pedal, Sally. Pedal.

BOTH pedal like mad as the LIGHTING slowly fades to BLACK OUT.

END—*Pedaling to Paradise*

SISTERS OF LITTLE MERCY

SYNOPSIS: 3W, No Set except a small table and 3 chairs. A bit of nun-sense about three nuns who are banished to Little Mercy, Colorado—an abandoned silver mining town high in the Rockies, to do penitence for conduct unbecoming the wives of Jesus. Their misfortune turns into a fortune found in the outhouse when Sister Mary Madeline discovers an unusual light shining between her legs.

AT RISE: The setting is high in the Rocky Mountains in a former silver mining camp town known as Little Mercy. There is a table with a single burning candle flanked by three chairs, a couple barrels and somewhere a crucifix hangs. Somewhere there is a shovel, a pail and a hammer lying about. The characters are three nuns, MARY MADELINE, PRECIOUS LITTLE and AMBROSIA who are seen sweeping, scrubbing and generally cleaning. They are whistling (perhaps something from The Sound of Music).

MARY: *(On her knees scrubbing the floor. Stops whistling.)* Jesus, Mary and Joseph. I don't remember signing on for this kind of manual labor.

PRECIOUS: *(Cleaning something.)* What kind of manual labor did you sign on for?

MARY: Something more useful to God, I should suppose.

AMBROSIA: Indeed, you should. Get off your knees, Mary Magdalene, and get closer to God.

MARY: Madeline. It's Mary Madeline. *(Rising.)* If you call me Mary Magdalene again I'll—

AMBROSIA: What?

PRECIOUS: Beat her with your rosary?

AMBROSIA: Not the rosary, Sister Precious Little—it was blessed by the Pope himself

PRECIOUS: That's her story.

MARY: It certainly was—when he came to Denver.

AMBROSIA: I don't remember the Pope coming to Denver.

MARY: Because you were doing penitence for having a conversation during the shrill murmur of Holy Silence.

PRECIOUS: Ah, yes—we both were.

MARY: Precisely. It takes a minimum of two to have a conversation. You were both caught whispering behind the Shrine of Mother Cabrini.

AMBROSIA: Another martini for Mother—

MARY: Don't start.

PRECIOUS: Does there really have to be two to have a conversation?

AMBROSIA: At least.

PRECIOUS: So, when we talk to God are we having a conversation?

MARY: Some of us are.

AMBROSIA: And some of us aren't. Some are just blowing stinky hot air out their behinds.

MARY: Sister Ambrosia, I never—

AMBROSIA: Of course you have. Every time Sister Flatulence cooks her cabbage casserole.

MARY: *(Giggles.)* I love her cabbage casserole. I always have seconds.

AMBROSIA: *(Snickering.)* We know.

PRECIOUS: How can you tell?

AMBROSIA: If she always has seconds?

PRECIOUS: If talking to God is having a conversation.

AMBROSIA: If you've got to ask, Precious Little, you're probably talking into a vacuum.

PRECIOUS: Surely, you don't mean—

AMBROSIA: An empty space—an abomination in the eyes of God.

PRECIOUS: Honestly. I know what a vacuum is. I'm not as dumb as all that.

AMBROSIA: That's your story.

MARY: I thought it was Mother Nature who abhorred an empty space?

AMBROSIA: Mother Nature is not a member of our Order. Besides, I'm not so gullible as to believe for a moment that Sister Mary Magneto had a private audience with the Pope.

MARY: Believe what you want. His Holiness blessed this rosary and that's all I've got to say in that regard.

PRECIOUS: Didn't stop her from trying to strangle Mother Bernardino with it.

MARY: Mother Bernardino is a witch!

AMBROSIA: Whatever she is or is not, your vile behavior got us banished to—where in perdition are we? It sure ain't home—is it, Sisters?

PRECIOUS: Little Mercy. We have been sentenced to Little Mercy, Colorado where the air is thinner than—air.

AMBROSIA: Air? Where the air is thinner than air?

PRECIOUS: Why not?

AMBROSIA: Hot air and hooey maybe. That's like saying water is wetter than water.

PRECIOUS: My point. Surely, there is something wetter than water.

AMBROSIA: Sister Mary McMuffin's Depends

(AMBROSIA and PRECIOUS giggle, do a high-five and a little jig.)

MARY: I don't wear Depends, Sister Ambrosia.

AMBROSIA: I remember differently, Sister Margarita.

MARY: Once. Just once, back in the convent—when I had that bladder infection. I haven't needed them since. *(After a pause.)* I suppose you two dancing penguins think you're funny. Unlike you, Precious Little, I don't suffer from short-term memory loss. So, let me repeat it once more before I do something, ladies, that all the Hail Marys said on all the beads in all the universe can't rectify: My name is Mary Madeline. Not Magdalene, mandolin, Metamucil, Magellan, magnesium or any other M-word you can conjure. Get it?

AMBROSIA: Got it.

MARY: Good.

PRECIOUS: *(Looking about—after an uncomfortable pause.)* Has anyone seen Brother Francis?

MARY: He's back at the convent where you left him.

PRECIOUS: No, I packed him.

MARY: I hate to be the bearer of bad news, Sister Precious, but Mother Bernardino confiscated him. I would have said something but she makes me afraid—afraid I just might accidentally kill her.

AMBROSIA: *(Aside.)* Uh-huh. Let's hope the Pope didn't bless any of her cutlery.

PRECIOUS: No she didn't confiscate him.

MARY: She certainly did. He was missing an eye and she said he looked demonic—probably possessed—and since our Order no longer performs exorcisms, she thought it best to burn him.

PRECIOUS: Demonic? She burned Brother Francis?

MARY: At the stake.

PRECIOUS: You're making this up. Please tell me you're making this up.

MARY: I'm so sorry.

AMBROSIA: I was there too—hiding behind the tree with Mary Magnet as Butch Bernardino danced in the altogether 'round the burning bear.

MARY: It wasn't a pretty sight.

PRECIOUS: I could cry.

MARY: You could. I would.

AMBROSIA: You certainly could. Why don't you?

PRECIOUS: I just might.

MARY: We ought to be cleaning, Sisters. As old Bernardino would say, "Let's have a little less jaw work and a little more claw work!"

AMBROSIA: Stop sucking up to Jesus, Mary!

MARY: I'm not sucking up to Jesus. What a terrible thing to say. The sooner we clean this . . . this . . . I don't know what to call this.

AMBROSIA: Try hovel . . . beaver hole . . . Satan's shanty—

PRECIOUS: Don't you know that a one-eyed bear is good luck?

AMBROSIA: Not for the bear.

PRECIOUS: Well, how am I supposed to get to sleep, huh? I can't sleep without Brother Francis.

MARY: You could always count sheep, I do. They're so cuddly—sheep.

PRECIOUS: Are there sheep in Little Mercy?

AMBROSIA: The air is—

MARY: Thin? Sheep need meadows.

AMBROSIA: You might see a mountain goat every now and again.

PRECIOUS: I'll be sure to keep my distance.

AMBROSIA: Then don't go spelunking, Precious.

PRECIOUS: They have horns—and cloven feet.

MARY: So does Mother Bernardino.

PRECIOUS: I need Brother Francis or I shall never sleep. I want my Frankie bear!

MARY: You mean teddy bear.

PRECIOUS: Whatever.

AMBROSIA: I hope you remembered to pack your lithium.

PRECIOUS: They're in the barrel.

MARY: The whole barrel?

PRECIOUS: Except for a few personal items, yes. *(There is a SILENCE as the other nuns stare at her.)* Well . . . we are going to be here for six long months, aren't we?

AMBROSIA: Thanks to Sister Mary Margarine.

MARY: I have heard it said that ambrosia is the food of God and all His saints and angels. Before I go to sleep tonight I'll pray to Jesus that He may find you deliciously edible!

PRECIOUS: He'd get a stinky behind after that!

AMBROSIA: Sister Precious, you're like a watch that runs backwards—every time one looks to you for the time it's much earlier than one thinks?

PRECIOUS: What's that supposed to mean?

MARY: Yeah, I don't get it, either.

AMBROSIA: Which one of you was bounced on your head in the marble baptism fount?

MARY: I don't remember. Was it you, Precious?

PRECIOUS: Mine was a baptism in a wading pool.

MARY: Was it inflatable?

PRECIOUS: I believe it was. Well, it could have been. It was yellow with little blue dolphins—and it was wet and blessed.

AMBROSIA: So was Mary Marshmallow's rosary when the Bishop had to unwrap it from around Mother Bernardino's throat. The beads had sunken so deep into her flesh, the blind could read their Hail Marys on her neck for weeks.

MARY: *(Fingering her rosary.)* I will pray to the Blessed Virgin to forgive you for that.

AMBROSIA: Why? You're the one holding the smoking gun, the object of terror, the blessed garrote—blessed by the Pope and drenched in the blood of the Holy Mother. That temper of yours needs . . . tempering.

MARY: Were I not a bride of Jesus, I think I might want to rip your heart out and stuff it up that never-used orifice of yours.

PRECIOUS: Sister Mary! Remember yourself! You are a bride of Jesus and that orifice belongs to God!

AMBROSIA: We're here to be disciplined, Sisters. May I suggest we get to cleaning this pathetic rat hole before winter sets in.

MARY: Remember your vow of poverty. Embrace nothing and there's nothing to embrace.

AMBROSIA: Why don't you embrace your inner nothingness, Sister Mango?

MARY: I'm simply reminding you that this humble cottage is only as bad as you make it.

PRECIOUS: Humble cottage? Mary, if I had brought more lithium I'd be glad to share it with you.

AMBROSIA: Since when has a vow of poverty included an outhouse abandoned by untold scores of silver miners doing God knows what behind the door.

PRECIOUS: You mean—

AMBROSIA: I certainly do.

MARY: Bless us and save us.

AMBROSIA: They're men being men, after all.

PRECIOUS: And men being men means—

AMBROSIA: They stand. And they don't always lift the seat and when they do they leave it up.

MARY: You don't need to worry about that. There are no seats in the outhouse—just a weathered old hole.

PRECIOUS: Oh my, I didn't know we had an outhouse.

MARY: We've been here for three days.

PRECIOUS: I've been holding it.

MARY: There's something shiny down there.

PRECIOUS: Down where?

MARY: You know—down below the old weathered hole.

AMBROSIA: You looked?

MARY: Something was catching the sun between my legs.

AMBROSIA: Stop! Stop right now! Not another word!

MARY: It's true. There was something reflecting up from down in the—the doodoo.

PRECIOUS: So you stuck your head in there?

MARY: Well, kind of. It looked silver. Lots of it—piles of it.

AMBROSIA: *(Mocking.)* Piles of it all right.

MARY: I'll check it out again later—see what's down there.

AMBROSIA: You do that, Sister Mary Manure.

PRECIOUS: I'll go with you, Sister Mary. We'll climb down there together.

AMBROSIA: *(To the heavens.)* Oh God! Deliver us! We'll never make it six whole months. *(To MARY.)* This is your fault! We could all be back enjoying a nice bowl of hot soup and cabbage casserole, instead of cleaning this filthy shack.

MARY: It's not all my fault. The two of you goaded me on. I'm sorry, Sister Precious, but the truth is the truth. None of us are perfect. The two of you were like the cheering section from asunder shouting, "When you can't transubstantiate, strangulate, strangulate, strangulate!"

PRECIOUS: I thought it sounded reverent—considering the nature of what was going on. The Bishop was leaving for Rome. You were strangling Mother Bernardino. Then a stray dog wandered over and was doing something unspeakable to the Bishop's leg.

AMBROSIA: He didn't seem to mind.

PRECIOUS: It was such a nice day—for awhile anyway.

MARY: I only wanted to show Mother Bernardino how mad she made me. She's always picking on me and I had enough. But you two had to egg me on. What choice did I have but to try and kill her? It really wasn't my fault.

Now, the two of you are condemned to share in my penitence—serves you right.

AMBROSIA: Well, what are we going to do for the next six months?

MARY: We could try behaving like the brides of Jesus we are.

AMBROSIA: That sounds somewhat hypocritical coming from the Butcher of the Abbey.

MARY: Put a muzzle on it, Sister!

PRECIOUS: Any of you ever think of getting a divorce?

MARY: You mean—

AMBROSIA: Leaving the—

MARY & AMBROSIA: Order?

PRECIOUS: Yes.

AMBROSIA: Watch your tongue, Sister.

MARY: Careful what you say while wearing the habit. He will hear you.

PRECIOUS: The problem is that when I hear Him instead of myself we can get this marriage consummated, or annulled. Didn't you say it takes two to have a conversation?

MARY: Yes.

AMBROSIA: Of course.

PRECIOUS: Well, I'm tired of doing all the talking.

AMBROSIA: Mary Mandolin, what does she mean?

MARY: I think she means she's tired of doing all the talking.

AMBROSIA: Mary Maudlin, this would be a good time to honor your vow of silence.

PRECIOUS: I think I want an annulment.

(AMBROSIA & MARY gasp.)

MARY: I'm worried for your precious soul, Precious.

PRECIOUS: Every time I pray to God I find that I am talking to myself.

AMBROSIA: If you'd shut up long enough and listened—

MARY: That's perjury.

AMBROSIA: You mean blasphemy, don't you, Mary Marxist?

(A flash of LIGHTNING followed by a loud clap of THUNDER.)

MARY: I think we should get on our knees and pray for God's forgiveness.

(The nuns fall to their knees, fold their hands, lift their heads heavenward and pray.)

PRECIOUS: *(After a long pause.)* I don't hear anything.

MARY: Listen with your heart, Precious.

PRECIOUS: I'm trying.

MARY: Well, what do you hear?

PRECIOUS: *Thump, thump, thump.*

AMBROSIA: *(A realization.)* Silver! This is an old silver mine, isn't it?

PRECIOUS: Abandoned years ago.

AMBROSIA: That's what the reflection was on Sister Mary Madeline's thighs—a sign from God in the outhouse?

MARY: That doesn't seem right.

AMBROSIA: We're rich! There's silver in the bottom of the well.

PRECIOUS: Hardly a well, Ambrosia. More like the pit of hell.

MARY: I can smell the sulfur now.

AMBROSIA: You're going to be smelling something else and it ain't gonna be sulfur. Let's go, ladies! We're rich!

(The nuns run about. AMBROSIA grabs a shovel and a pail. After a moment to consider, she hands off the pail to MARY, her new best friend.)

AMBROSIA: Follow me, Sisters!

(She heads for the door followed by MARY. They exit.)

PRECIOUS: *(Grabs a hammer and starts for the door, turns back and looks heavenward.)* Thank You, God. Thanks for the sign, even if it was between my legs. We don't need to have a conversation—I know You're there. (Moves to exit then turns around again.) Oh, and God, please take care of Brother Francis. He's only got one eye, but he sees better than most with two. And one more thing, if You don't mind, would You kindly take Mother Bernardino to Your bosom sooner than later. Thank you. *(She exits.)*

The *LIGHTING* dims to *BLACK OUT.*

END—*Sisters of Little Mercy*

TOUGH COOKIES

SYNOPSIS: 3W, One Set, One hour. Set in the formerly oil-rich desert Southwest, this play explores the lives of two generations of women living under one roof. The story centers on Jo who, after her father dies, takes in her feisty mother. The dialogue between them and with a long-time neighbor is, at once, outrageously funny and heart-breakingly tragic. These women tear and rip into each other's psyche with reckless abandon and something barely resembling love. The cookies in question may or may not be poisoned, but just beneath the surface these women hide a more potent poison—the deadly venom accumulated over years of unfulfilled dreams mixed with the sudden and bitter acceptance of a life unrealized. If you like your tragedies hysterically funny then take a bite of this.

THE CHARACTERS:
JO: A woman in her early fifties to mid-sixties.
BILLIE: Jo's friend and neighbor, the same age as Jo.
MAMMAW: (pronounced ma'am-ah) Jo's Mother.

THE SETTING: JO'S kitchen. It is clean and well-organized. The actual design of the set can be very simple, requiring only the following: Exits stage left and right, a kitchen table and three chairs, a curtained-window unit downstage left or right for the actors to look out, an ironing board and a basket of clothes downstage opposite the window unit. Upstage is cart with a coffee pot, a counter containing two standing plates, one with the face of Elvis and the other with the face of Jesus. There is also a telephone and somewhere a small trash can. This all works well against a black-curtained backdrop. That's the bare bones.

AT RISE – Perhaps "Don't Be Cruel" sung by Elvis Presley is playing on the radio.

BILLIE, a large bulk of a woman, her hair in rollers, is seated at the kitchen table, painting her toenails and sometimes knitting.

JO is slender by comparison and prone to move about the kitchen bird-like—pecking here and there, searching for something to clean, to polish, something to do. It is not JO's impulse to remain idle for very long. In her forever-scrutinizing eyes, it is her duty as a housewife to see that all the household chores are done and when they are, it is her duty to create new ones—however mundane they may be. She wears a cobbler's apron filled with all sorts of cleaning supplies that she uses, more often than not, throughout the course of the play.

JO: *(Running her hands down along the curtains hanging on the kitchen window—sighs and nods negatively.)* I don't know. Honest to God, I really just don't know.

BILLIE: *(Stops polishing her toenails.)* What kind of material did you have in mind?

JO: Don't know that I had any kind in mind, Billie. *(Crosses to turn off radio.)*

BILLIE: *(Sips coffee.)* You'll be wanting something cheery.

JO: Why?

BILLIE: All right . . . you want something gloomy and dingy and ugly as sin, right? *(Picks up her knitting.)*

JO: You go to such extremes.

BILLIE: You want my input or not?

JO: *Input?* I don't even like the sound of that! *(Dusting something.)*

BILLIE: Input is a perfectly good word. It means putting in ones—

JO: *(Cutting her off.)* Two cents?

BILLIE: *(Unruffled.)* Putting in ones ideas about a thing.

JO: You mean *opinion*.

BILLIE: Well, yes. You could say that.

JO: Why didn't you?

BILLIE: *(Sips coffee. After a pause.)* What's wrong with the ones you got, anyway?

JO: Whoever said there was anything wrong with them?

BILLIE: Excuse me, but I'm sure I heard somebody say not two minutes ago, in this very room, she wanted to change the curtains in that there window.

JO: That don't mean there's got to be something wrong with them. I'm just tired of looking at them, that's all.

BILLIE: *(After a pause to study curtains.)* Hmmm . . . oh . . . well . . . maybe you're right, Jo. I don't know.

JO: *(Polishing something.)* You don't know what?

BILLIE: I don't know if I'm tired of looking at them or not.

JO: Why should *you* be?

BILLIE: I see those curtains often enough, don't I?

JO: Not half as much as me.

BILLIE: No, not nearly so much.

JO: Then, who cares? I'm the one who's got to look at them day and night. Not you. You can go next door and look at your own curtains. You don't got to live with them like I do.

BILLIE: No. Not like you do. Sorry. *(Rises and goes to cabinet, looking for something.)*

JO: *Who cares* . . . that's all I've got to say. Who cares? *(Watching BILLIE.)* Now what?

BILLIE: Something to nibble on with my coffee. *Acid.* One should never drink too much coffee all on its own—too much acid.

JO: *(Reaches into a nearby cabinet and removes a plastic container filled with sugar cookies—handing BILLIE the cookies.)* Here. I made these yesterday.

BILLIE: *(Returning to table.)* Sugar cookies! My favorite.

JO: You say that about *all* cookies.

BILLIE: I do not.

JO: You do too. Last week peanut butter cookies were your favorite. The week before that it was tollhouse.

BILLIE: Oh, I love tollhouse.

JO: See what I mean?

BILLIE: Well . . . next to tollhouse, sugar cookies are my absolute favorite.

JO: Rats', too.

BILLIE: Rats?

JO: That's what I put down for the rats. (Gets coffeepot.)

BILLIE: You feed your rats?

JO: I don't have any rats—not anymore . . . *coffee?*

BILLIE: Please. Delicious. *(Polishing off a cookie.)* You must give me your recipe.

JO: *(Pouring coffee.)* The one for people or the one for rats?

BILLIE: For people, of course. I don't have rats.

JO: You don't?

BILLIE: No. The very idea—

JO: *(Returning coffeepot to counter.)* They had to come from somewhere.

BILLIE: If you're hinting that I have rats and that they somehow carpet bagged their way over here under my fence, you're sadly mistaken. What about Clara on the other side? They could've come from her, you know.

JO: Clean as she is? Don't be silly. *(Sits at table.)*

BILLIE: Well, I don't have rats. I never did have rats. And, I certainly don't intend to get any! But, if I did, I wouldn't be feeding them cookies. Poison. I'd feed them poison. *(Pauses to examine cookie.)* Jo, what's the difference between the people recipe and the rat recipe?

JO: Margarine instead of butter.

BILLIE: Practical.

JO: *Imitation* vanilla extract. *(Sips coffee.)*

BILLIE: Smart. Why waste the real thing on rats.

JO: And an extra cup of sugar.

BILLIE: *(Nibbling on another cookie.)* They like them sweet, huh?

JO: How would I know? The extra sugar counteracts the taste of the poison. *(Rises—starts dusting.)*

BILLIE: How would you know that? I mean, it could be sweet already. It seems to me, if you're going to make a poison, you're going to make it attractive to the thing you wanna kill. *(Nibbles on cookie.)* Maybe the extra sugar counteracts the taste of the cheese.

JO: What cheese?

BILLIE: In the rat poison.

JO: There ain't no cheese in the rat poison.

BILLIE: How do you know? Did you taste it?

JO: *(Through clenched teeth.)* No, I didn't taste it.

BILLIE: *(Slyly.)* Well, you ought to. (Nibbles cookie.) I bet it tastes like cheese.

JO: It could taste like chicken fried steak, for all I care.

BILLIE: That's it! I'll make chicken fry for dinner. Thanks, Jo.

JO: Don't mention it. *(Sits at table.)*

BILLIE: So, instead of sugar on the top, you sprinkle on a little rat poison.

JO: No. I mix it in with the batter—*a lot* of rat poison.

BILLIE: *(Spitting out cookie. The soggy crumbs fly across the table.)* What?

JO: Look at the mess you're making! *(Starts to wipe table with towel.)* You don't really think I'm going to feed my best friend cookies I baked for the rats, do you?

BILLIE: *(A moment to think.)* No.

JO: Then stop acting like a retard! Look what you went and did! You got coffee and crumbs all over my arrangement. *(Examines the arrangement of plastic flowers setting on the table.)* Something else to clean.

BILLIE: *(Starts to rise.)* I'll do it. JO: *(Motions BILLIE to remain seated.)* You just stay put. (Rises and crosses to drawer under counter.) I'll take care of it.

BILLIE: Okay. *(Begins to remove the rollers from her hair. After a pause.)* Any news about H.O.?

JO: *(Searching through drawer.)* Nothing more than I told you yesterday. *(Removes metal Bandaid container, closes drawer.)* They're going to send him home tomorrow. That's all I know. *(Crosses to table, sits and removes Q-tips from container—begins to clean plastic floral arrangement with meticulous care.)* Ugh . . . what a filthy mess.

BILLIE: That's not all me.

JO: Billie, did I say it was?

BILLIE: No.

JO: Then don't go putting words in my mouth.

BILLIE: Did they find out what made H.O. take such a fit?

JO: *(Uncomfortable with the subject.)* Some kind of stomach thing, that's all I know. *(Rises to get broom and dust pan.)*

BILLIE: Well, something ain't right. I mean, a man just don't start foaming at the mouth in the middle of Tootie's and take to ripping all the plastic off all the chickens in the meat case.

JO: He said he wanted to set them free. *(Begins sweeping crumbs around table.)*

BILLIE: *Free?* Free to do what?

JO: I don't know! Fly away, maybe.

BILLIE: Jo, frozen chickens can't fly away.

JO: *(More to herself.)* I suppose he'll be moping around the house all week expecting me to wait on him hand and foot.

BILLIE: They hop. *(Rises.)*

JO: What?

BILLIE: *(Demonstrates.)* Hop, hop! Chickens kinda run and hop. I'm sure they don't fly

JO: What on earth are you talking about?

BILLIE: Chickens. You said ol' H.O. took the plastic off so they could fly away.

JO: No, I didn't say any such thing.

BILLIE: *(Thinking back.)* Oh . . . I thought you did.

JO: Well, I didn't. 'Sides, they was quartered.

BILLIE: *Quartered?* That pretty much puts an end to hopping, too, don't it? *(Sits and brushes hair.)*

JO: What is wrong with you this morning? You take a stupid pill or something?

BILLIE: No. Took a water pill—bloat.

JO: Well, you better be careful. You're liable to end up with brain-rot! *(Returns broom and dust pan.)*

BILLIE: *(Slams down hairbrush.)* I know you don't mean to hurt me, Jo, but you do sometimes. You know that, don'tcha? *(No response.)* Jo, is something bothering you this morning—I mean, more than usual?

JO: *(Returns to table and sits and cleans plastic floral arrangement with Q-tip.)* Ain't nothing bothering me.

BILLIE: *(Watching JO clean the flowers.)* Well, you're not yourself.

JO: Who am I?

BILLIE: Don't you know?

JO: I know I'm someone who's tired. *Just tired.*

BILLIE: I didn't sleep well last night, either. Sanford dog barked all night. When Georgie's home, dogs don't bark all night.

JO: Course they do.

BILLIE: Oh, no. Georgie gets out there and yells once and you don't hear another yap all night.

JO: Well, it ain't got nothing to do with sleep. I'm just tired. Tired of taking care of people. Tired of living. Tired of *not* living. *Tired.* Just tired. Don'tcha understand?

BILLIE: I guess.

JO: When's my turn, huh? I thought when we retired we were gonna do things . . . travel maybe. Visit some of H.O.'s folks up north.

BILLIE: Well, you can still do that.

JO: *Sure* . . . with mother to take care of?

BILLIE: Mammaw can take care of herself. God! She's got more energy than any two people I know.

JO: *(Disregarding the last.)* And Howie Boy . . . sending him all our extra money so he can eat and pay his rent.

BILLIE: He's nearly forty, Jo. He hadn't ought to be drainin' you so.

JO: He's a songwriter. It takes time to break into the business.

BILLIE: Still, he's too tied to his mama, if you ask me.

JO: *(Warning.)* Ain't no one asking you, Billie.

BILLIE: *Sorry. (Pause.)* You got all the cotton plumb wore off that Q-tip. *(JO frowns and takes out a fresh Q-tip. After a pause.)* What do you suppose the "Q" stands for?

JO: *What?*

BILLIE: The "Q" in Q-tip. What do you suppose it stands for?

JO: It don't stand for nothin'.

BILLIE: It's gotta stand for something.

JO: Why? Because you say so?

BILLIE: *Quick.* Quick-tip, that's it!

JO: I got things to do, Billie. I can't sit around all day like some people I know.

BILLIE: What is that supposed to mean?

JO: What is *what* supposed to mean?

BILLIE: You think I sit around all day and do nothing, don'tcha?

JO: Why does the world always have to revolve around you, huh? You always think I'm talking about you. There are other people walking around this planet, too.

BILLIE: Then, who? Who, Jo? *Who?* Who did you have in mind?

JO: I don't know who! Honest to God—*Mix Astor!* That's who! *(Rises - throws down Q-tip.)*

BILLIE: You meant me. You had me in mind.

JO: *(Squirts back of chair with cleaner taken from out her cobbler's apron, then proceeds to wipe chair dry.)* I didn't have nobody in mind, Billie. Nobody. H.O.'s coming home tomorrow and there's things to get done. You know how men are. Get a little tummy ache and it's "get me this!" and "get me that!" There ain't nothing more helpless than a grown man outta sorts.

BILLIE: Still, it's nice to have a man around the house.

JO: Why don't you just die and stay stupid!

BILLIE: Abuse me all you like, Jo. What goes 'round comes 'round.

JO: So you say.

BILLIE: It's a fact, Jo. *As ye sow so shall ye reap.*

JO: Don't you quote to me, missy. You wanna do that kind of thing you go down the street corner and quote to somebody who cares. Not to me . . . not in my house!

BILLIE: *(Demurely.)* Elvis would have agreed.

JO: *(Controlled outrage.)* How dare you? How dare you?

BILLIE: Well . . . he would have.

JO: Don't you ever disgrace the name of Elvis Presley while you're sitting under my roof again. Elvis was a saint. *(Crosses to `Elvis' plate.)*

BILLIE: For God's sake, Jo, he weren't nothin' but a singer.

JO: A singer? A singer? *(Holding `Elvis' plate - with maniacal restraint.)* An instrument of God, Billie. A saint among men, martyred. Taken to the Lord's breast in his prime . . . *murdered!*

BILLIE: Nobody murdered him, Jo. He did it to himself.

JO: *How dare you?*

BILLIE: Drugs, Jo. He took drugs.

JO: He was murdered—cut down by the American Medical Association . . . a branch of the Mafia!

BILLIE: *(Resigned.)* All right. Whatever you say.

JO: No. No, it's not all right because I say it. It's all right because it's the truth—and I know it. *(Dusts `Elvis' plate.)*

BILLIE: Okay, okay.

JO: Don't you ever disgrace the good name of Elvis Presley in this house ever again.

BILLIE: All right. I'm sorry, okay?

JO: Never again. *(Replaces the `Elvis' plate and gives the `Jesus' plate a quick flick of the duster, almost as an afterthought.)*

BILLIE: *(Anxious to change the subject.)* I found a penny head's up this morning. That's good luck, isn't it?

JO: *(Returning to table - sits.)* It ain't nothin' but superstitious junk! How a grown woman can believe in that kind of thing is beyond me. *(Sips coffee.)*

BILLIE: I never said I believed in it. *(Gathers up her knitting and hair rollers.)* I think I'll be heading home.

JO: Why? Got something better to do?

BILLIE: Maybe.

JO: I'm sure it ain't housework.

BILLIE: *(Dropping her belongings back onto the table.)* Jo, my house is my business. You can clean and scrub and make a fool of yourself all you like. I don't care. Who've I got to clean for, huh? Georgie ain't home but three or four days a month.

JO: Well, that's what you get for marrying a rodeo man.

BILLIE: *Humph.*

JO: But, since you bring it up, you can't exactly eat off your kitchen floor, can you?

BILLIE: I don't know. Do you need an answer right away?

JO: You can eat off mine.

BILLIE: No, Jo. *You* can eat off yours. I'll stay at the table if you don't mind.

JO: It's just a figure of speech.

BILLIE: *(Stands.)* Of course it is. It's your quaint way of telling me I'm dirty.

JO: I never said any such thing.

BILLIE: Not directly, no. You don't know how to be that honest.

JO: *(Stands.)* Honest? You want honest? Your house is a pig sty.

BILLIE: That's not honest. That's rude. *(Sits.)*

JO: You asked for it. *(Sits and starts on flowers with Q-tip.)*

BILLIE: This compulsive addiction you have for house-wifery is a sickness, don'tcha know.

JO: So is living in filth.

BILLIE: Look at yourself.—polishing that there bunch of plastic flowers with a Q-tip. That's sane?

JO: It's my job.

BILLIE: Only because you make it so. Why don'tcha just dump it in the sink and run water over it?

JO: Because that's not the way to do it.

BILLIE: That's the way I'd do it.

JO: Well, that's your problem, isn't it?

BILLIE: *(Suddenly.) Cushion!*

JO: *What?*

BILLIE: Cushion-tip! That's what the "Q" stands for, *cushion-tip.*

JO: Cushion don't start with a "Q", it starts with a "C", stupid.

BILLIE: *Oh,* that's right. I wonder what I could've been thinking of?

JO: There's no telling.

BILLIE: You're turning into an old lady, you know that?

JO: I'm fixing to say something spiteful. 'Sides, I am an old lady. *(Stands and crosses to ironing board -- begins ironing a pair of H.O.'s boxer shorts.)*

BILLIE: By choice. You don't need to be. *(Bites into cookie, sips coffee.)* You were the sweetest thing in grade school.

JO: Weren't we all!

BILLIE: *(Resumes knitting.)* No, Jo, you were different. Everybody liked you then. And in high school you were a regular hell-raiser and, still, everybody liked you. All those boys chasing after you. You. Not me. *You—always you.* I didn't even have a date for the prom.

JO: Yes, you did. H.O. took you, as I recall.

BILLIE: I took him.

JO: Same difference.

BILLIE: No, it's not. Do you know how humiliating that was? I had to buy my own corsage.

JO: He was broke.

BILLIE: He was saving up to marry you come the end of June.

JO: You knew we was engaged. And if I hadn't broke my leg falling off the running board of that stupid Packard of yours, you wouldn't even have had H.O. to go to the prom with.

BILLIE: Well, who asked you to go and try to jump on it just as I was pulling out of the driveway?

JO: You always put on the brakes before.

BILLIE: Maybe I was in a hurry that time.

JO: Ain't never been in a hurry before.

BILLIE: Look, we've been over this before and we already decided it was your fault.

JO: I'm not saying it wasn't and I'm not saying it was.

BILLIE: Well, it was.

JO: I'm just saying be thankful you had somebody to go to the prom with—considering. You know, Billie, you ought to count your blessings.

BILLIE: Easy for you to say.

JO: If you had the good sense to push yourself away from the table a bit more often, maybe some of the boys might've taken a keener interest, if you know what I mean.

BILLIE: Oh, I know what you mean all right. Maybe I just didn't want to end up an old lady, waxing and polishing and Q-tipping my life away.

JO: You married George Patterson, didn't you?

BILLIE: He's different. We're more friends than anything else.

JO: *Friends?*

BILLIE: *(Defensively.)* That's right—friends.

JO: Billie, a husband ain't supposed to be your friend. He's supposed to be someone you cook for and clean for.

Wash for and iron for. Mend for. Call the boss up and lie for. Raise children for. Get your hair done for. If you want friends, you join the Mormons.

BILLIE: Georgie never expects anything from me but *me*.

JO: And that's how you picked up your filthy habits.

BILLIE: He doesn't want a house-slave, if that's what you mean.

JO: Is that what you think I am?

BILLIE: Well, I wasn't referring to the First Lady.

JO: *Humph.* You're dumber than the day you were born.

BILLIE: Then, so are you!

JO: *(After a pause to glare, she turns toward the window.)* Yellow.

BILLIE: What?

JO: Yellow! Yellow! Something wrong with your hearing? I think I want something in yellow.

BILLIE: What? A dress?

JO: No, stupid! *Curtains.* We was talking about curtains, weren't we?

BILLIE: Oh . . . well . . . yellow's nice. *(The PHONE RINGS.)* Telephone.

JO: I got ears, don't I? *(Crosses to phone.)* I wonder who could be botherin' me now?

BILLIE: Maybe it's H.O. calling from the hospital.

JO: *(Into phone.)* Yeah? Yeah. Yeah. No. No. No. C. C. B. No. Wouldn't you like to know. Suppose I don't want to have a nice day? Goodbye to you, too. *(Hangs up phone.)*

BILLIE: *Who was that?*

JO: Computer.

BILLIE: Didn't think it was H.O. What did it want?

JO: Information.

BILLIE: What kind of information?

JO: The nosey kind!

MAMMAW enters. Maybe in spite of her age - maybe because of it - it is her spunky youthfulness that strikes us first.

MAMMAW: *(Entering.)* Was that for me?

JO: Was what for you?

MAMMAW: The phone.

JO: No, mother, it wasn't for you.

MAMMAW: *(To BILLIE.)* She wouldn't tell me if it was.

JO: You know that's a lie, mother.

BILLIE: Good morning, Mammaw.

MAMMAW: *(To JO.)* You never tell me when Howie Boy calls. *(To BILLIE.)* Mornin'. Stuffin' your face again, I see.

JO: I do too. Only sometimes he don't ask for you. Sometimes he only wants to speak to his mother.

MAMMAW: Funny thing when a boy don't want to talk to his Mammaw.

JO: Well, sometimes he's in a rush.

MAMMAW: *(To BILLIE.)* That's *her* story. Gained some weight since I seen you last.

JO: It ain't a story, mother.

BILLIE: That was only yesterday. I took a water pill. I lost some since yesterday.

MAMMAW: That's *your* story. *(To JO.)* Then, who called?

JO: For your information it was a computer that called.

MAMMAW: Did it ask for you?

JO: No, mother. It didn't ask for nobody.

MAMMAW: Then how do you know it wasn't for me? *(To BILLIE.)* She does this all the time.

JO: No, I don't, mother.

MAMMAW: *(To BILLIE.)* She hordes all the mail what comes for "occupant". *(To JO, while going through discarded mail in waste basket.)* Now don't lie about *that*, sister.

JO: I don't know what you're talking about.

MAMMAW: That's never stopped you before. *(To BILLIE.)* She's got something to say about everything. Don't know a dang thing—never did. Knows more than Walter Cronkite, she does. *(Pours herself some coffee. After a pause.)* Pit bulls are eating people up left and right, don'tcha know.

BILLIE & JO: *What?*

MAMMAW: Munchin' people up to beat the band.

JO: Mother, they ain't doing any such thing.
MAMMAW: Don't tell me! I got eyes, don't I? *(To BILLIE.)* She thinks I'm senile. She'll be senile long before me, I'll tell you that. *(Pulls her `special' chair to the table and sits.)*

JO: You never saw a pit bull eat nothing or nobody. You don't even know what a pit bull looks like.

MAMMAW: *(To BILLIE.)* See how she talks to me? Showed the kid being eaten right there on TV in front of God and everybody.

BILLIE: Really? Why didn't somebody do something about it then?

MAMMAW: They was busy takin' pictures. That's show biz, don'tcha know.

JO: No, mother. They never showed anything like that on TV.

MAMMAW: How do you know? Were you there? They show people gettin' eaten up by all kinds o' things all the time on TV. *(To BILLIE.)* It was on the news last night.

JO: I saw the news last night and there wasn't anything about pit bulls eating people.

MAMMAW: You got up.

JO: No I didn't.

MAMMAW: *(Sips coffee. To BILLIE.)* She got up.

JO: I didn't get up.

MAMMAW: You got up and went to relieve yourself.

JO: I did not relieve myself during the news, mother.

MAMMAW: Oh, you relieved yourself all right—just when they was about to show them pit bulls eating that little kid. Now, don't tell me different 'cause I know better.

BILLIE: Seems to me I heard something about that.

JO: Now don't *you* start!

BILLIE: Up in Roswell, wasn't it?

MAMMAW: That's right. And then there was that ball player what got himself hit by lightning and it never did come back out.

JO: Mother, you don't know what you're talking about.

MAMMAW: I do too!

JO: I saw it too, mother, and they took him off the field where he was playing that there new kind of game they got—soccer, they call it.

MAMMAW: Baseball.

JO: No, mother, they don't kick a baseball.

MAMMAW: That's right. They use a bat. And they got him under lock and key just in case that lightning decides to come out and strike a nurse or something. He's in the hospital up in Albuquerque. *(Rises and searches about the kitchen.)* I'll tell you, the moral fiber of America is worn thin and that's the truth.

JO: What are you prowling around for?

MAMMAW: *(Finds loaf of bread.)* Something to eat. *(To BILLIE.)* She never feeds me.

JO: Oh, for pity's sake.

BILLIE: Would you like a cookie, Mammaw?

MAMMAW: I don't eat rat food. *(Sits - peels the crust from a slice of bread.)*

JO: It ain't rat food, mother.

MAMMAW: It's why H.O.'s in the hospital, ain't it?

JO: *(Through clenched teeth.)* No, it isn't, mother.

MAMMAW: *(To BILLIE.)* I wouldn't eat those cookies if I was you.

BILLIE: (Rises.) Excuse me.

JO: Where are you going?

BILLIE: To the bathroom.
JO: There ain't nothing wrong with those cookies, Billie!

BILLIE: It's the water pill. *(She exits.)*

JO: Now see what you've done.

MAMMAW: I don't know what you're talking about, sister.

From OFFSTAGE we hear the SOUNDS of BILLIE throwing up.

JO: You made her sick.

MAMMAW: *(Rises - crossing to window.)* Well, you make me sick.

JO: Sometimes I could strangle you with my bare hands!

MAMMAW: You could chew on a Brillo pad for all I care. *(Examining curtains.)* Thought you was going to change out these curtains today?

JO: Yes, mother. Billie and I are going to the fabric store soon as I get 'round.

MAMMAW: Can I come?

JO: If you want.

MAMMAW: No. Maybe I'll just stay to home . . . in my room . . . all alone.

JO: Do what you want, mother.

MAMMAW: You'd like that, wouldn't you? Leave me alone so I can fall and break my bones while you're out galivantin'.

JO: Then come with us for God's sake!

MAMMAW: The way you drive? Be safer on roller skates. *(Looking out window.) Utt!* That ol' Tom's in the backyard again. *Shoo, shoo!* Remember the McGreevy boy?

JO: Tommy Lee?

MAMMAW: That's the one. He died of cat fever.

JO: He had the croup.

MAMMAW: From sleepin' with cats.

JO: You don't get the croup from sleeping with cats.

MAMMAW: Are you a doctor now?

JO: He had weak lungs, mother. He was born with weak lungs and that's what killed him. *Weak lungs.*

MAMMAW: Sleepin' with cats didn't help. (Out window.) *Shoo, shoo!* Go home! Scat! *Utt!* There's that black boy. *Shoo, shoo! (Yelling out window.)* Don't you go climbin' over that fence! I'll get the police on you. See if I don't! *(Turning back to JO who is crossing to window.)* Call the police, sister.

JO: *(Looking out window.)* Oh, mother, he's just getting his ball.

MAMMAW: He ought to keep his balls on his side of the alley!

JO: There. He got it.

MAMMAW: What's that hangin' outta his pocket?

JO: I don't know, mother. Looks like a stick.

MAMMAW: Bet it's a jackknife!

JO: It's not a jackknife, mother.

MAMMAW: Looks like a jackknife to me. Liable to cut your throat in the dead of night.

JO: For God's sake, mother! Nobody's gonna cut anybody's throat. *There.* He's gone now. *(Crosses to ironing board.)*

MAMMAW: He'll be back. And the next time he'll bring the whole gang with him.

JO: What gang?

MAMMAW: They run in packs don'tcha know. Robbin' and killin' and rapin'. Wanna get raped?

JO: No, mother, I don't want to get raped.

MAMMAW: Then, call the police before he gets back here with his gang.

JO: Where on earth do you get this stuff?

MAMMAW: It's the truth, Utt! There's that ol' Tom again doin' his duty. Better be careful when you go to hangin' out the wash, sister. Pile of cat shit big enough to bury your shoes in.

BILLIE: *(Entering.)* Do you have any Lysol?

JO: Now what did you do?

BILLIE: A little accident.

MAMMAW: Rat food.

JO: Honest to God! If it ain't one thing it's another! *(Exits.)*

MAMMAW: *(After a pause.)* Is she gone?

BILLIE: *(Sits a table.)* Yes.

MAMMAW: *(Crossing to BILLIE. Urgently.)* They beat me.

BILLIE: No.

MAMMAW: *(Showing BILLIE the bruises on her arms.)* See these? They didn't get there by themselves.

BILLIE: I can't believe—

MAMMAW: Believe it! It's true! Call the police!

BILLIE: *What?*

MAMMAW: Does that stomach of yours effect your hearing?

BILLIE: No. Of course not.

MAMMAW: Then, call the police.

BILLIE: I can't do that.

MAMMAW: Fingers gone bad? Arthritis, huh?

BILLIE: No.

MAMMAW: Oh, don't talk to me about arthritis. Look at these. *(Showing BILLIE her fingers.)* Sometimes they like to get knotted somethin' awful. I'll never play the harp, I'll tell you that! Let me see yours. *(BILLIE holds out her hands.)* Fat little piggies, ain't they? Call the police.

BILLIE: Mammaw, if what you say is true, why don't *you* call the police?

MAMMAW: I did. They don't believe me. Some know-nothin' woman cop came to investigate and ended up siding with sister. When you reach my age you don't have any rights, don'tcha know.

BILLIE: Well, what makes you think they'll believe me?

MAMMAW: You're my witness.

BILLIE: But, I never saw them beat you.

MAMMAW: That don't make no nevermind. Tell them you did.

BILLIE: That would be a lie, Mammaw.

MAMMAW: Have it your way. One day when you come over here, stuffing yourself with rat food, I'll be layin' in my room all beat up and broken . . . dead, maybe. How are you gonna feel then?

BILLIE: I'd feel— Is this the truth?

MAMMAW: You want it on the Bible?

BILLIE: No. Of course not.

MAMMAW: Don't believe in the Good Book, *huh?*

BILLIE: Look, I'll have a word with Jo about it.

MAMMAW: What good do you think that'll do?

BILLIE: I'll ask her if she's ever done what you said.

MAMMAW: Sure. Go ahead and sign my death warrant!

BILLIE: I won't ask her directly, of course.
MAMMAW: I'm telling you they beat me! They kick me! They punch me! The slap me! They— *(JO enters with Lysol and bucket.)* Have a nice day.

JO: What?

MAMMAW: I said, "have a nice day."

JO: *(Hands BILLIE Lysol and bucket.)* Here.

BILLIE: Sorry. *(Exits.)*

MAMMAW: She's sorry all right. If that ol' gal had to haul ass, it'd take her two trips.

JO: Now, mother, she's a child of God just like you and me.

MAMMAW: If you're a child of God, sister, I'm throwin' in with the one downstairs!

JO: Did you *ever* love me, mother?

MAMMAW: *(After a pause to think about it.)* No.

JO: I thought not.

MAMMAW: They drown female babies in Africa.

JO: What are you talking about?

MAMMAW: Unwanted offspring. They drown 'em in Africa.

JO: Well, thank God they don't do that in America.

MAMMAW: Yeah. . .aren't you lucky.

JO: Mother, what exactly are you saying?

MAMMAW: Got time to give me a perm this week, or do I got to go to that sissy-man on Gibson? *(Goes to ironing board and refolds JO's ironing.)*

JO: You don't need a permanent. You only had one a month ago. *(Gets scissors and magazine, clips coupons.)*

MAMMAW: Grew out.

JO: It didn't do no such thing!

MAMMAW: It did. I always was a fast hair grower.

JO: Oh, mother! Your hair grows like everybody else's.

MAMMAW: No, it don't!

JO: It most certainly does.

MAMMAW: It grows faster when you're older. The older you get, the faster it grows.

JO: Then how come mine don't? I'm getting old, too, mother.

MAMMAW: You ain't normal, that's why. When you're normal it grows faster. Maybe yours is retarded.

JO: It ain't retarded, mother!

MAMMAW: They say when you get old enough you can hear it growin'. *(Crosses to counter, searching.)* It don't even stop when you're dead. Hair's awful funny that way.

JO: Are you looking for an excuse to be silly this morning?

MAMMAW: No. I'm looking for my teeth. Where did you hide them?

JO: I suppose they're where you left them, mother—in the bathroom.

MAMMAW: She probably threw up on them.

JO: She didn't throw up on them.

MAMMAW: People do, you know. *(Returns to ironing board.)*

JO: She didn't throw up on your teeth, mother.

MAMMAW: How do you know? Were you there? That doctor in Juarez what fitted me with those teeth said not to get foreign objects on them.

JO: Your teeth are just fine. When Billie comes out you can go in there and get them.

MAMMAW: Make me sick! *(Spits on iron.)* This ol' iron ain't puttin' out steam again. *(Looking up toward ceiling.)* And that seems to be all that ol' swamp cooler's puttin' out—steam.

JO: When H.O. gets home I'll have him take another look at it.

MAMMAW: What about the iron?

JO: I'll have him look at that, too, mother.

MAMMAW: That's all he ever does is look. He ain't mechanical minded, I'll tell you that. Run some vinegar through the iron. That ought to break down the corrosion. *(A beat.)* What did you poison him for?

JO: *What?*

MAMMAW: You heard me.

JO: It was an accident!

MAMMAW: That's *your* story.

JO: I did not poison H.O.!

MAMMAW: Somebody did.

JO: Now you stop that! I didn't do no such thing!

MAMMAW: He got into the rat food just like you intended.

JO: *(Genuinely hurt.)* How can you say such a thing?

MAMMAW: True, ain't it?

JO: No! It isn't true!

MAMMAW: How'd they get switched, then?

JO: Suppose you tell me. I'm not the only one who lives in this house.

MAMMAW: You're the only one in all of Hobbs who bakes cookies for the rats.

JO: To get rid of them, mother, not *for* them.

MAMMAW: What's the difference?

JO: There's no use trying to make sense with you.

MAMMAW: No. Not when you're retarded. *(Re-ironing and "correcting" all of JO's ironing and folding.)*

JO: I'm not retarded!

MAMMAW: Doc Sears said you was.

JO: Then, Doc Sears was a quack.

MAMMAW: Oh, you shouldn't speak ill of the dead, sister. Poor man, killed himself. Treated Dickie Keefer for hemorrhoids—big as grapes, they were—then he went into the closet and hung himself. Tongue swelled up like an eggplant—big and purple. Terrible thing—hemorrhoids. That's why I don't eat eggplant.

JO: You don't eat eggplant because it gives you gas, mother.

MAMMAW: There was this travelin' show with a two-headed rattle snake come through whiles I was carryin' you and it liked to scare me to death. Give me nightmares, it did.

JO: Oh, mother, you're making this up.

MAMMAW: Am not. It had two heads big as your fist.

JO: Well, what's that got to do with me?

MAMMAW: Told you. It marked you and that's why you're retarded.

JO: *I am not retarded, mother.*

MAMMAW: Not all the time, no. Just some of the time . . . like when you poisoned H.O.

JO: I didn't poison H.O.

MAMMAW: Tell it to the judge.

JO: You stop it! Stop it right now! *(Stops clipping coupons. Rises, with scissors in hand, and crosses towards MAMMAW.)*

MAMMAW: Sure is lucky Tootie ain't gonna sue. All that good chicken gone to waste.

JO: *(Shaking her fist, with scissors, at MAMMAW.)* Sometimes I could . . . could . . . *(BILLIE enters.)* kill you!

MAMMAW: *(To BILLIE, with great satisfaction.)* There. See?

BILLIE: Jo, what's going on?

JO: Nothing!

MAMMAW: Don't say you didn't see that, Billie Patterson. *(Slams down iron and starts to exit -- turning back.)* There better not be puke on my teeth. *(Exits.)*

BILLIE: *(After a pause.)* What was that all about?

JO: She thinks I poisoned H.O.

BILLIE: Did you?

JO: You can go lay down on the highway right now, Billie Patterson!

BILLIE: I don't mean on purpose.

JO: On purpose or otherwise, I did not poison H.O.

BILLIE: Does this have something to do with rat poison in the cookies?

JO: I'm going to tell you something and I don't want it to leave this house.

BILLIE: What?

JO: You better sit down.

BILLIE: *(Sitting.)* What?

JO: I think my mother switched the cookies.

BILLIE: *(Covering her mouth, with panic.)* Oh my God! I'm going to die, aren't I?

JO: No, stupid! Not on you, on H.O.

BILLIE: Then, *I'm* all right?

JO: Yes, Billie. You're perfectly fine. I already threw the poisoned batch out. She's trying to kill me, Billie. She wants me dead.

BILLIE: But, *I'm* all right?

JO: Yes. You're just fine. It's me she's trying to kill, not you.

BILLIE: Jo, I can't believe that.

JO: She's been trying to kill me for over fifty years!

BILLIE: She couldn't have been trying very hard.

JO: Would you shut up and listen to me? I think she switched the cookies around knowing I like a snack every now and again. Only, she didn't count on H.O. getting into them since he's always braggin' on not having a sweet tooth.

BILLIE: Surely they would have discovered that at the hospital, wouldn't they?

JO: Not if they weren't looking for poison.

BILLIE: What are you going to do?

JO: I don't know. I can't go to the police because she's my mother. 'Sides, I'm the one who baked them in the first place. She's an evil woman, I'm telling you that.

BILLIE: I'm sure it's all just an innocent mistake.

JO: You really want to die stupid, don'tcha!

BILLIE: What proof do you have?

JO: She murdered my father. What more proof do you need?

BILLIE: Jo, Pappaw died of heat stroke.

JO: Who knitted him that sweater in the middle of July, huh?

BILLIE: That's hardly murder.

JO: Not in the eyes of the law, maybe. But, murder just the same. She knew what she was doing.

BILLIE: I think you're being a bit unfair.

JO: You think so, huh? Daddy always loved me better than her and she knew it. She knew it and that was her way of getting back at me.

BILLIE: Jo, that is the most ridiculous thing I ever heard you say.

JO: You think so, huh?

BILLIE: I've heard you say some pretty dumb things, but that takes the blue ribbon, best of show, hands down.

JO: Side with her all you like, it don't change a thing.

BILLIE: I'm not siding with anybody, Jo.

JO: As soon as H.O. gets out of that hospital, she's going in a home. I don't care if it takes every last cent we've got she's not staying here!

MAMMAW: *(Entering.)* My mouth tastes like Lysol.

JO: What are you on about, mother?

MAMMAW: Those motor vehicle people took my license away!

JO: What has that got to do with anything?

MAMMAW: I could get in the car and get out of here, that's what! Go somewhere where people don't go throwing up on other people's teeth! *(To BILLIE.)* I drove a covered wagon 'cross Texas and now they won't even let me drive across the street.

JO: It's for your own protection. You'd only get yourself killed like you almost did last time.

MAMMAW: Because you went and bought me them slippy shoes for my birthday. I told you they was no good. Slipped right off the brakes and onto the gas pedal. Who told you to buy me them anyway?

JO: Nobody, mother. I just thought I was doing something nice.

MAMMAW: Why?

JO: What do you mean, *"why?"*

MAMMAW: You ain't never done nothin' nice in your life.

JO: How can you say such a thing?

MAMMAW: You want me dead, don't tell me. You bought me those slippy shoes on purpose.

JO: I bought you those shoes because you was complaining about how you didn't have any shoes to wear.

MAMMAW: I had plenty of shoes.

JO: That's what I told you. Only you went on and on about how nobody ever does anything for you.

MAMMAW: Well? Do they?

JO: I've given up my life for you, mother, and I've had about all I can take!

MAMMAW: *(To BILLIE, who is nervously knitting.)* They was cheap, slippy, catalog shoes. 'Sides, they never fit me right, anyhow.

JO: Can't you let me love you?

MAMMAW: Now you stop that! You stop that right now. You hear me, sister?

JO: *(Pleading.)* I just want to love you.

MAMMAW: Stop it, I said! Don't you go play-actin' for Billie's sake. She knows better.

JO: I gave up my life for you.

MAMMAW: And I gave you life. Remember that, sister.

JO: *(Holding back her tears.)* Then, why are you trying to kill me?

MAMMAW: You got it backwards, sister. *(To BILLIE.)* Don't let her kid you. She knew they was slippy shoes when she bought them.

JO: I didn't know any such thing, mother!

MAMMAW: Sister, you can stand there and lie all you like. It don't change a thing. God knows how you hate me. *(Crosses to window.)*

JO: *(Wiping her eyes.)* I don't hate you.

MAMMAW: Oh, yes, you do. Ain't no doubt about that. *(Shouting out window.)* Get outta that apricot tree, you Mexican hoodlum! Go! *Shoo, shoo!* Damn wetbacks!

JO: *(Crosses to look out window.)* That's the Martinez boy, mother.

BILLIE: Dorella's boy?

JO: That's the one.

MAMMAW: *Wetbacks.*

BILLIE: Oh, no. Dorella's a teacher.

JO: No, she ain't. You're thinking of Manny's wife. *(Crosses to ironing board and refolds the laundry that MAMMAW had previously refolded.)*

BILLIE: No, I'm not. Manny's wife is a secretary over at the high school. Dorella teaches.

MAMMAW: *(Yelling out window.)* Go back to Pango Pango!

JO: Mother! Will you stop making a spectacle of yourself!

MAMMAW: Thievin' hoodlum.

JO: He ain't but six or seven years old.

MAMMAW: They teach them young. They got three year old pickpockets roaming the streets of Juarez. Steal everything you got if you don't keep an eye on 'em. Knife you for a chew of bubble gum.

JO: Nobody knifes anybody for bubble gum, mother.

MAMMAW: No? *(To BILLIE.)* What do you say?

BILLIE: Well . . . I think that's a bit extreme, Mammaw. Don't you?

MAMMAW: *(Sits and rearranges the order of JO's coupons.)* If I did, I wouldn't have brought it up. Remember the Flowers girl?

JO: Peggy?

BILLIE: June.

JO: Peggy. Peggy Flowers.

BILLIE: No. It was June. I'm certain.

JO: I'm certain it was Peggy.

MAMMAW: Christie Mae. Christie Mae Flowers.

BILLIE: Ah, yes, that was her name.

JO: Well, whoever! Died of scarlet fever.

BILLIE: Measels.

JO: *Scarlet fever.*

MAMMAW: Bubble gum. She swallowed bubble gum.

JO: Oh, mother!

MAMMAW: She did! She swallowed bubble gum. Got herself bound. All stuck up. Died. Some say it was suicide. *(To BILLIE.)* What do you say?

BILLIE: I don't know enough to say anything, Mammaw.

MAMMAW: Of course you don't. Never thought you did.

JO: Mother, why don't you go and lay down for awhile?

MAMMAW: No! You're gonna sneak out to the fabric store while I'm not looking.

JO: No, I'm not, mother. *Please* . . . just for a little bit while I fix us some lunch.

MAMMAW: I don't want any lunch.

JO: Then, lay down anyway!

MAMMAW: I might not wake up.

JO: Of course you'll wake up.

MAMMAW: You don't know that.

JO: *(Crossing towards MAMMAW.)* Go and lay down!

MAMMAW: *(Rises. Backing away.)* No! I'm afraid.

JO: There's nothing to be afraid of.

MAMMAW: People die in their sleep. I'm not going.

JO: Nobody's gonna die in their sleep, mother.

MAMMAW: *(Crosses to ironing board.)* How do you know? Are you a fortune teller now? *(Proceeds to, once again, refold the ironing.)*

JO: Oh, for God's sake— *(BILLIE rises.)* And just where do you think you're going?

BILLIE: *(Feigning an excuse to get out of the room -- away from the mounting tension.)* Well . . . I thought . . . ah . . . the bathroom.

JO: Sit down!

BILLIE: I . . . I took a water pill and I—

MAMMAW: She's not going to pee on the floor, is she?

BILLIE: I really need to—

JO: SIT DOWN! *(BILLIE sits.)* Thank you.

MAMMAW: Sister, if she's got to pee, let her pee.

JO: She doesn't have to pee.

BILLIE: I do. I really, really do, Jo.

MAMMAW: You hear? She does. She really, really does.

JO: She don't!

BILLIE: I do.

MAMMAW: She does.

JO: She don't gotta pee! She wants to get away from you! You're making her crazy! *(Sits and proceeds to rearrange the order of the coupons.)*

MAMMAW: *(Crossing to BILLIE.)* Am I making you crazy?

BILLIE: No, Mammaw. It's these water pills I've been taking for the bloat.

MAMMAW: See, sister? Bloated like a blimp. It's those water pills making her crazy.

JO: It's not the water pills. It's you!

MAMMAW: I ain't never in all my life made anybody have to pee. Remember Harvey Monroe? He had bladder problems, too. They had to hook a plastic bag to him.

JO: Mother! Go and lay down!

MAMMAW: No! And you can't make me. You just don't want me around when Howie Boy calls.

JO: Howie Boy ain't gonna call today.

MAMMAW: How do you know?

JO: 'Cause it's Monday. He never calls on Monday. 'Sides, he called last night.

MAMMAW: Liar.

JO: He called last night, mother.

MAMMAW: *Liar.* He didn't call last night.

JO: He did too. After you went to bed.

MAMMAW: *You called him.*

JO: No, I didn't.

MAMMAW: Yes, you did.

BILLIE: *(Trapped between them.)* I have to pee.

MAMMAW: You thought I was asleep, but I wasn't. *You called him.*

JO: He had a right to know that his daddy was in the hospital, didn't he?

MAMMAW: You waited for me to go to bed so you could have him all to yourself.

JO: That's not true.

MAMMAW: It's true all right. You don't want him to talk to his Mammaw.

JO: You're crazy. You don't know what you're saying.

MAMMAW: Because you know he loves me more than he does you.

JO: How can you say such a thing?

BILLIE: *(Rising.)* Look, I really need to—

JO: *(Stopping her.)* Sit down! *(BILLIE sits.)*

MAMMAW: *(To BILLIE.)* Do you know why Howie Boy never comes around?

BILLIE: I just want to go to the bathroom, Mammaw.

JO: *(Warning.)* Mother, stop it. *(To BILLIE.)* Go to the bathroom. *(BILLIE rises to leave.)*

MAMMAW: Stay put! *(Blocks BILLIE's way.)*

JO: She's got to go to the bathroom.

MAMMAW: I don't care if she's got to go to the emergency room. Sit! (BILLIE sits.)

JO: Mother, I'm gonna have you put away!

MAMMAW: Put a zipper on it, sister! *(Picking up the plastic floral arrangement. To BILLIE.)* See this ugly plastic flower thing?

BILLIE: Yes.

MAMMAW: I'm gonna bust it over your dumb skull if you budge one inch! *Now.* Do you know why Howie Boy never comes around here anymore?

BILLIE: No, Mammaw. Why?

JO: That cinches it! You're going today!

MAMMAW: *(Putting floral arrangement down.)* He told me.

JO: Mother, stop it! Stop it right now!

JO and MAMMAW begin a pattern of going 'round and 'round the table like two cats about to pounce.

MAMMAW: Told me how sister runs around in front of him in her under things.

JO: That's not true!

MAMMAW: In front of a grown man in her bra and panties.

JO: That's a lie!

MAMMAW: Trapping him in her bedroom.

JO: You goddamn liar!

MAMMAW: Seducing her own son.

JO: You're crazy.

MAMMAW: Spider! Spider! What did you think you were doing, sister?

JO: You crazy old bitch!

MAMMAW: Taking baths with him till he was fifteen years old.

JO: That's a lie!

MAMMAW: Sleepin' with him when H. O. was workin' nights.

JO: You're crazy.

MAMMAW: Crazy like a fox, sister!

JO: How dare you?

MAMMAW: No wonder he prefers men to women.

JO: You don't know what you're talking about!

MAMMAW: I know what I'm talking about all right. *(Sits.)*

JO: You'd do anything to get between us! You was always interfering—trying to poison him against his own mother just like you tried to poison daddy against me! Well, he's *my* son, not yours! You wanted a son, but you had me and you couldn't stand that, could you? So, when

I had a son you tried to take him away—poison him against me—make him your own.

MAMMAW: I should've drowned you.

JO: *I know.* You've been telling me that all my life! Why didn't you, huh? Why, mother, why?

MAMMAW: Because you're my daughter!

JO: Since when has that ever meant anything to you?

MAMMAW: You ain't nothin' but an ingrate!

JO: Me? *Me?* Who takes care of you, mother? Who took you in when daddy died? You sat over in that old drafty shack and didn't eat a thing for nearly a week. You'd be dead now, if it weren't for me.

MAMMAW: It weren't no shack! It was good enough for you at one time, wasn't it?

BILLIE: *(Timidly.)* Can I go now?

JO: Shut up! *(Crosses behind MAMMAW who is seated at the table.)* I should have left you there to die.

MAMMAW: Why didn't you?

JO: Because you're my mother and I . . . I—

MAMMAW: *(Venomously.)* You what?

JO: I love you! (Grabs towel and begins to strangle MAMMAW.) I love you! I love you! I love you!

MAMMAW: *(Sinking to the floor.)* Help! Help! *(Obviously struggling to breathe.)*

BILLIE: *(Pulling JO off MAMMAW.)* Jo! Stop it! You'll kill her! *(The PHONE RINGS.)* Stop it, Jo! Stop it! (Manages to get JO off MAMMAW.)

BILLIE comforts MAMMAW. JO, staggers around in a rage. She grabs the coupons and rips them up. She grabs the plastic flowers and hurls them across the kitchen. She throws the folded ironing in all directions - things fly: The laundry, the ironing board, the iron, this & that, etc.

JO: *(While in her rage.)* When's my turn, huh? When's my turn?

MAMMAW: *(To BILLIE.)* She never was any good. Now, will you call the police?

(The PHONE continues to RING.)

BILLIE: Nobody's gonna call the police, Mammaw.

JO: Oh, she's had the police here before. Don't think she hasn't.

BILLIE: Are you all right, Mammaw? *(Helping her back into the chair.)*

JO: Is *she* all right? Is *she* all right? What about *me*, huh? What about *me*? Jesus Christ! What about me?

BILLIE: *(Grabbing JO - trying to calm her.)* Jo, get hold of yourself. *(JO pulls away.)* Why don't you answer the phone, Jo?

JO: When I'm good and ready! I'll answer the goddamn phone when I'm good and goddamn ready! *(Picks up the phone.)* Yeah?

BILLIE: *(Comforting MAMMAW.)* You want to go to your room?

MAMMAW: No. Now do you see what I have to put up with?

BILLIE: Yes, Mammaw. Do you want something to drink . . . eat?

MAMMAW: Is that Howie Boy she's talkin' to?

BILLIE: I don't know, Mammaw.

JO: *(Into phone.)* When? Are you sure?

MAMMAW: I bet that's Howie Boy. *(To JO.)* If that's Howie Boy, you better let him talk to his Mammaw!

JO: *(Into phone.)* Yes, I understand.

MAMMAW: Don't you hang up that phone without me talkin' to him! JO: *(Into phone.)* Thank you. *(Hangs up phone.)*

MAMMAW: *(To BILLIE.)* See? She did it again.

JO: Did *what,* mother?

MAMMAW: Talked to Howie Boy and pretended I didn't exist.

JO: That wasn't Howie Boy, mother. It was the hospital.

MAMMAW: Was it for me?

BILLIE: Is everything okay?

MAMMAW: I bet it was for me.

JO: It's H.O. They're operating on him right now.

MAMMAW: Now what did you do to him?

JO: I didn't do nothing, mother. That stomach thing turned out to be appendicitis.

BILLIE: Oh, dear.

JO: Will you drive me to the hospital, Billie? My nerves have had all they can stand for one day.

BILLIE: Certainly. You want to go right now?

JO: If you don't mind, yes.

MAMMAW: Since you're not driving, can I come?

JO: Yes, mother. If you want to come, come.

MAMMAW: *(Rises to exit.)* Just let me get my bag. *(Turning back.)* Remember Piggy Smith?

JO: No, mother. Who's Piggy Smith?

MAMMAW: Oh, just someone I knew once. He used to charge a nickel to let you see his appendix scar.

JO: *Mother.*

MAMMAW: All right, all right. I'll just be a minute. *(Exits.)*

BILLIE: *(Gathering up her knitting and her hair rollers.)* Is H.O. going to be all right?

JO: Yes, I think so.

BILLIE: And you?

JO: I'm fine, Billie. Just fine. Let's go. *(BOTH start to exit - JO turns back and looks toward the window.)* Maybe next year. We'll wait till next year, Billie.

BILLIE: Next year? What are you talking about, Jo?

JO: *Curtains.* We were talking about curtains, weren't we?

BILLIE: Yes. We were.

JO: Well, we'll hold off on new ones. For awhile, anyway.

BILLIE: Sure, Jo. Anything you say. I'll get the car. *(Exits.)*

JO: *(Alone. She crosses to window and gently touches the curtains.)* Maybe . . . maybe in the spring. I mean, they're no bad. Not really. Not *all* bad. A little worn, perhaps. A little frayed. But, they're familiar—comfortable. Easy to come home to. Easy on the eye. I mean, they still have some wear in them. Some life. Don'tcha think?

Slow FADE to BLACK perhaps to the music of Elvis Presley's "Don't Be Cruel."

END *Tough Cookies*

VAMPYRE HOLIDAY

SYNOPSIS: 1M/1W, No Set except a loveseat. Approx. 10 minutes.
Bambi has applied for the job of nanny to Santa's elves. Santa isn't all he seems and neither is Bambi. There's mystery and comedy afoot for the Holidays.

AT RISE: The set consists of a loveseat. SANTA is dressed in his traditional red suit. BAMBI wears a frilly, girlish dress. She's a bit of an air-head.

BAMBI: *(Standing somewhere.)* Thank you for coming all this way just to see me.

SANTA: No problem.

BAMBI: You saved me from schlepping all the way to Poland.

SANTA: Poland!?

BAMBI: Isn't the North Pole in Poland?

SANTA: It's an easy mistake. It must be a challenge being you.

BAMBI: Gracious. It is, Mister Clause.

SANTA: *(Sitting on loveseat. Correcting her.)* Klaus. Herr Klaus.

BAMBI: I beg your pardon.

SANTA: The Klaus family hails from the Black Forest of Deutschland. We changed the family name during the first half of the twentieth century—for obvious reasons.

BAMBI: Of course. Obviously. *(After a confounded pause.)* So, what were the obvious reasons?

SANTA: Letters from children dropped off considerably, especially from Eastern Europe—two letters and they were poison pen letters.

BAMBI: How could you tell the pen was poisoned?

SANTA: *(A pause to size her up.)* I couldn't till the goat ate them and died.

BAMBI: That's really sad.

SANTA: Yes . . . it was. Tragic, Bambi dear. I was almost demoted from a Christmas icon to a Halloween bogyman.

BAMBI: *Oh, dear,* Mister Herr Klaus.

SANTA: Santa. Just call me Santa. *Ho-ho-ho.* Your house was on my delivery route so I thought I'd make a quick stop.

BAMBI: How very thoughtful. I really want to make a good first impression—Santa.

SANTA: You already have, Bambi. What a lovely name, my dear.

BAMBI: Thank you. My parents gave it to me.

SANTA: Did they? How very generous.

BAMBI: Yes. When I was born, I think.

SANTA: As early as that?

BAMBI: I'm not sure, but it must have been a long time ago since I don't remember not being Bambi.

SANTA: That's hard to imagine.

BAMBI: What is?

SANTA: It was that long ago.

BAMBI: Although they did call me Bam for short—until I got taller, that is. Well, I never did get tall, but enough not to be called Bam anymore. Then it was Bambi all the way.

SANTA: Remarkable.

BAMBI: It is, isn't it?

SANTA: It definitely is. Tell me, Bambi, what is your experience with elves?

BAMBI: I've always liked elves—little people. I've always had a fondness for little people. They make me feel tall. You know, without having to wear uncomfortable heels. I have such tender feet. That's why I applied for the position.

SANTA: Because of your tender feet?

BAMBI: Because of being short.

SANTA: Short. Yes, it is a position that calls for someone not too tall, but not too short. You seem to fit the bill. They need someone to look up to. Ceilings are low in the elf quarters. They hide in all sorts of places.

BAMBI: Who hides in all sorts of places?

SANTA: The elves. It might come in handy to wear heels when they get into the cupboards and such. Otherwise I'd say you're the right height for an elfin nanny.

BAMBI: That's so good to know because I've always wanted to be an elfin nanny. Ever since I can remember that's been my life's dream.

SANTA: Good, good. We must follow our dreams, mustn't we?

BAMBI: If we must, we must.

SANTA: Do you really think you have what it takes to be a nanny to the elves?

BAMBI: Whatever it takes, I've got it.

SANTA: Yes, I can see that. You will be required to sleep days and work nights. The elves work only in the night. They are my children of the night—so to speak.

BAMBI: Goodness gracious. I don't have a problem with that.

SANTA: They can get pretty rambunctious. They can be difficult. Test your nerves. *Ho-ho-ho.* Do you still want the job? Have you the nerves for it?

BAMBI: Oh, I do. I really do. I mean, I've got some.

SANTA: Quite obvious, indeed.

BAMBI: Oh, Santa. I'd love working for you. More than ever. You know what?

SANTA: That depends on the nature of the *what.*

BAMBI: I could sing the elves to sleep every morning.

SANTA: I'm sure they would like that.

BAMBI: *(Sings – badly.)* Jingle bells, jingle bells/jingle all the way/oh what fun it is to ride in a one horse . . .

SANTA: *(Cutting her off.)* Thank you, thank you. *Humming.* The elves really like humming.

BAMBI: I'll hum like a bird—a humming bird.

SANTA: Indeed you will.

BAMBI: Where are my manners? Would you care for some coffee, Santa?

SANTA: No, no, my dear. I love coffee, but I can only drink it when the world is asleep.

BAMBI: The world? Asleep? Surely there is always somebody awake in the world. *Goodness.* I mean, the world is a big place.

SANTA: Most assuredly. *Ho-ho-ho.* But I am Santa and Santa needs a safe haven from the sound of Human thought. Human minds are never still and their sounds confound and destroy the creative process.

BAMBI: That pretty much rules out coffee, doesn't it? *(A beat.)* Creative process?

SANTA: Toy design. Delivery routes. Organizing the elves. Managing the whole Christmas thing. Reindeer flying exercises. Dry runs in the snow. Dry runs when there isn't any snow. Dry runs in the rain.

BAMBI: Dry runs in the rain?

SANTA: The reindeer wear rain coats.

BAMBI: That's so sweet.

SANTA: And so are you, my dear.

BAMBI: *Gracious me.*

SANTA: One must be prepared for all kinds of weather. Testing the atmosphere for friction. Avoiding hot spots —trying not to get shot down. It all takes a tremendous amount of talent and creativity. There are so many things to do—it's all very draining.

BAMBI: Draining? Yes, I imagine it is—draining.

SANTA: *Ho-ho-ho.*

BAMBI: There must be something I can offer a big strapping, red-blooded man like you. A candy cane? A ginger snap? Perhaps some eggnog?

SANTA: No, no, my dear Bambi. They all sound delightful. 'Though eggnog has been known to give a body heartburn.

BAMBI: I can leave out the nog.

SANTA: You can do that?

BAMBI: *(A pause to think about it.)* I don't know. Maybe not. I'll Google it. *(Sits on loveseat next to SANTA.)* I feel like a terrible hostess. There must be something you would like.

SANTA: *(Moving closer to her. Hand on her knee.)* There is.

BAMBI: Are you making advances towards me, Mister Herr Klaus?

SANTA: *(Sternly.)* Santa.

BAMBI: Santa—are you making advances towards me?

SANTA: Well—if you want the job . . .

BAMBI: *(Removing his hand.)* Isn't there a Missus Herr Klaus?

SANTA: There was a Frau Klaus—as I recall.

BAMBI: Was?

SANTA: She wanted to get as far away from me as possible. That's why I put the notice on Craig's List for a nanny. She moved to the South Pole.

BAMBI: And that's not in Poland, is it?

SANTA: It certainly is not. It's at the furthermost bottom of the world.

BAMBI: *Goodness.* That's about as far away as a body can get. How come she wanted to get away, if you don't mind me asking?

SANTA: There's some bad blood between us.

BAMBI: Bad blood?

SANTA: Really bad, if you know what I mean.

BAMBI: I'm sure I ought to, but I'm not so sure that I do. *(A ponderous pause.)* Are you telling me you're—free?

SANTA: *(Moves closer to BAMBI.)* As free as a bat. Ho-ho-ho.

BAMBI: A bat?

SANTA: As I said before, in my line of work I'm only up when the world sleeps—checking my list then checking it twice. It takes me nearly a year just to get through the list. I hate lists. And then, of course, there is my annual long night of deliveries. *(A big sigh.)* My nights are filled with lists, bats and flying reindeer.

BAMBI: How awful it must be for you.

SANTA: And that is why I need a nanny for my elves.

BAMBI: *(A pause to observe SANTA.)* There's something wrong with this picture.

SANTA: What picture?

BAMBI: *(Dubiously.)* Are you really Santa?

SANTA: *Ho-ho-ho.*

BAMBI: Something just isn't right. *(She tugs on SANTA'S beard and it comes off in her hand.)* There. Just as I thought! You're not Santa.

SANTA: Of course I'm Santa.

BAMBI: You're not real!

SANTA: Am to. As real as you.

BAMBI: With a fake beard?

SANTA: I've always had a fake beard.

BAMBI: Get out of here.

SANTA: It's true. My long white beard is an urban myth—suburban and rural too. I never could grow a beard—genetic. In the old days I used to pluck Donner and Blitzen's white tail hairs and the Missus would weave them into a beard. Donner hated getting plucked. Blitzen didn't seem to mind. In fact, he seemed to like it.

BAMBI: I pluck my eyebrows, but that's not quite the same, is it?

SANTA: Not in the least. I'll tell you this.

BAMBI: What's that?

SANTA: Those tail hairs made me itch. They didn't smell too good either.

BAMBI: I can imagine. Although I'd prefer not to.

SANTA: Now I order my beards online. Suits too—since the little woman went south.

BAMBI: *Goodness gracious.* Little Bambi's head is spinning like a top from all this new information. I seem to be over-stimulated.

SANTA: *(Moves closer to BAMBI and removes his cap.)* Over-stimulated, you say?

BAMBI: *(Takes a long, hard look at SANTA. Nearly swooning.)* Oh, dear. Gracious me. I'm in a tither and I'm so confused.

SANTA: Of course you are.

BAMBI: Does it show?

SANTA: Not at all. That's the great thing about tithers and dithers. No one is ever sure when you're in one.

BAMBI: I never knew that.

SANTA: It's not something most folks talk about. Most like to keep it to themselves—and take pills for it. *Ho-ho-ho.*

BAMBI: Well, I have no intention of taking any pills.

SANTA: Good for you. Leave them alone and they'll go away wagging their tails behind them.

BAMBI: That's funny, *(Sizing up SANTA. After a pause.)* You're so much younger than I expected.

SANTA: You were expecting a geezer?

BAMBI: Well, sort of. A big jolly man whose belly shakes like Jello.

SANTA: *(Squeezes his belly.)* See. All padding. *Ho-ho-ho.*

BAMBI: Ho-ho-ho indeed. But nice, really nice.

SANTA: Live and learn, I say. Live and learn.

BAMBI: Tell me the truth. Who are you?

SANTA: I'm Santa.

BAMBI: But you're so young, so good looking, so—

SANTA: Unexpected?

BAMBI: Yes. How is it you're so unexpected—I mean young?

SANTA: Fat, jolly and old—another myth. I never age.

BAMBI: You don't age?

SANTA: Not in over a hundred and fifty years.

BAMBI: I find that hard to believe.

SANTA: Is it easier to believe a jolly old fat man hasn't aged in over a hundred and fifty years?

BAMBI: Since you put it that way—

SANTA: *Ho-ho-ho.*

BAMBI: It must be nice not to age.

SANTA: Nice, indeed. *(Snuggles up to BAMBI.)*

BAMBI: You *are* making advances towards me, aren't you?

SANTA: Well, the wife went south and . . . I was thinking about it—yes.

BAMBI: You stop it right now. I'm not the kind of girl you think I am.

SANTA: *Ho-ho-ho.* What kind of girl is that?

BAMBI: *Easy.* I'm not easy, Mister Herr Klaus, or whoever you are. Stop seducing me. I only wanted to be your nanny. I mean, nanny to your elves. I will have no seduction going on around here, sir.

SANTA: The seduction is the most pleasant part of the game, isn't it?

BAMBI: What game?

SANTA: The magical game of love and life.

BAMBI: You have much experience with the seduction?

SANTA: I seduce the elves and the muses.

BAMBI: The elves? *Yuk!* No wonder Missus Frau Klaus went south.

SANTA: It gets lonely at the North Pole.

BAMBI: What do you use for bait?

SANTA: Bait?

BAMBI: For the seduction.

SANTA: For the elves I use cookies. Chocolate chip. They do love their chocolate chip cookies. And for the muses I simply use my enormous talent. *Ho-ho-ho!*

BAMBI: You have an enormous talent?

SANTA: Immeasurable.

BAMBI: *Immeasurable?*

SANTA: Too big to measure.

BAMBI: *Oh, my. Oh, dear. Oh, goodness.*

SANTA: I am considered by many to be endowed with

BAMBI: *(Swooning - expectantly.) Yes? Yes?*

SANTA: Genius.

BAMBI: *(After a pause to exhale.)* Seductive bait, indeed. Alas, I shall never get the opportunity to see your —genius in action. *(After a pause to regain her composure.)* Delivering your stuff to all those good little girls and boys.

SANTA: Of course you will. It's almost midnight. You could come with me tonight. Have you ever wanted to fly?

BAMBI: Hasn't everybody?

SANTA: Absolutely. Let's take to the sky.

BAMBI: No. Not tonight. Tonight is out of the question.

SANTA: There's always next year. *(Puts his hand on her knee.)*

BAMBI: *For some.* Other than wooing me with your lovely smile and those beautiful coal-black eyes of yours, not to mention your enormous genius I'll never get to see in action.

SANTA: I could show you if you like.

BAMBI: I'll just have to take your word for it, Santa. *(After a gimlet-eyed pause.)* Just how many unsuspecting women have you seduced?

SANTA: I really can't say.

BAMBI: *That many? (Removes his hand. Rises and moves about the room.)*

SANTA: I'm afraid you're the first—since the Missus went down under . . . deep down under.

BAMBI: Poor Santa baby. It must be so lonely for you.

SANTA: Well, there are the elves.

BAMBI: Are they good company?

SANTA: Only when they're drinking.

BAMBI: How sad.

SANTA: It's not all bad. Only sometimes—it sucks.

BAMBI: I'm sure it does.

SANTA: *(Checking watch.)*   Well, it's about time to make my delivery. *Ho-ho-ho and Merry Christmas!*

BAMBI: *Humbug.*

SANTA: *Huh?*

BAMBI: Goodness gracious, Mister Herr Klaus. You're not going to like this, but—

(BAMBI has positioned herself behind the loveseat. She bares her deadly fangs and with one quick swoop she sinks her teeth into his neck. THE LIGHTING dims to the sound of SANTA'S screams.)

BLACK OUT.

END—*Vampyre Holiday*

WHISKERS

2M, No Set. Timtu Chatterley, a finicky Siamese, and Tom, the street-smart alley cat, meet in the parking lot of a hospital where Timtu's mistress, Lady Chatterley, is a patient. A clash of cultures ensues between the haves and have-nots, the entrapped and the free spirit.

The TIME is early evening. The ACTION takes place in the parking lot of a city hospital—in and around parked cars.

TIMTU is sitting on a ladder overlooking TOM, who is rummaging through a garbage can. TIMTU surveys his surroundings from atop the ladder. They take their time and go about their business before TOM speaks.

TOM: *(Turns from garbage and spots TIMTU.)* Hey! You in the car!

TIMTU: *(Reluctant.)* Are you meowing to me?

TOM: *Yeah.* I'm meowing to you.

TIMTU: Well, *um* . . . hello.

TOM: *(Crossing toward TIMTU.)* Come out of that car.

TIMTU: I'm afraid I can't do that.

TOM: Yes you can. Get on outta there.

TIMTU: I can't.

TOM: Kitty kitty *can't?*

TIMTU: I can, too. I'm just not supposed to.

TOM: You always do what you're 'sposed to?

TIMTU: I try.

TOM: How hard?

TIMTU: Hard enough.

TOM: Hardly enough.

TIMTU: I do what is expected . . . most of the time.

TOM: You look like an "all the time" cat to me.

TIMTU: I don't like to brag.

TOM: Ain't that grand.

TIMTU: If I didn't do what they expected, they wouldn't keep me around, now would they?

TOM: You tell me.

TIMTU: No, they wouldn't. So I maintain a low profile. Below the radar. Keep to myself. Don't make waves. Respect the status quo. Give them no excuse to . . .

TOM: To . . . ?

TIMTU: I don't want to find out.

TOM: What kind of people they are?

TIMTU: They're good people.

TOM: That kind of people, *huh?*

TIMTU: They're not *that* kind of people.

TOM: They certainly are that kind of people.

TIMTU: You tell me what kind of people!

TOM: Unforgiving. Go to church on Sunday so's they can gossip about who wasn't there and how short So-and-So's skirt was and how hung-over Old Such-and-Such looked . . . that kind of people.

TIMTU: The best kind of people. Upright. Upstanding.

TOM: Uppitty. Uptight.

TIMTU: They pay their bills on time. They go to party caucuses.

TOM: Of caucus they do.

TIMTU: They do what's expected of them, and I do what's expected of me because they expect me to do it.

TOM: Gotta love the logic. What exactly do they expect?

TIMTU: Use the litter box. Stay off the coffee table, the furniture, the laps of others. Never stray . . . De-clawed.

TOM: Oh, man!

TIMTU: You get used to it.

TOM: Neutered, too, right?

TIMTU: Naturally.

TOM: Unnaturally, you mean.

TIMTU: Twice, in fact.

TOM: Don't tell me you have... had...

TIMTU: First time didn't take.

TOM: *Phew.*

TIMTU: They cut the wrong thing.

TOM: What thing?

TIMTU: I don't know. They never mention it.

TOM: *(Losing patience.)* Are you going to come out of that car?

TIMTU: *Why?*

TOM: So we can meow like brothers.

TIMTU: I can meow from here.

TOM: *Nah.* We can't have no confidentiality with you in there and me out here. 'Sides, we don't want to disturb the hospital patients, now do we?

TIMTU: I didn't think of that.

TOM: Time to start thinkin', brother. *(A pause to wait for him to come out of the car.)* Well?

TIMTU: Well what?

TOM: You coming out or you want me to come in? *(Approaching him.)*

TIMTU: *No!* You can't come in here. This is my mistress's car.

TOM: Whose?

TIMTU: The lady of the house . . . Lady Chatterley.

TOM: Some lady. She drives last year's model . . . and foreign, to boot.

TIMTU: Honey Buns gave it to her when he got the new Cat-ill-ac.

TOM: You mean Cad-ill-ac.

TIMTU: I mean, Cat-ill-ac.

TOM: You're a real laugh riot, ya know that? I take it Honey Buns is her awful lawful wedded?

TIMTU: He's the man of the house. Lord of the manor, he calls himself. But I belong to Lady Chatterley.

TOM: Cats ain't 'sposed to belong to nobody.

TIMTU: She pets me and grooms me and calls me "Lady Chatterley's poody cat."

TOM: *Whoa.* She's out of it, huh?

TIMTU: She's very affectionate.

TOM: No doubt. *(An introspective pause.)* I've been called worse.

TIMTU: By whom?

TOM: Get you. *By whom.* Ain't you the royal puss.

TIMTU: I am, actually. Siamese, you know. Descended from royalty.

TOM: But of course, your highness. The night you were born the stork took a detour. *(After a pause.)* So. You coming out or am I coming in?

TIMTU: I can't have guests getting fur all over the seats. Besides, you're not declawed.

TOM: You better believe I'm not. So come out.

TIM: Only for a short while.

TOM: As long as you like.

TIMTU: *(Prepares to jump.)* Here I come. I'm going to jump. *(Hesitant.)*

TOM: OK . . . so jump already.

TIMTU: I'm trying.

TOM: Come on. Piece o' cake.

TIMTU: I can't.

TOM: Reason being…?

TIMTU: Suppose I can't get back in?

TOM: You'll get back in.

TIMTU: You don't know that. There's a certain probability that once I'm out I won't be able to get back in. Then where will I be?

TOM: Where do you think you'll be?

TIMTU: Stranded. I'll be stranded.

TOM: No sweat. I'll help you.

TIMTU: How?

TOM: *(Losing patience.)* I don't know how because it ain't happened yet.

TIMTU: How can you help me if you don't know how?

TOM: I'll think of a way.

TIMTU: When?

TOM: When I need to.

TIMTU: Suppose Honey Buns comes back before you think of a way?

TOM: He won't.

TIMTU: You can't know that. Suppose he does? Suppose he leaves without me? Suppose some stranger finds me and picks me up for a stray before Honey Buns discovers I'm missing? Or suppose no one at all finds me? Oh, Feline! Nobody finds me and then I'm lost. Out in the cold. No hearth, no home, no Fancy Feast. Suppose when he comes back to find me I'm not here? Suppose he doesn't come back . . .

TOM: *(Harshly.)* Suppose the world ends tomorrow!

TIMTU: The world couldn't possibly end tomorrow!

TOM: Right. And you couldn't possibly get lost. *(Relents)* OK, look. If you jump out and stay near the car -- as soon as you hear Honey Buns coming, you jump on the hood, then to the roof, and then you slip back in through the window. How's that sound?

TIMTU: Sensible.

TOM: Never been called that before.

TIMTU: OK. Here I come. *(Jumps from ladder.)*

TOM: Doesn't that feel better?

TIMTU: No.

TOM: Sure it does! You're free now.

TIMTU: I don't feel free.

TOM: You do. You just don't know it yet. It'll grow on you, you'll see. (Observing collar.) Nice collar. Real rhinestones, I bet.

TIMTU: Probably. I don't know.

TOM: Of course, you don't. *(A beat.)* So, what's your handle?

TIMTU: Pardon me?

TOM: Your name. What's your fuzzle-lovin' name?

TIMTU: You don't have to swear. It's Timtu Chatterley.

TOM: Tim Two?? Oh. I get it. Cuz of those two operations. They shoulda called you Tim Zip.

TIMTU: *Huh??*

TOM: *(A pause to stare at TIMTU expectantly.)* OK. Thank you for asking, *Tim Two.* My name is Thomas Q. Hunnicut the Third.

TIMTU: Impressive!

TOM: Get real. I ain't swanky like you. Just plain Tom. That's me.

TIMTU: Hi, Tom.

TOM: Hello, Tim Two. *(Licks his fists and wipes them on TIM's head. Proudly.)* Now you're 'nitiated. Do you know what I am?

TIMTU: *(Pause)* Domestic?

TOM: *(Angered)* Why are cats so quick to judge? *(Mimics)* Domestic? Why can't you meow what you really think?

TIMTU: What do I *really* think?

TOM: You should know.

TIMTU: Apparently, I don't.

TOM: What was it they snipped 'fore they got it right? All right, all right. I'm an alley cat! A great big, filthy, garbage-pickin' alley cat! You got a problem with that?

TIMTU: Most assuredly not.

TOM: Meow me alley.

TIMTU: I would never meow such a thing.

TOM: Meow it.

TIMTU: You're a bully, and I don't negotiate with bullies.

TOM: Meow it, I said, meow it! *Alley!*

TIMTU: *Alley.* Happy now?

TOM: Do I look happy?

TIMTU: I'm not judgmental, not in the least.. I was brought up better than that.

TOM: Oh, man. You are . . . yes, you definitely are. You are indeed . . .

TIMTU: What? What?

TOM: Whipped. That Lady Chatterley, she owns you, cat.

TIM: Of course she does.

TOM: And you're cool with that?

TIMTU: Better than living in an, an . . .

TOM: An, an, an . . . alley? Is that what you're trying to meow?

TIMTU: I'm sorry.

TOM: For meowing alley? Or thinking alley?

TIMTU: I don't know?

TOM: Maybe you need to figure that out.

TIMTU: I will. OK?

TOM: I got nothin' but time. *(After a pause.)* Do you want to do it?

TIMTU: Do what?

TOM: A little sniff . . .

TIMTU: Certainly not!

TOM: Don't want to fuzzle?

TIMTU: *No. No fuzzling.*

TOM: How come?

TIMTU: I told you I was neutered.

TOM: Twice.

TIMTU: Besides, it wouldn't be right, now would it?

TOM: Excuuuuse me. I forgot that you're Siamese and I'm common domestic.

TIMTU That's not it.

TOM: Rat droppings!

TIMTU: It's simply not done.

TOM: Think you're too good?

TIMTU: No. It's just that you're . . . well, you're a male and I'm a male.

TOM: *Hello!* I get that!

TIMTU: It's simply not done, that's all.

TOM: Not done by . . . *whom?*

TIMTU: By anybody. By proper, well-bred cats.

TOM: *Well-bred, indeed.* It's done all the time. You're a cat and nobody cares what cats do.

TIMTU: They most certainly do!

TOM: Garbage! It's different when you're a cat. If you were people and I were people, they might say, "Look at the public fuzzilators!" But we ain't. We're cats. No one cares. Instead, they say things like, "Aren't they naughty" or "Isn't that cute?" They never say, "Look at the fuzzilators."

TIMTU: You may have a point. I never thought about it that way.

TOM: Tim Two, there's a lot you haven't thought about.

TIMTU: You needn't be rude.

TOM: No. I *must* be.

TIMTU: *(After a pause.)* OK. I have given the matter some thought.

TOM: And?

TIMTU: If you want to.

TOM: Are you sure? You're not gonna get bent out of shape or somethin'?

TIMTU: I won't, but I don't want you to think I'm . . . you know.

TOM: Prejudiced?

TIMTU: I wouldn't meow that.

TOM: Of course you wouldn't. You're royalty. You're Lady Chatterley's royal little poody cat.

TIMTU: That's unfair.

TOM: I don't have your hang-ups, pretty poody. I can tell you that. Us alley cats don't strut around with our noses higher than our tails.

TIMTU: I don't, either. I don't think I'm any better than you. We're just different. I'm Siamese and I've never come face to face, nose to nose, paw to paw with . . . a member of the domestic family. I mean, alley.

TOM: Now you have. *(Taking a sniff.)*

TIMTU: Now I have. *(Sniffing back.)*

TOM: *(Sniffing.)* You smell like television, wax paper and fish from a can.

TIMTU: *(Insulted. Sniffing himself.)* I don't smell anything.

TOM: Nobody smells their own stink. *(A beat.)* We happen to be the majority, you know. *(Sniffing.)*

TIMTU: I didn't know.

TOM: That's a fact, Jack! *(Stops sniffing.)*

TIMTU: Strange, your being in the majority. I never really thought that domestic . . . I mean, *alley* cats were all that common. Not *common*. That's not what I meant at all. Oh, some days there are simply too many words with too many meanings. I only meant . . . there are a lot of you, aren't there?

TOM: What of it?

TIMTU. I'm merely making an observation.

TOM: Wanna know why there's a lot of us?

TIMTU: Does it matter?

TOM: Not to you, apparently.

TIMTU: I don't think it matters, period. If you're in the majority, you're in the majority and that's all there is to it. That's lovely. You have no end of company.

TOM: *Yeah* . . . no end of starving, mangy, lice-infected, homeless company!

TIMTU: I didn't mean it that way. You don't make the best of what I say.

TOM: Fuzzle you, nobody's poody cat!

TIMTU: I'm sorry.

TOM: For not caring?

TIMTU: I care! Don't misjudge me. I care! I care for cats all over the world, whoever or whatever they may be.

TOM: Rat droppings!

TIMTU: Don't blame me. I had nothing to do with your station in life. You chose it.

TOM: Did I now?

TIMTU: I'm not responsible.

TOM: You got that right.

TIMTU: You make me sound . . .

TOM: Insincere?

TIMTU: Unfeeling.

TOM: Imagine that. Imagine if you really cared. Imagine how there might be less of us mangy domestics and more of you sleek fat cats with sharp blue eyes. *Yeah, you care all right.* I can smell the care all over you. Hoo-eee! what a stench! But chew on this, Mr. Tim Two Chatterley. One day it will all be ours. Tomorrow belongs to the dregs, the outcasts! One day you'll look out from your warm cozy home and you'll see us snarling on your doorstep for everything you have. You, Lord Honey Buns and Lady Chatterley!

TIMTU: Fine, fine! Can we meow about something else?

TOM: We can. What would you like to meow about?

TIMTU: Something pleasant.

TOM: Avoidance.

TIMTU: There's no sense in talking about what I can't do anything about.

TOM: You're a prince. *(A beat.)* Do you want to hear a story?

TIMTU: If you've got one.

TOM: I got one all right. I got one. Let's see . . . I have this friend. Well, more than a friend. I love her.

TIMTU: A love story. How divine.

TOM: Don't start purring too soon 'cause it ain't a love story -- no way.

TIMTU: It isn't?

TOM: She's a dog.

TIMTU: I'm sure she's not as bad as all that.

TOM: You dumb mouse brain! Not *that* kind of a dog! A real dog. *Arf, arf.* She's a genuine, first-class canine. Don't you get it? Oh, what's the use? Nobody cares -- especially cats!

TIMTU: The story. What about the story?

TOM: That's it. I told you the whole fuzzilating story in a nutshell. Weren't you listening?

TIMTU: Of course I was listening.

TOM: You don't hear much, I'll tell you that! *(A beat.)* We'd be barked at and meowed at wherever we went by dogs and cats just like yourself!

TIMTU: I'd never meow at you.

TOM: Rat droppings! *(A beat.)* So, how's life?

TIMTU: Life?

TOM: Keep up.

TIMTU: I don't follow.

TOM: Of course you do. I said, how's life on your side of the fence?

TIMTU: Pleasant enough.

TOM: What's ol' Honey Buns like?

TIMTU: He's OK. He feeds me regularly. Empties the litter box. But he leaves me alone most of the time . . . since my mistress took ill. Perhaps he's depressed. Honey Buns thinks she is going to die. I heard him talking to somebody named Insurance.

TOM: Insurance ain't a name.

TIMTU: I know what I heard.

TOM: I doubt that.

TIMTU: He'll probably take it hard if she dies. She's always telling him he has a weak backbone. I guess if she passes -- *it* and *he* will break.

TOM: So he's visiting her in the hospital?

TIMTU: Yes. He comes every night. This is the first time he brought me. I sensed that he was very lonely.

TOM: He should have brought Insurance with him.

TIMTU: No. I heard him tell Insurance if anything should happen, he'll get in touch.

TOM: And anything means?

TIMTU: You know . . . in case she dies. But I don't like to think about that. How about you? Did you ever have a mistress or a master?

TOM: Once. Not exactly. It was my mother who did. A master *and* a mistress. After I was born they kept me for awhile; the master and the mistress.

TIMTU: Awhile?

TOM: Not long. Some of the other cats think I don't remember my mother. But, I do. A cat don't forget his mother. I remember my mother and my brothers and my sisters. What I remember most is my master and mistress. I mean, my mother's master and mistress and how they . . . it wasn't that long ago, you know.

TIMTU: I can see you're not that old.

TOM: What the fuzzle do you know? *Huh? What the fuzzle do you know about anything?*

TIMTU: I like to believe I know a thing or two about the world we inhabit.

TOM: You know rat droppings! You're one dead pussy!

TIMTU: I'm not dead.

TOM: Coulda fooled me.

TIMTU: If you wish me to return to the car, I will.

TOM: No. You need to hear this. You need to hear how us *domestic* types live and die. *(After a pause.)* My mother. All that pain.

TIMTU: I'm afraid I don't understand.

TOM: Try listening! *(Dreamy)* I remember her purring. She had a beautiful purr . . . so warm, so loving. I can still hear it. When she was begging behind the super market, eating from the dumpsters, running from vicious brats with rocks and firecrackers, dodging cars trying to run her over ... she purred. She fuzzling purred. She had that kind of disposition. From inside the pillowcase I heard my mother purring . . . until she realized . . .

TIMTU: Forgive me, but now I am truly lost. Pillow-case?

TOM: Never mind. Fuzzle off.

TIMTU: Realized what?

TOM: Fuzzle you!

TIMTU: Pardon me, but you started this. If you're going to tell me, then kindly tell me!

TOM: She stopped purring when she realized they had put us in a pillowcase, tied it up and held us underwater in the bathtub. There's a master and a mistress for you. There were eight of us. We were pretty big by then, so when that sack hit the water we fought to get out. Scrambling and scratching and clawing onto one another's backs. We can be cruel that way. And me, well, I was the biggest. So I managed to claw my way to the top. That's the only way when you're fighting to stay alive . . . you claw your way to the top or you die.

TIMTU: *(After a pause.)* They drowned?

TOM: Of course they drowned, you stupid know-nothing!

TIMTU: There's no need for you to get personal.

TOM: There ain't no other way. It's all personal. What's a life if it ain't personal?

TIMTU: I really couldn't say. Pray, continue with your story.

TOM: The story of a life. My personal life. Where were we?

TIMTU: You clawed your way to the top and your poor siblings drowned.

TOM: Then, the master or the mistress -- I could only hear their whispers -- carried the sack to the garbage can and dumped us all out. Did you ever smell death?

TIMTU: Most assuredly not!.

TOM: *(Musing)* I guess they needed the pillowcase back. Personally, I can't imagine sleeping on a pillowcase that was used as a death chamber. But then, I'm a mighty finicky cat. Anyway, I could hear my mother back in the house, screeching and meowing something terrible. I don't know what ever happened to her. But I was alive. I'd managed to crawl my way to the top. Over the dying bodies of my brothers and sisters.

TIMTU: *(After a thoughtful pause.)* How would you like to come home with me? We have a lovely big apartment, and it does get lonely sometimes.

TOM: I doubt Lord Honey Buns and Lady Chatterley would take to the likes of me. For one thing, I'm not Siamese. No royalty here.

TIMTU: No, but you're my friend. If you get in the car with me and purr and beg most beseechingly when he comes, how could he possibly say no?

TOM: Easy. You and your ilk are too swell for the likes of me.

TIMTU: You shouldn't put yourself down like that.

TOM: Is that what you think I'm doing? For the love of Feline, get fuzzled!

TIMTU: I think you need a proper home. One with delicious, nutritious food. Canned tuna. Canned sardines. The real thing.

TOM: What do you know about the *real* thing?

TIMTU: I'm attempting to be nice.

TOM: I get great food, too, you know. You're not the only one. It's mostly catch as catch can, though, if you know what I mean. Hey! How would you like to join me in a *real* dinner, some *cuisine de allee?*

TIMTU: I just ate. I'm not . . .

TOM: It's on me. *(Crosses to garbage can.)* I was going to save this for later, *(He pulls out the skeleton of a large fish.)* but I'd rather share it with you.

TIMTU: *No.* No thank you.

TOM: You ain't gonna share a meal with me?

TIMTU: Really I . . . I ate just before we left home.

TOM: Wait.

TIMTU: What?

TOM: *Shhh. (He slowly sneaks around the garbage can, then pounces on a mouse.) Got ya! (Holds the mouse by the tail and displays it like a trophy to TIMTU.)* Like it?

TIMTU: What is it?

TOM: Good Feline, cat! It's a nice big, tasty mouse.

TIMTU: *Ugh.* I wouldn't eat that if I were starving.

TOM: *(Taunting TIMTU with the mouse.)* Mousey, mousey.

TIMTU: Stop it! Get that filthy, disgusting thing away from me.

TOM: *(Throws mouse at the garbage can.)* Better?

TIMTU: Yes.

TOM: Who the fuzzle do you think you are!? You're mouse droppings if I ever met one. Feline, you make me sick!

TIMTU: *(Sotto voce.)* I really did eat, you know.

TOM: Sure.

TIMTU: I didn't mean to offend you.

TOM: You couldn't. Don't get your whiskers in a twist.

TIMTU: My whiskers?

TOM: *Yeah,* those nice, long whiskers of yours.

TIMTU: All cats have whiskers.

TOM: Well, sport, maybe we got something in common after all. *Whiskers.* Only mine's a bit scruffy.

TIMTU: Not too scruffy. A bit shorter than most.

TOM: That's because I actually use 'em. They serve a purpose, you know. There's lotsa times you gotta squeeze through narrow places when somebody's chasing you or throwing water on you. Then there's all those other cats who just want to fight you.

TIMTU: Why?

TOM: I ain't figured that one out yet. Some cats just like to fight. It's their nature.

TIMTU: I want you to know that I think your whiskers are perfectly fine. They get the job done. That's all that matters, isn't it?

TOM: Ain't you sweet. They kind of make us brothers, don't they?

TIMTU: I think it takes more than whiskers.

TOM: You think? *Hallelujah!* The poody cat thinks!

TIMTU: After all, it's not as if we all come from the same litter. We can't go around calling every cat with whiskers our brother, now can we?

TOM: Why not?

TIMTU: It's just not . . .

TOM: What? *(Gazing out beyond parking lot.)*

TIMTU: Realistic.

TOM: I came to that conclusion long ago.

TIMTU: Nor practical.

TOM: Nope.

TIMTU: There you have it.

TOM: Darn tootin'.

TIMTU: You don't have to be sarcastic. You could show more appreciation for one who is trying to give you a paw up in this world.

TOM: A paw up? *Wow.* Ain't you something.

TIMTU: I don't see what you're . . .

TOM: *(Cutting him off.)* What makes you think I need a paw up in this world? *Huh?* Fuzzle off, poody cat! You got to be the dumbest pile of rat droppings I ever met. No! *Never* met. You're so deep into yourself there's nothing for anyone to meet. And if they did meet you, really see you for what you are, they'd puke.

TIMTU: That's it! I've had quite enough. I've listened most politely to you. I've been kind and considerate. I invited you to my home, and you insult me.

TOM: Did I?

TIMTU: You and your type. Vile vagrants. Utterly useless. You terrorize well-bred, well-meaning cats, and then you blame everyone but yourselves for your station in life! You make me sick!

TOM: Wow, that's a hundred and eighty-degree turn if ever I saw one. *Whoops,* I just got a glimpse of the poody cat wonder.

TIMTU: You think you can take advantage of our friendship!

TOM: What friendship? You don't know the meaning of the word.

TIMTU: Do you know what you are? You're a nothing. A zero. A transient. Nobody wants you in their neighborhood.

TOM: *Ouch!* That's telling me.

TIMTU: You want other cats to feel sorry for you. You've intimidated and insulted me, and now you want me to feel sorry for you. This was your choice and your choice alone. I won't feel sorry for you.

TOM: Wait a minute, I don't want no cat feeling sorry for me! *(Pause.)* You're the pathetic low life, not me!

TIMTU: I have nothing against you, personally.

TOM: Here it comes.

TIMTU: But we are not brothers. We never were and we never will be.

TOM: And friends? I suppose that's out of the question.

TIMTU: Tom, I don't think it's going to work.

TOM: You mean, you don't want me to come home with you.

TIMTU: You wouldn't like it.

TOM: You got that right. Why, I've got the whole outdoors. That's where I belong. Where a cat with claws and other parts can roam at will. Outdoors. Not in some stuffy apartment with a deodorized litter box. Trust me, Tim Two, I understand.

TIMTU: Do you?

TOM: More than you want to know.

TIMTU: *(After a Pause. He's sensing something.)* He's coming. *(Sniffing the air.)* I best be going back in the vehicle now.

TOM: *(Watching him in the distance.)* So that's ol' Honey Buns.

TIMTU: Yes. The lord of the manor.

TOM: Looks like he's crying.

TIMTU: It does, doesn't it. Oh, dear.

TOM: Reminds me of my mother. No purr left. I guess he'll be calling his friend Insurance. Lady Chatterley has left the building.

TIMTU: That means . . . that means I'm all he's got.

TOM: *(With a smirk.)* Isn't he lucky?

TIMTU: Such a responsibility! I don't know if I can… Oh, dear. *(Crosses to ladder and starts to climb)* Hood . . . roof . . . in the window. There! I made it. *(Sits on top of ladder.)* That was touch and go.

TOM: Safe and sound now.

TIMTU: A cat could get himself killed in this neighborhood! With all due respect, of course.

TOM: Some cats are already dead. They just don't know when to stop meowing. With all due respect, of course. Anyway, smooth sailing, *bon voyage,* have a nice day and goodbye, Tim Two Chatterley.

TIMTU: Oh, dear. So now it's just me and Honey Buns. I do hope I can handle the responsibility. I do hope we can make this transition . . . I do hope . . .

TOM: You'll make a cute couple. *(Starts to walk away then he bursts out laughing)* Too fuzzling funny!

TIMTU: Whatever are you purring about?

TOM: Everything. The whole fuzzling idea of it. You.

TIMTU: What did I say? What's so funny?

TOM: I haven't a clue.

TIMTU: So?

TOM: So, what's expected of you now, Tim Two?

TIMTU: I wish I knew. Oh, the uncertainty . . . I'll just have to buck up and do the best I can. Show him how dependable I am. I'll meet -- no, I'll exceed! -- his every expectation.

TOM: You do that. *(Moves toward exit. Turns back.)* Hey!

TIMTU: What?

TOM: I'd avoid the pillow cases! *(Exits laughing.)*

TIMTU stares toward the emptiness where TOM once stood. LIGHTING dims to BLACK OUT.

END Whiskers

MONOLOGS

21 TODAY

21 TODAY (1M, No Set, 15-20 Minutes.) An edgy, chilling, adult monologue given by a serial killer. The audience, however, is never aware that the man is a serial killer until all the unsuspected pieces that had been hiding in plain sight fall together. Since you've already been told, much of the thrill and the shocking ending will be somewhat of a necessary spoiler.

The CHARACTER is a young man who can easily be taken for twenty-one. He should be charming and likable. He is surrounded in dark, addressing the audience.

I'm a regular guy. Regular things . . . sports, football, baseball, the ladies. I'm a regular lady killer, know what I mean? I watch my share of TV, but I'm no couch potato. I eat fast food, sometimes to excess, have a beer now and again, but never to excess and I'm into cars. Regular guy stuff, know what I mean? I'm really into traveling, seeing what there is to see, meeting folks along the way . . . especially the ladies.

Drove coast to coast in my Jeep exploring the wonders of America. Lots of wonders out there . . . New York City . . . not as bad as you heard. Disney World, not as good as you heard. The mighty Mississippi . . . big, but mighty muddy. The Rio Grande's not a river at all. Not by a long shot . . . a trickling stream, if you was to ask me. Las Vegas . . . that was a whole lot like Disney World, but with a lot of hookers. The Grand Canyon . . . that's a big hole in the ground, but it's pretty grand alright. And L.A., the City of Angels. If there be angels in Las Angeles they're not from where most people think they're from. You know, from upstairs. They're the other kind, from another place altogether, if you know what I mean.

So, here's the big news: *Twenty-one today.* A magic number, *huh? Twenty-one.* I like the sound of that.

Sure seemed to take a long time. It takes a lot of years when you go to adding them up. Know what I mean? And all the stuff you've got to get through to make it from there to here.

There are so many moments in a life you can never forget no matter how hard you try. They don't let loose. They're like scars. You look at them and you remember how you got every one of them. There's no forgetting. Nope. They're there and they never go away. The most indelible scars, those fucked up moments in your life, are the ones you come face to face with when somebody close to you dies . . . somebody you care about. You don't ever forget those moments. They're tattooed deep beneath the skin, those moments of death. They're always right there, staring you right in the face. *Scars*.

For instance, my mother. My mother and her fucking enemas. *Fucking enemas.* That's funny, isn't it? I mean, it's funny when you come to think about it, if you know what I mean. Ain't nobody that constipated. What the hell was she looking for? You'd think I'd swallowed gold nuggets or gold plated Cheerios or something. We all have our quirks, our little eccentricities, don't we?

I hadn't yet reached puberty when I got my first taste of death . . . my mother, the enema lady. You can be sure you'll never forget that sweet and pungent smell associated with death . . . the perfume of flowers mingling with the unmistakable odor of dead flesh into one overpowering scent. It stunk up the air in the parlor filled with strangers I never saw before and some family I never saw before, and they were all in mourning . . . all with their great big phony crocodile tears. *People* . . . they treat you like shit when you're alive and the minute you bite it they go all mushy and teary-eyed . . . then they go home, watch a little TV, go to bed, get up the next day and they can't remember your face or where they met you or who you were or why you were in their life in the first place. Just another day in Deadwood. You can't help but love them, can you? No man's an island, right? Some of the best times I ever had involved people.

What are you going to do without them, *huh?* You can't eat them, so you might as well love them.

So, there they all were wearing their solemn faces and such when somebody came up from behind and escorted me to the coffin to kiss my mother goodbye. Well, I didn't want to kiss that corpse, who the hell would? The hands that administered the enemas lay crossed upon her bosom. No way was I going to kiss them. Suddenly, a fat ham hock of a hand forced my head to bend and my lips to press hard upon her cold, waxen cheek . . . and there it was. There was that smell, sweet and pungent. Nobody is going to forget a thing like that. Nobody . . . and I can guarantee it. There's no forgetting decay.

After her death I went to live with my grandparents 'cause the old man was still in the army. They were good people, my grandparents. They tried to love me, but they never quite got 'round to it. I figure they never really felt it deep in that place that makes it real. You see, they couldn't accept that my mother committed suicide. They refused to believe it and so they could never bring themselves even close to saying the word "love" when it came to me. Not once did they ever say that word. I guess I was a constant reminder of what they wanted to bury in the back of their thoughts and so, at best, I became an object of their ambivalence. What the hell, love's nothing but a word used so often, over and over, it no longer means a thing . . . just another four letter word. But, we cry waiting for somebody to say it anyway.

Two weeks after the old lady went to greener pastures, if you believe in that kind of stuff, the old man was discharged from the army. That man would sooner kick you in the head than rub it. He really got off on torturing me. Tied me up, beat me up and bloodied me up. No respect for kids, if you know what I mean. I sure as hell don't know what made him so cruel, but he was one mean sonofabitch. So getting his comeuppance wasn't a surprise or a sad affair to anybody. He must have really rubbed somebody the wrong way 'cause his battered body with its smashed-in face not even a mother could recognize was found less than half a mile from the house . . . down by the watercress pond. Anyway, he was beaten to death with the bloody rock the police found a few feet from his body. His killer was never found. They looked alright, but he hasn't yet been found. And that's how I became acquainted with death and the smell of it.

Love, too, has a smell of its own. There was a blond girl with emerald eyes in junior high. One fall day after school she lured me down to the brook where the high school kids went to smoke during lunch hour. Nobody ever went there after school. Said she had something to show me. I told her I had something to show her too. She smelled like bubble gum and soap, yet her skin tasted like salt and freshly mowed grass. I know, 'cause . . . well, I don't have to tell you, do I? And her eyes . . . oh boy, those eyes . . . wide and unblinking, trying to figure me out, I guess. Her watery eyes with tiny golden flecks sparkled in the light of the setting sun as I watched her watching me. She was twelve. That's another magic number, isn't it?

Anyway, where was I? *Oh,* telling you about love. Years later love was in a clearing in the woods behind the old tire factory, long since closed and boarded up. The raven-headed girl lay on the ground silently as my hands reached under her dress and pushed her legs apart. She was trembling and she started to cry, but willing . . . maybe she was scared. You can never tell about a thing like that. This was all new to her and she wasn't sure what was going to happen next. You could smell the blood between her legs . . . like rusty iron. And the taste . . . *tinny.* It's a taste you don't forget. She was fifteen.

Year after year passed on my way to twenty-one and the girls became more frequent. The years were filled with the scent of sweet breath, peaches, moss, straw, cheap perfume and the tinny taste that lingers and, if only in the mind, never quite goes away.

All the girls had their own scent. That's how I remember each and every one of them. Every now and again I catch a whiff of *déjà vu*.

The girl without a smile, with the twisted foot and braces, was the saddest of all. I don't think anybody had ever touched her before. She gave herself over to me as if I were an angel come to save her . . . to take her away to a fairy castle and love her forever after. I like the thought of me being an angel, but I know better. Anyway, it didn't turn out that way. No castle, I couldn't save her and no love forever after. Fantasies and dreams of forever after never do come true, do they? I felt her sadness and pain and I almost told her that I loved her and, even though I did, I couldn't bring myself to it. She smelled like medicine . . . like the smell of a hospital room where a body lays waiting to be discovered. She was twenty.

Finally, late last night, early morning really, there was the tattooed girl who reeked of beer, urine, sweat and crack. What a shame. How does a person fall that far? What causes a person to care so little for themselves? She stumbled out the bar and I saw that she needed somebody to comfort her, to give her a sense of worth, but when I tried she ran like a wounded rabbit . . . screaming all the while, trying to get away, but she never did. They never do. When I caught up with her in the stench of the alley I grabbed hold of her . . . offered her my arms . . . and with a gripping embrace and a quick twist of her neck until you could hear it snap . . . breathlessly, her head fell forward . . . her dead body went limp and I let it fall to the ground. Then I shoved it into a dumpster and closed the lid. She was number twenty-one . . . *twenty-one today.*

Well, that's the story of my life. I'm just a regular guy who loves the ladies. Would you repeat that back to me?

"Regular guy, honest, dependable and never lies, loves moonlit walks, sports, traveling and good times, looking for same to share mutual interests. Willing to relocate for the lady of his dreams and to kill her with kindness." Perfect. That'll run in tomorrow's classifieds, right? What? No…that's it. Nothing else. Thank you very much.

END—*21 Today*

PINK GIN FOR THE BLUES

SYNOPSIS: 1M, Minimal Set. A monologue for a mature drag queen. Trick, a sadder but wiser drag queen, in her cups, sits at a bar where she pours her heart out about lost love and lost innocence.

The CHARACTER is Trick. Fifty-plus. Dressed in drag.

The SETTING is a bar counter with a stool facing the audience.

AT RISE – TRICK, a mature drag queen, sips a pink gin while seated on a stool at a bar, speaking to an invisible bartender.

TRICK: I don't know. Crime has become institutionalized, hasn't it? From the bottom to the top — everybody is doing it. Now, it's mostly white-collar, isn't it? That's a kind of drag, don'tcha think? White collar, silk tie and pin stripes or tweeds — it's all drag, sweetie. It's the CEOs and the politicians getting caught in the act now, isn't it? Of course, they've always been doing it, but most folks are pretty slow to catch on. We're either raping or looting or we're being raped and looted. We're either politicians or we're political prisoners.

No, no, no. This has nothing to do with anything, darling. Absolutely nothing to do with anything. Just the ramblings of an old drag queen. *I'm sorry.*

Some days I just get wrapped up in the world — this sorry, sorry world. Drag queens shouldn't be taken seriously, should they?

Oh, my dear, *you're looking particularly well this evening.*

(Sips gin.) Gin with a touch of bitters. It's called a pink gin. You don't get much call for it, I suppose. *Oh, the first?* Well, there you go. Maybe you won't soon forget me, *huh? The drag queen who rambles and drinks pink gins.*

What? I don't remember. Perhaps, it was something by Noel Coward. You know. They were all sitting around in lavishly appointed digs, posed in fabulous gowns and in elegant tuxedos, in glorious black and white and every shade of gray in between. There would always be one — and that one would be me — casually anchored to the fireplace, taking turns between sipping smoke through a long cigarette holder and inhaling gin and bitters, in a white satin gown with a plunging neckline. *Be still my heart! How posh is that?*

(Sips gin.) Tastes like pond scum! Well, at first, I mean. Then, one gets used to it and, before you know it, you like it. Like so many things, we just get used to them. You know, like friends and lovers we learn to hate.
Is there a show tonight? Or am I it? Just you. Just me. And I wore my Shelly Winters. Ah, yes. All my wigs have names. This is late Shelly Winters — post-*Poseidon.*

It's all post-something nowadays, isn't it? What comes after post-modern? Well, whatever it is, I'm sure I'm already there. Fashionable, fashionable, fashionable. Fashion is always *fashionable*, isn't it? You ought to see me in my Ava Gardner. Now that is the most beautiful woman there ever was!

(Looking around room.) Well, I guess it's early yet.

You know queens. Always fashionably late. Not me. I make it a point to be fashionably early. It doesn't matter where. I'm always fashionably early.

I hate to walk into a room already filled with people. I'd much rather hold court. I like to greet the guests as they enter. It elevates my level of comfort. I like to grow into the evening . . . to feel more a part of it . . . more at one with the crowd. And, oh, my dear, I hate to leave early. I hate to feel compelled to do the rounds — to say my good byes while trying to think of something clever, some final parting gem that will endure and endear me in their memories. One must think of something clever. When you're an old queen dressed in feathers and beads, one must *always* think of something clever.

When it is time to break the balloons and go home . . . I like to sit and smile at each and everyone as they stop by to wish me well before departing. That's the proper way to treat a lady, isn't it? It really doesn't matter if it's sincere or not. It's the illusion of sincerity that carries the day.

Still, sometimes it would be nice to be invisible . . . and other times . . . just not to care.

You seem like a bright young man. Have you grand plans for your life? Why not? You certainly strike me as someone who could go the distance . . . someone capable of doing whatever he damn-well pleased. You have that air about you, that undeniable charm. You appear . . . *intelligent.* Oh yes, indeed you do.

Some intelligent people, who ought to know better, have minds like steel traps. You know the kind. You say one thing, anything, and they bite you on the butt by responding to what they imagine, whether it's real or not. That's when you pray for divine intervention. Something clever . . . something to inspire you with the amazing grace to say something totally appropriate and sage-like. One must do that in the moment. It cannot be rehearsed.

A mind is like a trap. It brings stuff in. Some of it, it holds. Some of it, it casts aside. Some of it moves on all on its own. The nasty thing about steel traps is that they damage the thing they are designed to catch. They crush it out of existence. Darling, I love the mind of a gentler soul. I much prefer the mind that is more a cardboard box, a stick, and a length of yarn. Pull the yarn and you catch the moment . . . like a trembling rabbit, unharmed, beneath the box.

Somebody once said . . . to me . . . that there was nothing quite so sad as a woman in her cups, but I don't know. Except for the obvious, I don't know the difference between a woman and a man. Do you?

Do you know who is beneath all the grooming and the clothes . . . behind the eyes? We're equally sad in our cups . . . a woman and a man . . . out of control, out of our minds. I think there are far sadder things. Like the soul of the man behind the drag . . . helplessly watching from behind the mask while trying to control the performance, simultaneously. Now, that's the trick, isn't it? And, that's my name. *Trick.* Just Trick. And, I've still a few up my sleeve.

(A long pause to stare.) You have beautiful eyes. No, really. You do.

I'm forever trying to believe that there is some element of God in there . . . inside . . . behind the eyes . . . in you . . . in me.

Oh, God! Bless my soul. The things we do for love. The things we say . . . *Now, how sad is that?*

I had a live-in houseboy. I was his John. I kept him in booze and cigarettes between odd jobs. He was mostly between jobs and they all seemed odd to me. But he was a clever boy . . . until the day he said he had to find himself. He said I was smothering him and he had to get away. *"All right, go,"* I said. So he went.
An hour later he came back, slammed the door, and ran into the bathroom. *"That was quick,"* I said. And he said he had just come back to use the John and then he left again. *Humph!* Sort of gives new meaning to the word "John," doesn't it? He used me alright. But that's what happens to a queen in lust.

We never really learn, do we? They walk into our lives, glorious and new, bright as pennies and we take them into our hearts along with their terrible, all-consuming, self-absorbed pain . . . exquisite pain . . . like no one's ever felt pain before.

His pain could be felt from the next room. And his pain could be seen in his smile. His was a most fatal kind of pain. A gorgeous, unquenchable pain that glowed like coals behind his eyes. A pain so attractive that it can turn the best of us into moths. We throw ourselves into their beautiful fire . . . and we are consumed.

It's a different world now, isn't it? Nowadays, you'd do better to keep your thoughts to yourself. Hide your soul — your spirit. Nobody cares. *No.* I take that back. They do care. *They care* when they hear thoughts that run counter to their own. *They care* when they don't like what they see. *They care* and they care enough to make you want to run and to hide behind every available mask. So, here I am — behind mascara.
(Takes a sip of gin.) It's called a pink gin. We used to drink them together through the night and into the wee hours — my houseboy and me.

He didn't want to be touched. Yet, he'd make you think you were the only one. You'd want to believe him because not to believe him would force you to face the fool you've become . . . utterly, hopelessly in lust. Ah, well. *Pink gin . . . don't it sound grand?*

(Looking around room.) Are you sure there's a show tonight? You'd think there'd be more here by now.

Isn't life just plain weird sometimes? Inexplicable. I'm sure you meet them all. I don't know how you do it. It takes a very special kind of talent to be a bartender. And you certainly seem to have *a very special talent.*

This is where we met, you know — my houseboy and me. Right here, right here in this bar, about a year ago. One glance and that's when I fell into his eyes and the liquid that gave them their sparkle. Then, something happened. *Something always happens.*

Something happens to your sense of self when you discover that it is the drunk you love and not the drinker. *Something happens* when you discover that it wasn't the man in you he loved, but rather the woman with a penis . . . the enabler in lust. That's a tough one, darling. That's a tough one.

I had the strangest experience this morning. I had just finished with my douche. I'm just kidding. I was letting the tap water run hot so I could make myself a cup of instant coffee. Suddenly, everything stopped. I stood there, frozen. I disappeared. I was completely gone from my body. I was out of my mind, literally.

My only sensation was that of my body's recognition that nobody, so to speak, was home. You could have asked me my name and I would have had no idea what you were talking about.

Slowly, I began to re-enter my self, but something had changed . . . like a wheel had turned for the first time . . . and something was gone . . . and it had left an empty space in my mind . . . and I knew I would never remember it again. Oh, well. Maybe, there's room in there . . . under the old Shelly Winters . . . for something else now . . . something new . . . something better. There must *always* be something better.

Now, after my disappearing act, what I remember is that I never really got what I was looking for in the arms of another . . . someone to touch me down there . . . to touch my heart, my soul . . . my being . . . and . . . to kiss me on the lips . . . and mean it.

The world is a sad place, isn't it?

Please come home with me. Nothing is the same without you. I'm sorry. I don't know what I'm saying. What

am I saying? Is there a show tonight? I'm here for the show. You know . . . for the laughs.
Please, I'd love another. If I could have another, I'd surely love another. And while you're at it . . . why don't you have one on me?

END—*Pink Gin for the Blues*

DRAMAS

CORNERED

SYNOPSIS: (2M) BLACK is accused of the gruesome murder of his longtime companion and WHYTE is conducting a psychological assessment to determine whether or not he is fit for trial.

AT RISE: BLACK, an elderly gentleman in an orange jumpsuit and in handcuffs, sits in a chair next to a desk where WHYTE, a much younger man sits, wearing a suit. WHYTE taps his pencil on the desk and on his note pad. A full minute of WHYTE tapping his pencil while BLACK remains silent, exploring his surroundings. They exchange glances and frowns and WHYTE appears exasperated waiting for BLACK to say something.

WHYTE: *(Breaking the silence.)* Well? I'm waiting.

BLACK: I'm not what you think I am.

WHYTE: And what is that?

BLACK: *(Hesitantly.)* You know.

WHYTE: You tell me.

BLACK: *(Difficult to say.)* A murderer. *I am not a murderer.*

WHYTE: That's for a jury to decide. If you're fit to stand trial, that is.

BLACK: My life.

WHYTE: What about your life?

BLACK: *(Strangely distant and addressed to no one—the ceiling, maybe.)* It hit me. Yes. That's when it hit me.

WHYTE: What? What hit you?

BLACK: My life . . . it just came down upon me.

WHYTE: And how was that . . . when it hit you?

BLACK: At first, I felt a lump in my throat. Then, all of a sudden, there was a white flash. Bright flash. Heat. Like a bomb went off in my head. I was frightened. And then . . .

WHYTE: *(After a pause to wait for BLACK to continue.)* Then?

BLACK: Nothing. *(A long sigh.)* Nothing. Absolutely nothing. And then there was the man across the street.

WHYTE: What man?

BLACK: Just a man. He was on the corner.

WHYTE: And you?

BLACK: I was across the street.

WHYTE: Doing?

BLACK: Watching. Waiting. Just watching—and waiting.

WHYTE: Tell me about the man on the corner.

BLACK: He was sitting. Begging. Cradling somebody in his arms. It could have been a man.

WHYTE: You're not sure?

BLACK: I wanted it to be a man.

WHYTE: You wanted it to be a man? Why is that?

BLACK: I don't know. Perhaps I'd feel more . . . pain.

And, if the man were dead, the pain would be merciless. Pure. Sharp. Exquisite.

WHYTE: I see. You like to feel pain.

BLACK: No. I don't. I just thought pain might take me away from it.

WHYTE: It?

BLACK: My life, I needed to feel something . . . *anything.* Something that would take me away from my life! *Nothing.* I felt nothing. *There must be something better.*

WHYTE: And you thought the man . . . or the woman might help you feel something?
BLACK: It was a man. *He* was a man.

WHYTE: You've decided it was a man.

BLACK: Yes. I decided. He was a dead man . . . draped across the man who held him.

WHYTE: *Dead?*

BLACK: Decidedly.

WHYTE: But it could have been a woman.

BLACK: Yes, it could have been.

WHYTE: It could have been a woman and she could have been alive.

BLACK: Yes, but it was a man and he was dead.

WHYTE: What made you decide he was dead?

BLACK: Desire. My desire to cry for someone other than myself. He was across the street sitting on the corner . . . with his dead friend. I was on a bench waiting for a bus. I wanted to cry. I needed to cry. I felt nothing.

WHYTE: Do you often feel sorry for yourself?

BLACK: I disappoint myself. It saddens me. But the man with his friend comforted me in a most distressing way. There was someone worse off than me—two worse off. It gave me pleasure.

WHYTE: Pleasure?

BLACK: In a convoluted sort of way, yes.

WHYTE: Where were you?

BLACK: When?

WHYTE: Just now.

BLACK: Here. Watching the man on the corner. Across the street. Watching people pass. Watching them move more quickly as they came upon the scene of the accident. An accident of fate. Breathing a sigh of relief because it wasn't them. They, too, felt nothing, *(A long SILENCE.)* I thought, maybe he is me. Maybe that was my life . . . across the street. Maybe it was my death. Outside myself. Waiting. On the corner. Across the street. Living and breathing within that stranger.

WHYTE: What did you do?

BLACK: What could I do?

WHYTE: I don't know.

BLACK: I watched. I watched as I sat on the bench at the bus stop with two full shopping bags at my side. Waiting. Just waiting. *(A pause. A sigh.)* The minute I get there everyone seems to have moved on. It's always been that way. So now I wait—hoping to catch the sun. Waiting for the sun . . . some warmth . . . a tender touch.

The Age of Aquarius. Whatever happened to that? The sun forgot to shine. So I stay in one place—*my place*—and wait. Hoping to catch the first glimmer. Hoping they'll come to me . . .

(A glance from WHYTE.)

BLACK: *(Continues.)* . . . the partygoers, the revelers who are glad to see me—really glad. The kind of glad I can see and feel. *(A deep breath. A pause before exhaling.)* The sun. God. Sometimes there's God, but only sometimes. Then He disappears. Like everybody else. They disappear. Sometimes—most of the time—there is nothing. And—

WHYTE: Do you know why you are here, Mister. Black?

BLACK: Because they think I killed—

WHYTE: *(After a long SILENCE.)* Who, Mister Black? Who did you kill?

BLACK: Nobody.

WHYTE: You don't remember?

BLACK: I don't know.

WHYTE: Why did you dismember the body?

BLACK: I don't remember.

WHYTE: Of course you do. It didn't cut itself up.

BLACK: Oh, God. *(Looking heavenward.)* Why, why, why? *(After a pause to remember.)* Ah, yes. I needed to get rid of it.

WHYTE: After you killed him.

BLACK: No! *I loved him.* Do you think it was easy?

WHYTE: I don't know. Was it?

BLACK: He was dead. My life was dead. I was dead! Dead . . . like the friend of the man on the corner. What was I supposed to do?

WHYTE: Why don't you tell me?

BLACK: *(Coldly, deliberately and without emotion.)* I wrapped his body in the drop cloth. The one we used to paint the living room wall green. Just the one. He had fabulous taste. I couldn't look at him while doing what I had to do. I began with the arms—*his arms.* I tried the electric carving knife, but it broke. I should have known —it barely carved the Thanksgiving turkey. *Thanksgiving.* There won't be another, will there? I took a bus to the hardware store. Number fourteen. I bought a sturdy saw with big teeth. All the better to see you with. Funny, I don't know where that came from. The things that rattle through the mind. Anyway, you could cut down a redwood with that saw . . . with the big teeth. I removed his arms. I had to cut them into . . . oh, maybe ten-inch pieces so they'd fit into shopping bags. I had to cut off his hands too. He had nice hands, always did. Piano hands, you know? He didn't play the piano. We had one. Once. Neither of us could play. How pretentious is that? We tried to sell it. Ended up giving the thing away. So much of our lives . . . we gave away. The saw with the big teeth inched its way through his bones. I thought I'd never finish. The kitchen was covered with blood. I was covered with blood. I saved the head for last. It rolled across the floor. His head. I knelt there. I couldn't touch it—*him*—*his head. I went to sleep.* When I awoke, I thought about keeping the head—*his head*— preserving it somehow. He was his head. He was my friend, my brother . . . my lover . . . my everything—

WHYTE: *(Interrupting.)* Stop it! Stop it right now! You disgust me! What in hell is wrong with you? I've seen my share of wackos, but you're one sorry sonofabitch!

BLACK: You don't find that a bit judgmental? I mean, for a psychiatrist?

WHYTE: Did it never occur to you that what you were doing was wrong, Mister Black? Did you know it was wrong?

BLACK: What else was I supposed to do? He was dead. I was alone. Totally, completely—*alone.*

WHYTE: You could have called the police.

BLACK: *(Visibly shaken.)* And how was I supposed to live? He had a heart attack in our bed. I could feel him next to me as he died—side by side, arms touching, legs touching. What was I supposed to do? How was I going to live? How, Doctor Whyte? *How?*

WHYTE: Husbands and wives live on after their loved ones die every day.

BLACK: Husbands and wives. Yes. But we weren't married, were we? We couldn't be, could we?

WHYTE: Parts of him were buried all across town.

BLACK: I took the bus. I used shopping bags. It took me over a week. *(A pause to remember.)* The stench. That God-awful stench!

WHYTE: For six months you've been living off his Social Security.

BLACK: I had no choice.

WHYTE: Everybody has choices.

BLACK: And live like that man on the corner—an accident of life—in life?

WHYTE: That's not the only alternative.

BLACK: For me it was. I'm too much a coward for suicide. There was no way I could support myself. My Social Security doesn't even cover the rent.

WHYTE: Why did you?

BLACK: What?

WHYTE: Kill—

BLACK: *I told you I didn't kill him!*

WHYTE: I understand you not wanting to talk about it.

BLACK: There is *nothing to talk about!*

WHYTE: Maybe later.

BLACK: All I did was steal a dead man's Social Security. So I broke the law. He was my lover—my lover. We were together forty-five years! I had every right to it! *I loved him!*

WHYTE: That has nothing to do with anything?

BLACK: *Everything. Everything, God damn it! It has everything to do with it!*

WHYTE: Calm down. *(Threatening.)* The guard is just outside the door.

BLACK: Don't you understand?

WHYTE: What do I need to understand, Mister Black?

BLACK: They put us in a corner. Everyone put us in a corner. Everyone . . . *you.*

WHYTE: You put yourself there, Mister Black..

BLACK: *(After a long SILENCE.)* Well? What's the verdict? Am I fit to stand trial?

WHYTE: *(Calling to door.)* Guard.

BLACK: Well? Am I?

WHYTE: *(Calling again as LIGHTING dims to BLACK OUT.)* Guard . . .

END—*Cornered*

EMPIRE

SYNOPSIS: (4M/3W). Barroom set with juke box. EMPIRE is set in the Empire, a run-down tavern in Upstate New York; the Empire State. The characters are a group of individuals who have reached the bottom of their lives, in their cups, beyond middle-age, suffering the depression of closed factories and joblessness. From the torrential rains, water begins to rise and threatens to flood the town and the captives in the Empire. Enter the angel Michael who forces each to face the reality of themselves, but can he save them from the flood? He gives each of them an intriguing choice. The metaphor, or allegory, is meant to draw a comparison between the decay of the Empire Lounge and the decay of the Empire that is America. Situation and language make this play unsuitable for younger audiences.

The Characters:

BETTY: Over fifty. Owner of the Empire.
LARRY: Fat. Over fifty.
MARTHA: Over fifty
HARVEY: Over fifty. Walks with an exaggerated limp.
BILL MONROE: Over fifty.
JENNY HILL: Somewhat fragile. In her twenties.
MICHAEL: An angel. Any age.

AT RISE: The Setting is the Empire, a barroom with a juke box. LARRY, MARTHA, BILL and HARVEY, all beyond their prime and in their cups, are seated at separate tables. Palm down, BETTY, the owner of the Empire, is slapping the table where LARRY sleeps with his head buried in his arms.

BETTY: Hey, lard ass! Get it in gear.

LARRY: *(Waking.)* Huh?

BETTY: Closing time. Time to haul it.

LARRY: *(Raising his head.)* C'mon, just kiss it. Give it a little touch.

BETTY: I ain't Irene, Larry. Touch it yourself.

LARRY: What? Irene? *(An uncomfortable realization.)* Of course you're not. You couldn't be.

BETTY: You're not going to crash here, again. Irene's probably right where you left her.

LARRY: Sleeping like a log.

BETTY: Exactly what you ought to be doing, but not here.

LARRY: It's raining.

BETTY: You ain't made of salt.

LARRY: You got a sweet tit for me, darlin'?

BETTY: I got the back of my hand! Drink and git. *(Sniffing the air.)* What the hell is that? Jesus H. Christ. You didn't go shit on another o' my chairs, did you?

LARRY: I didn't shit. Geez, Betts.

BETTY: God help you if you did. Jesus, Mary and Joseph. What in hell did you eat?

MARTHA: *(Calling from the shadows.)* Give the poor slob a break. He lost his job. Laid off, for God's sake.

BETTY: Do I look like the Salvation Army?

MARTHA: *(To everybody and nobody in particular.)* Men . . . more sensitive than ya think, believe me. They break and they die just like *(Tries snapping her fingers, but can't.)* that. Like . . . that. Shit. My Harry got the bum end when the plant went and closed up in Scum City. That's what killed the sonofabitch and don't you go tellin' me different.

BETTY: Nobody's sayin' nothin', Martha. You shouldn't blame yourself. The jury said you wasn't guilty and that's good enough for me.

MARTHA: *(To BETTY.)* Don't ya just hate regrets?

BETTY: *Huh?*

MARTHA: Regrets, don't you hate 'em?

BETTY: Yeah, every day. Usually somethin' I ate.

LARRY: Me too. I hate feeling regrets all right. Ain't a thing you can do about 'em.

HARVEY: No shit, lardo.

MARTHA: Regrets'll eat ya up from inside out.

BETTY: So will bad Chinese.

MARTHA: Wong's?

BETTY: Ain't none other from here to Scum City.

MARTHA: I don't go to Wong's no more. It ain't been good for my system, if you know what I mean.

BETTY: *Yep.* Only so many sweet and sour cockroaches a body can eat. *(A pause to sigh.)* Martha, fillin' your life with regrets can't be good for you, either. Think about tomorrow.

MARTHA: Scares me.

BETTY: Ain't no stopping it. It's gonna come until it don't no more.

MARTHA: They'll come and I'll still be . . . A woman alone ain't natural. I see how they look at me.

BETTY: You were acquitted.

HARVEY: She had a good lawyer. Bamboozled the jury.

BETTY: That ain't got nothin' to do with it, Harvey. So why don't you shut up or take your little dick outta here?

LARRY: *(Bursts with laughter.)* You tell 'im, Betts!

HARVEY: C'mon, she did it and everybody knows it.

BETTY: I don't know any such thing.

MARTHA: Innocent. Godfuckingdamnit innocent. That's what they said and that's what I am.

HARVEY: Go on believing that, sister. They said you was "not guilty." They never said nothin' 'bout innocent.

MARTHA: I wish I was dead. *(She downs her liquor, slams the glass on the table and retreats into herself.)*

BILL: Is it last call yet?

BETTY: I believe it is. *(Shouting to ALL.)* Last call! Speak now or forever hold your peace. *(Crosses to behind bar.)*

HARVEY: Why don't you come over here and hold my piece, Betts?

BETTY: I thought your piece got blown off in Iraq?

HARVEY: Just a couple inches. There's plenty to spare and it's got your name written all over it.

BETTY: You sure it ain't B.M.? *(Pouring drinks.).*

HARVEY: B. M.? What the fuck are you saying?

BETTY: My initials, dumb butt.

LARRY: Maybe it's written in short hand.

BETTY: Everybody havin' the same? Bill, ain't it time for you to switch to Sterno?

BILL: Amusing. I'll put that in my journal.

MARTHA: Hey Bill, what the hell's in that book o' yours? *(Jumps out of her seat and rushes over to BILL and grabs his journal)* Huh? What you got in here?

BILL: You, for one. Please give it back.

MARTHA: Me? Am I pretty?

BILL: Beautiful, Martha . . . as a sweet lily of the field.

MARTHA: Go on . . .

BILL: True.

MARTHA: I wanna read it.

BILL: You're in no condition.

BETTY: *(Comes out from behind bar where she had been pouring drinks.)* C'mon, honey. Let me help you back to your seat. Give me the book. *(She gently takes it out of MARTHA'S hand and passes it to BILL.)*

MARTHA: *(While being escorted.)* Said I was beautiful. A lily of the field.

BETTY: Yes, I heard. Here we are. You sit down, sweetie, and I'll bring you another Scotch.

MARTHA: Thank you. I didn't kill him, you know.

BETTY: I know, Martha. *(Goes to bar to get tray of drinks.)*

HARVEY: What about me? What do I look like in that book o' yours?

BILL: A soldier.

HARVEY: You bet your ass I do! I gave up the best part o' me for my country. Don't none o' you forget it!

BETTY: Who could forget it, Harv? You won't let us.

LARRY: Harvey saved America by giving it dick!

HARVEY: Fuck you! And your farts! Go home to Irene. She's the only one who can tolerate you. You lard ass sack of shit!

BETTY: Okay, boys, play nice. *(Delivering another round of drinks.)* This one's on the house.

MARTHA: Last call's always on the house. Every night since I can remember, last call's been on the house.

BETTY: This one's special. So, enjoy 'cause I'm thinking of changing that tradition pretty soon. Don't get the Scum City boys no more . . . now that the base is closed . . . everything's gone to hell—

HARVEY: One day there won't be nobody left to protect this great land o' ours; closin' bases to save a buck to give to Public Radio and Hollywood liberals; They send jobs t' India to get cheaper prices and sooner or later we're looking for work and we can't even afford to go to Walmart.

LARRY: Ain't no Walmart no more. Scum City's a ghost town 'cause Walmart up and hauled ass.

HARVEY: *(Sotto voce.)* And fag marriages.

BILL: *(To LARRY.)* Something will come to fill the void. Something always does

MARTHA: Sometimes nothin' does. Nothin'. Nothin' on the half shell. As far as ya can see -- just a whole lot o' nothin'.

LARRY: And I didn't get fired—got laid off. There's a difference, you know.

HARVEY: *(To LARRY.)* Either way you cut it, the paycheck's the same. *Nothin'. Nada. Zero. Shit. (Sniffing the air.)* What the? I can smell you from here. No wonder they fired your sorry ass.

LARRY: One of these days I'm gonna put a bullet through that thick gimp skull o' yours.

HARVEY: You better bring an army, fatso. *(Rises.)* I gotta take a leak. *(Limping towards the men's room.)* Hey, Bill! You wanna come hold it for me?

BILL: Not today, thank you.

HARVEY: Betts, you're gonna need somethin' real potent to fumigate this place.

BETTY: What do you suggest, Harv?

HARVEY: Agent Orange—it always worked for me. *(Limps into the men's room.)*

MARTHA: You shouldn't egg 'im on like that. He got that way protecting folks like you and me. He's a decorated war hero—Purple Heart and all.

LARRY: Don't make no nevermind. What the hell do you suppose he pisses out of?

BILL: From what I understand they managed to reconstruct enough to urinate through.

LARRY: He has to sit. I hear it's about the size of a baby's thumb. *(Directly to audience.)* Larry is ashamed of the size of his own penis. He hates it almost as much as he hates himself. *(Back into scene.)*

BETTY: Ain't the size what matters—

MARTHA: Bullshit! Harry had one the size of Montana. Ride 'im cowboy!.And I loved every inch of it! Tell the truth, Betty. Size matters and you damn well know it. The bigger the better!

BETTY: You got me on that one, Martha.

BILL: Have you ever been to Montana, Martha?

MARTHA: I ain't never been out o' New York State.

BILL: Big country out there.

(JENNY HILL rushes in from out the pouring rain, carrying luggage and trying to close her umbrella. She is cold and dripping wet. There is a long SILENCE while ALL stare at her.)

BILL: *(Breaking the silence.)* Jenny Hill, what are you doing out in this weather, this hour of the morning?

BETTY: Good God, girl— *(Quickly exits to backroom.)*

JENNY: The water—it's over the sidewalk. I've got three more hours.

MARTHA: Three more hours for what?

JENNY: The bus.

LARRY: No bus comes through here no more.

JENNY: Five-thirty. Sometimes it won't stop unless you flag it down.

MARTHA: Not if it's washed out, honey. Where ya headed?

JENNY: Albany.

BETTY: *(Enters carrying a blanket and a towel. Crosses to JENNY.)* Albany, huh?

JENNY: Yes, ma'am.

(During some of the dialogue to follow, BETTY helps JENNY out of her raincoat. Takes it, her umbrella and her luggage and places them somewhere. She wraps the blanket around JENNY'S shoulders while JENNY uses the towel to dry her face and hair.)

JENNY: My sister is a teacher there . . . in Albany.

BILL: How is Nancy these days?

JENNY: Married.

BILL: A local boy?

JENNY: She met him in her senior year at New Paltz—Bobby Standish. She's teaching high school English—in Albany. He teaches art at the university. She's always asking about you, Mister Monroe.

BILL: She was one of my brightest students. Come sit over here, Jenny.

JENNY: Thank you, Mister Monroe. *(Goes to his table and sits.)*

MARTHA: *(Watching BILL writing in his journal. To JENNY.)* Watch what you say, Missy. He writes it down.

LARRY: He writes all the shit down. Hey, you writin' all this shit down?

BILL: All that is fit to write.

BETTY: *(Delivering a drink to JENNY. To LARRY.)* That leaves you out, Larry. *(To JENNY.)* Here ya go, sweetie—on the house. Scotch, all right?

JENNY: Yes, ma'am. Thank you.

(BETTY returns to the bar.)

LARRY: Very funny, Betts . . . very funny. Did he write that down? Was that fit enough for 'im?

BILL: I'm keeping a record for posterity, Larry.

LARRY: Posterity? Bullshit. You're a sorry ass schoolteacher they won't let near a classroom no more?

BETTY: *(Holds up a bottle from behind the bar. To LARRY.)* Careful. I'd hate to bust a brand new bottle o' Black & White over that thick skull o' yours. Apologize.

LARRY: Why?

BETTY: 'Cause I said so!

LARRY: *(Mimicking, effeminate.)* Sorry, Mister Monroe. Okay?

BILL: Sure.

LARRY: *(Directly to audience.)* Larry will be arrested the day after tomorrow for the murder of his wife. After his trial he will spend the rest of his life behind bars in Ossining, New York. Eleven years from now he will be found on Christmas morning hanging in his cell. His last thought before committing suicide will be this barroom and how his nights at the Empire Lounge were the "good old days." I could not stop his murder. *(Back into scene.)*

JENNY: The water—it's over the sidewalk.

BETTY: *(Goes to see for herself.)* I hope it ain't—

LARRY: They say it could flood the valley. Hudson's up.

BETTY: *(At window.) Christ!* Looks like we're gonna be here for the duration. Put that in your journal, Bill.

BILL: Got it. Maybe we'll have a few more last calls.

MARTHA: Sounds good to me.

BETTY: If we do, they won't be on my dime.

LARRY: You got me in that journal?

BILL: I'd rather not say, Larry.

LARRY: It better be nice.

BILL: It's the truth. I only write the truth.

HARVEY: *(Entering from men's room.)* What's the truth?

BETTY: The truth is it looks like we're all stuck here for awhile.

HARVEY: *(Looking toward JENNY.)* Who do we got here?

JENNY: Jenny. Jenny Hill.

HARVEY: You sure you're in the right place?

JENNY: Yes, sir. Only place open. I'm waiting for the bus.

HARVEY: Ain't no bus coming through here this morning.

JENNY: It's got to. It's just got to.

BETTY: Got to or not, I don't think it'll be able to get through till the rain lets up.

JENNY: It'll come.

MARTHA: Don't set your heart on it, honey. Don't never set your heart on nothing.

LARRY: I hope he shook it good. Did you shake it good, Sergeant?

HARVEY: I thought I'd let Bill do that for me.

BETTY: Don't you be payin' them no mind, Jenny. Every last one of 'em is pigs. Put that in your book, Bill.

BILL: It's already in the book, Betty. It's been in every entry for the last twelve years.

BETTY: Well, put it in again. Some things can't be overstated. *(Still at window.)* Nope. Don't look like anybody's goin' anywhere.

JENNY: Oh, dear— *(Directly to audience.)* Jenny needs to get out of town. She is desperate and in fear for her life. There must be a bus, she thinks. There must be a bus. *(Back into scene.)*

HARVEY: So what's the truth, Bill? Do ya know? Do ya know anything?

BILL: This moment—right now. That's all I know, Harv. And, the Empire Lounge—the best watering hole outside of Scum City.

MARTHA: I'll drink to that.

BETTY: You'll drink to anything.

MARTHA: I thought you was my friend?

BETTY: I am. I'm just joshin' ya, sweetie.

JENNY: This? This is the best watering hole in town? I'm sorry. I didn't mean to make it sound like that.

BETTY: I've heard a lot worse.

BILL: It's the only one left since Chuck Murphy closed the Shamrock.

MARTHA: What about that, Betty? Where'd all the Shamrock crowd go?

BETTY: Well, let's see. Jimmy Vogel died and his wife moved to Watertown. Verge Vandersteer died from a rotten liver. The Babcock brothers are down in Ossining doing hard time. Oh, and Sal Turco went on the wagon. Let's see . . . *yup,* that's about it.

JENNY: *(Finishing her Scotch. To BETTY.)* May I have another, Miss . . . Miss—

BETTY: Betty. Betty works just fine.

JENNY: Thank you . . . Betty. *(Directly to audience.)* Jenny will give birth to a baby girl eight months from now. Three months later, Von Dixon will break into her sister's apartment in Albany and beat Jenny so badly she will go into a coma for seven months before dying. Von

Dixon will be charged with murder. He will be acquitted. I have no control over justice. I am not God. I am — *(Back into scene.)*

BILL: What are you covering under that makeup, Jenny? Is that a black eye?

JENNY: You can see it?

BILL: It looks like a nasty bruise to me.

BETTY: *(Delivering a fresh drink to JENNY.)* You sure look like you could use another.

JENNY: Thank you, ma'am . . . Betty.

BETTY: That's some shiner you got there. Is that why you're headed for Albany?

JENNY: Yes.

BETTY: Poor kid.

HARVEY: What do ya tell a woman with two black eyes?

BETTY: I don't know, Harv. What do ya tell her?

HARVEY: Nothin'. Ya already told 'er twice! *(He roars with laughter.)*

BETTY: That's funny, Harv. You hear anybody laughin' but your own fool self?

MARTHA: Ain't no man ever git a second chance with me. Give me a black eye and I'll blow his head off.

HARVEY: What else is new?

MARTHA: I didn't mean it that way. Why don't all o' you just go fuck yourselves!

LARRY: 'Cause the gimp ain't got nothin' to fuck himself with.

(HARVEY jumps up. Suddenly a knife appears poised to slit LARRY'S throat. Screams are heard. BETTY rushes over.)

LARRY: Help—

BETTY: Give me the knife, Harvey.

HARVEY: Not till this sonofabitch learns a little respect.

BETTY: *(Holding her hand out.)* The knife.

HARVEY: *(To LARRY.)* You done talkin' 'bout my dick?

LARRY: From what I hear, there ain't much to talk about.

HARVEY: *(Pushing knife firmly against his throat.)* I said, are ya done talkin' 'bout my dick?

LARRY: Yes.

HARVEY: What?

LARRY: I said yes!

MARTHA: Give Betty the knife before ya hurt somebody, Harv.

JENNY: Shouldn't somebody call the police?

BILL: No. Every other night Harvey pulls a knife on Larry and then he hands it over to Betty. It's old news. I don't even put it in my journal anymore.

BETTY: *(With her hand out to HARVEY.)* The knife.

HARVEY: *(To BETTY, handing her the knife.)* Here. *(To LARRY.)* Ya better thank Betty 'cause one o' these nights I'm gonna slit your throat for real.

LARRY: Well, it ain't gonna be tonight.

BETTY: *(Returning to bar with knife.)* You boys are gonna die miserable and stupid. I ought to throw you all out into the weather.

BILL: Who gave you the black eye, Jenny? That is, if you don't mind my prying?

JENNY: Do you remember Von Dixon?

BILL: A troubled student, I recall—quit school to join the air force?

JENNY: He never did go. I guess they didn't want him. Anyway, we moved in together—about a year ago.

BILL: I see.

JENNY: Big mistake.

BILL: And now you're heading for your sister's in Albany.

MARTHA: That five-thirty don't go to Albany.

JENNY: I know, ma'am.

HARVEY: Ma'am? Hey, Martha! Somebody's confused you with a lady.

MARTHA: Go to hell!

JENNY: I'll need to transfer in Scum City.

BILL: I wonder when we all started calling Scum City Scum City?

LARRY: It's always been Scum City. We called it Scum City since I was a little boy.

HARVEY: You were never a little boy.

LARRY: Ha-ha, very funny.

MARTHA: I'm still Here. Here! I hate here.

LARRY: You was here the last time I looked.

MARTHA: Ain't what I mean. *Here, here.* I don't want to be here no more!

LARRY: Hear, hear! Let's drink to that!

JENNY: *(To BILL.)* Did you feel that—the silence? They say that an angel passes through that silence.

BILL: Yes, I have heard that, Jenny.

MARTHA: Angels my ass! Harry—lyin' in his grave, head blown clean through. How the hell do I get out of here? Would somebody tell me how to get out of here?

HARVEY: Through the front door for Christ's sake!

BETTY: It's okay, sweetie.

MARTHA: No. It's not. Ever regret somethin'—somethin' so bad it cripples ya? Worse than Harvey it cripples ya—inside, ya know? Why? Huh—why? *(Directly to audience.)* Martha is thinking she wants her life to be over. Yet, she has rarely allowed herself to live. What she really wants is to be once again the girl—the girl with dreams, longing to be the woman—the woman with children, a porch and a white picket fence. As do so many Human dreams, they seldom come to be. Nothing happens all on its own. One day, many unhappy years from now, Martha will die without the memory of joy—without ever knowing me. *(Back into scene.)*

BETTY: I don't know why, sweetie. I wish I did but I don't—plain and simple. There just ain't no rhyme nor reason to anything. *(After an awkward SILENCE.)* Hey, c'mon. Let's cheer this joint up. You're all a bunch of sorry excuses. *(Crosses to the juke box and plays something.)* C'mon, cheer your sorry asses up.

LARRY: Mine's cheery enough.

HARVEY: That's a laugh—

MARTHA: Anybody wanna dance? *(Looking around.)* Anyone? Betty?

BETTY: Not tonight, sweetie.

JENNY: I'll dance with you, ma'am. *(She rises and meets MARTHA who stumbles from her seat.)*

BILL: Patsy Cline. There's a woman who felt the weight of the world.

(JENNY and MARTHA dance for awhile until LARRY pushes MARTHA aside and begins to dance with JENNY. He is clumsy and is squeezing her tightly.)

JENNY: Please . . . I can't . . . breathe . . . .

BILL: Larry, let her go!

HARVEY: Leave 'im be. The bitch asked for it.

BILL: *(Rising.)* You crazy sonofabitch!

BETTY: Bill, sit!

JENNY: Stop it! *(Wiggles free. She then attacks him with the full force of her flying fists.)* I hate you! I hate you! You're just like every other man!

LARRY: You don't even know me, girl.

JENNY: Yes, I do. I know you. I've known you all my life.

(BETTY crosses to the dance couple and pulls them apart. JENNY falls to the floor and BETTY pushes LARRY into his chair. BILL rushes to help JENNY onto her feet.)

BILL: *(To JENNY, escorting her back to the table.)* You okay?

MARTHA: Anybody wanna dance with Martha?

BILL: *(To LARRY and HARVEY.)* The both of you are the stupidest sonsofbitches I have ever known!

HARVEY: *(To BILL.)* Shut the fuck up! I didn't get the Purple Heart so people like you could eavesdrop and fill up your filthy book with other people's lives. *(Rises.)* You make me sick! *(Crosses to jukebox.)* You all make me sick! *(HARVEY pulls the plug on the jukebox and the MUSIC comes to an abrupt stop. Speaks directly to audience.)* Harvey will die six months from now in a ward at the Veteran's Hospital from a severe infection of the pancreas. He will die owing nothing to anybody and regretting nothing. He will die alone. No one will attend his funeral, but Bill Monroe. Through Bill I will watch Harvey's body as it is lowered into the ground. *(Back into scene.)*

LARRY: You shouldn't o' done that, Harvey. You really shouldn't o' done that.

HARVEY: Blow it out your ass!

MARTHA: I only wanted to dance.

BETTY: Harvey, sit!

HARVEY: I'll do what I please. *(Crosses to BILL.)* You wanna see my dick?

BILL: Nobody wants to see your dick, Harvey.

HARVEY: I'll bet otherwise. I'll bet you like seeing every dick you can get your eyes on, faggot!

BETTY: I said, sit down!

HARVEY: *(Ignoring BETTY. With his back to the audience, or not, he shows BILL his penis. JENNY turns away.)* Take a look! Look at it, fucker! You like that, sweetheart?

BILL: I'm underwhelmed.

BETTY: I said, sit!

HARVEY: *(Zipping up his fly.)* I'm sittin'. *(Crosses to his table and sits.)* I'm sittin' but it ain't 'cause of you. You hear me?

BETTY: I hear you loud and clear, Harvey.

HARVEY: Good—'cause I can't stand on this leg for very long.

LARRY: I always thought Harvey didn't have a leg to stand on. *(Roars with laughter.)*

BILL: I don't think that's funny, Larry.

LARRY: *(Mimicking.)* I don't think that's funny, Larry. You let 'im show you his dick and you get mad at me. So, how big was the gimp's dick? MARTHA: Can I see it, Harvey?

BETTY: Would all of you shut up! I got something to say and I'm only going to say it once. Tomorrow there will be no more Empire Lounge.

ALL: *What?*

BETTY: You heard me.

BILL: Why, Betty? I thought everything was going well. You don't have the boys from the base or the Scum City crowd anymore, but you still got your regulars.

BETTY: Not as regular as you think. Besides, it's something else. I'll need to—What's the use?

MARTHA: What is it, Betty?

BETTY: It's female stuff. I'm supposed to start chemo in the morning.

BILL: That's—I'm truly sorry, Betty.

LARRY: So, what's the chemo for?

BETTY: What do you think? *(A pause to think about her response.)* For what's left of my pussy—that's what for.

MARTHA: I don't know what to say—

HARVEY: Then don't say nothin'.

MARTHA: *(Nodding off, in her own world.)* They break so easy—men.

HARVEY: Yeah—'specially when you shoot 'em in the head.

MARTHA: What? *(To anybody but HARVEY.)* What did he say? What did he say?

BILL: He didn't say anything, Martha. That type never do.

HARVEY: She heard me all right. Put that in your book, faggot!

BETTY: How did all this suddenly become about you!? *(Going from one to the other.)* Or you? Or you? Or you—any of you? No wonder I'm sick of the lot of you.

They ripped out my uterus—my goddamn sticky—and God knows what else, and the big C just keeps on growing!

MARTHA: I'm so sorry to hear that, Betty.

BILL: All of us are.

BETTY: Then drink up, kids. This is your last drink on the Empire Lounge.

MARTHA: What will I do. Where will I go? It just ain't the same without Harry.

HARVEY: Then you shouldn't have shot him.

MARTHA: I didn't shoot him! I helped him. I helped him get out of here. *Here.* He didn't want to be *here.* He couldn't pull the trigger all by his self. That old rabbit riffle was just too long for his little short arms. So, I pulled the trigger for him.

BETTY: Martha, don't say another thing.

BILL: They can't try her again—double jeopardy.

BETTY: *(Directly to audience.)* Betty will close the doors of the Empire Lounge. She will begin chemo therapy and she will survive. Betty came to me during her chemo therapy and we've been one until the day she will die in a car accident while visiting her sister in Syracuse, New York. She will feel no pain and she will die happy. Her last words will be— *(Back into scene.)* Oh God! I can't wait.

MARTHA: Can't wait for what, Betts?

BETTY: To get the hell out of here. Close the doors on this dump for once and for all.

BILL: *(Directly to audience.)* Bill will publish his novel about life in a small, dying town in rural America. He will move to New York City where he will celebrate the rest of his long life as a successful novelist. Bill will die a very old man of natural causes—in the arms of his lover. I am the river that flows through every life that ever....

BETTY: *(Ibid.)* ... was ...

MARTHA: *(Ibid.)* ... or is ...

LARRY: *(Ibid.)* ... or will ever be.

HARVEY: *(Ibid.)* I am—

ALL: *(Ibid.)* I am.

(ALL go back into scene.)

LARRY: Holy shit! I just had one of those ... you know, like when ya feel you've been here before ... exactly the same.

BILL: It's called *déjà vu.*

LARRY: So real.

BETTY: *(Runs to the front door.)* The water!

JENNY: It's coming in.

HARVEY: Under the door.

MARTHA: Oh my god!

ALL: A flood!

The LIGHTING dims to BLACK OUT.

END—*Empire*

LEAVING TAMPA

3M, Minimal Set, One-Act. This play examines gay self-hate, abusive relations, the role of the gay male in relationship to his father and in relationship to Christianity. Roy, bitter about childhood abuse by his father, sits with his lover in an airport restaurant on their way home from Roy's father's funeral. At another table sits the ghost of the father, whom only Roy can see. The dialogue between Roy and his lover overlaps with that of his father—building to an unexpected and emotional climax.

THE CHARACTERS are ROY and MARC, a gay couple in their thirties. And WAYNE, Roy's father, a ghost.

THE ACTION of the play takes place in an airline terminal restaurant in Tampa, Florida.

THE SETTING can be as simple as two tables covered with tablecloths with accompanying chairs. One table is center stage and the other is downstage left or right. There is the SOUND of soft music in the background as well as the din of restaurant sounds. Every-so-often, some kind of airline arrival and departure information is heard over the terminal speakers.

THE TIME is around noon, the present.

ROY and MARC sit opposite each other at the center stage table eating their lunch. Every so often, MARC will busy himself by writing something on a yellow legal pad. There is a carafe of wine on the table and only one wineglass—it is MARC'S. Next to the table or on an empty chair is some hand luggage belonging to ROY and MARC. Facing the audience, WAYNE sits by himself at a downstage table. WAYNE can be seen and heard only by ROY.

MARC: *(Looks up from writing something on his yellow legal pad.)* You're not eating.

ROY: I'm not hungry. *(After a pause.)* I mean, he lay there in that hospital for six months dying and not a word. Not one stinking word.

MARC: Maybe, he didn't want to worry you.

ROY: He loved to worry me.

MARC: That's absurd.

WAYNE: And it isn't the truth.

ROY: *(To himself.)* Isn't it?

WAYNE: I tried very hard to show you love, monkey.

ROY: *(Ibid.)* That's a laugh.

MARC: No, Roy. I really think he didn't want to worry you.

ROY: When did he ever show me anything other than contempt?

MARC: I'm sure there must have been a time.

ROY: Are you? Why? What do you know that I don't?

MARC: People. I know people.

ROY: And I don't? I'm a playwright, remember? Besides, you didn't know him. You didn't know a thing about him.

MARC: Only what you've told me.

ROY: And that's supposed to mean something? What I've told you? He was an overbearing bully. He hated us and he deserted us. A long-distance truck driver in love with the road.

MARC: I know nobody's all bad.

ROY: Do you? Then, please illuminate me with that brilliant legal mind of yours.

MARC: Please. I don't want to argue. *(Drinks some wine.)*

ROY: Nobody's arguing. Nobody's threatening. I just want to know what makes you think you know so much.

MARC: I never said I thought I knew so much. Forget it.

ROY: No. I'm not going to forget it. I want to know.

MARC: I don't have an answer for you, Roy.

ROY: Well, you seem to have an answer for everything else.

MARC: That's not true.

ROY: I'm a liar now? Is that it? Are you calling me a liar?

MARC: I'm not calling you anything. Would you please just stop it? I just don't want to argue.

ROY: Nobody's arguing. There are people that way you know.

MARC: What way?

ROY: Rotten. Evil. Worthless.

MARC: Not completely.

ROY: Yes. Completely. Some people are just born rotten and he was one of them.

MARC: No. I don't believe that.

ROY: Have another glass of wine. That'll make a believer out of you. It always does, doesn't it?

MARC: What is this all about?

ROY: What would you like it to be about?

MARC: Over. I'd like it to be over.

ROY: Us? Is that what you'd like to be over, huh?

MARC: It's not about us. It's about you. Your interminable anger and hostility. I'd like it to be over.

ROY: Over. Right. Sure. What else would you like? Your own winery?

MARC: Stop it! You stop that right now? I'm not your father and I won't be the brunt of your anger against him. It's unfair and you have no right.

ROY: He was born rotten and worthless . . . and he died rotten and worthless.

MARC: You of all people know differently. Nobody's born that way.

ROY: No?

MARC: No. Life. Circumstances. They turn a person.

ROY: Simpleminded. You're so fucking simpleminded. He hated me!

MARC: I'm sorry. *(Nervously, drinks more wine.)*

WAYNE: I wrote. For years I sent you letters.

ROY: I'm not listening.

WAYNE: I poured my heart out to you.

ROY: Can't hear you.

WAYNE: You never answered one of them . . . never answered me.

ROY: Never read a one.

MARC: But I don't think he hated you. He never really knew you.

ROY: How could he? Deserted us when I was eleven. We had to go on welfare. Do you know what it's like on the public dole?

MARC: I can imagine.

ROY: No, you can't. You can't imagine. It was a small town. Everybody knew. Some felt pity. Some felt contempt. Some probably just laughed their fucking heads off.

MARC: I understand.

ROY: Bullshit. My clothes were secondhand. Some of the kids recognized them as discards their parents had donated to the Salvation Army. I had to wear a girl's overcoat one whole winter, for God's sake!

MARC & WAYNE: I'm sorry.

ROY: Nobody's sorry.

WAYNE: I had to leave. I had no choice.

ROY: You had a choice. You had a choice alright. But you were just an irresponsible sonofabitch . . . in love with the road. *(To MARC.)* He deserted us and it drove my mother crazy.

MARC: So you've said.

WAYNE: She was crazy long before I ever left that house.

ROY: No! That was your doing. You gave her nothing to live for.

WAYNE: I gave her you.

ROY: Obviously, I wasn't enough.

MARC: I'm sure it was difficult for you.

WAYNE: She tried several times. Tried to kill me . . . herself. And you. Let's not forget that. The sleeping pills, the gas stove, the knives . . .

ROY: She's dead and you killed her.

WAYNE: I'm not responsible.

ROY: You got that right.

WAYNE: She did it to herself. She took the pills and killed herself. You're not going to pin that one on me, monkey.

MARC: *(Looking up from his plate.)* Eat something, Roy.

ROY: I told you I'm not hungry! And stop calling me monkey!

MARC: Monkey? What are you talking about?

ROY: What?

MARC: Monkey. You said to stop calling you monkey.

ROY: Wayne. He used to call me monkey. Did I ever tell you who I was named after?

MARC: No. Who?

ROY: Roy Rogers.

MARC: You're kidding.

ROY: Nope.

WAYNE: We could've named you after Dale Evans. That's a boy's name too, you know.

MARC: Well, look at the bright side. He could have named you after Dale Evans.

ROY: That seems to be everybody's opinion.

MARC: Eat something, cowboy.

ROY: Why must you keep harping on a thing? If I were hungry I'd eat! Stop acting like a faggot!

MARC: I'm sorry, but I am a faggot.

WAYNE: What a shit you've become.

MARC: I don't mean to harp. It's just that . . . well, you know the stuff they'll serve us on the plane. You'll be starved by the time we get back to Denver.

ROY: How do you know what I'll be?

MARC: I know you, Roy.

ROY: You know shit!

MARC: I know you're upset. You have a perfect right to be. I understand. Tomorrow you'll see things differently.

ROY: You think so?

MARC: Yes, I do.

ROY: I don't.

MARC: Well, you've got to do something to help yourself feel better. You're just upset now. You're upset about the funeral and you're upset about the play.

ROY: Oh, I was waiting to see just how long it would be before you brought that up. You have no empathy. My feelings are of little consequence to you, I'm sure. They slaughtered me, Marc, and you don't give a shit.

MARC: That's not true.

ROY: No? Look what they did to me! There's no way I deserved that kind of venom.

MARC: No, you didn't deserve it. Your play is good and it was a fine production. That was just one critic, Roy. Just one.

ROY: That's all it takes.

MARC: One man's opinion. The other notices were pretty good.

ROY: "Scrap the whole first act." You call that good? The public humiliation. How can I ever write another play?

MARC: Oh, give me a break. That's the nature of the business. If you really feel that way, maybe you should think about doing something else.

ROY: Fucking sonofabitch! I'm not good enough, am I?

MARC: Roy, I never said that. You can't expect everybody to love everything you do. Nobody's perfect.

ROY: *Platitude.* Nobody but you, right?

MARC: Why can't you learn to listen? Why can't you just feel when others are trying to say something for your own good? *(Drinks some wine.)*

ROY: When I hear something profound I'll let you know.

MARC: Do that.

ROY: The years . . . the years of love I poured into that play.

WAYNE: Love? You're a funny man. Excuse me while I bust a gut, will you? Love. You don't know the meaning of the word, monkey.

ROY: Re-writing . . . over and over . . . time and time again.

MARC: Why don't you put some of those feelings that anger—into your writing? Give it to one of your characters. Look at it. See it for what it is.

WAYNE: Because it would probably scare the tar out of him. Maybe even help him pass for something human.

MARC: Think about it.

ROY: Sure, sure. I'll think about it.

MARC: Good. *(Resumes writing.)*

ROY: I'm a human being. I'm doing the best I can. I've got feelings . . . pain.

WAYNE: Right . . . and when you're pricked you bleed . . . .

ROY: When did you suddenly get literary? God, how I hate you. I hate everything about you.

WAYNE: Including your *self?*

ROY: No.

WAYNE: Could've fooled me.

MARC: Why don't you write a play about us . . . and your relationship with your father?

ROY: Well, that'll be the shortest play ever written.

MARC: So? Make it a one-act. It'll help you work through some of this, this. . . .

ROY: This what?

MARC: I don't know. These negative feelings that seem to be getting in your way, crippling you.

ROY: Right. I'm sure that's just the world is waiting for; a play about a dead child-abuser and a couple of psychologically crippled faggots. Or, do you think we're only emotionally crippled?

MARC: Speak for yourself. If it's honest and true, I'm sure you'll make it great.

ROY: It'd be like looking at a bloody accident. They'd hate it and me for writing it.

MARC: People are more forgiving than you give them credit for. *(Nibbles on salad. After a pause.)* I love fresh tomatoes.

ROY: What?

MARC: Try the tomato. Fresh, I think. Not hothouse. Well, maybe. But certainly not gas ripened.

ROY: For God's sake, Marc, what are you on about?

MARC: I heard somewhere they pick the tomatoes green and just before they go to market they're exposed to a gas which ripens them.

ROY: A gas? What kind of gas?

MARC: I don't know.

ROY: Where did you hear that?

MARC: I don't remember.

ROY: Then, you're not sure?

MARC: No. Not for certain. I seem to remember hearing it though.

ROY: What a piece of work! That's called disinformation, Marc. Disinformation.

MARC: I'm just not sure, that's all. Jesus, Roy. Sometimes you're like the Spanish Inquisition.

ROY: *Disinformation.*

MARC: Taste your tomato. It's wonderful. Organic, I bet.

ROY: How would you know a thing like that?

MARC: I said, I'd bet. Fully aware of the potential for loss. *(After a thoughtful pause.)* The taste. Natural things just taste better. You know the difference without anybody telling you. When I was a kid I used to go out into the garden and pick them fresh. Big beefsteak tomatoes. Pop loved his beefsteak tomatoes. Big as two fists. God, they were good. You know something?

ROY: What?

MARC: When was the last time you saw a big beefsteak tomato?

ROY: I don't remember.

MARC: Me either. Maybe they don't grow them much anymore. I wonder why?

ROY: No market, maybe.

MARC: Maybe. *(Drinks some wine. Returns to legal pad.)*

WAYNE: That's a swell mate you got there, monkey.

ROY: Swell mate? He's my lover!

WAYNE: Lover? Odd. One would think he was your whipping boy.

ROY: Just butt out, all right?

WAYNE: Sure, kid. Whatever you say.

ROY: I've been waiting a long time for you to die.

WAYNE: Have you? I trust I made it worth your while.

ROY: I couldn't wait till you were dead.

WAYNE: Here I am. Dead. Disappointed?

ROY: I wanted to spit on your corpse.

WAYNE: You've been watching too many old movies, monkey.

ROY: I had it all worked out in my mind. I'd walk into the funeral parlor. All eyes would be on me as I'd walk down the aisle towards your coffin. I'd stand over your body, sneer and spit. I'd run it over and over in my mind and it felt better each time . . . every time.

WAYNE: What an image! Is that from some old Bette Davis movie?

ROY: What would you know about movies? I don't recall you ever taking me to one.

WAYNE: I was on the road, monkey. I'm sorry you feel short-changed.

ROY: Go to hell.

WAYNE: How do you know I'm not there already?

ROY: I didn't . . . .

WAYNE: Of course you didn't. The thought of me frying is too much even for you, isn't it?

ROY: I meant . . .

WAYNE: Of course you did. So what happened?

ROY: About what?

WAYNE: You didn't sneer and spit. Why didn't you? Lost your nerve?

ROY: I played it out in my mind so many times there just wasn't any joy left in it any longer.

WAYNE: Sorry. I seem to disappoint you at every turn.

MARC: The service was very nice.

ROY: What?

MARC: The service . . . it was very nice.

ROY: Was it?

MARC: I thought so.

ROY: Nobody was there. Didn't he have any friends?

MARC: If he was the way you say he was . . . .

ROY: I don't know how he was, Marc. Not in the end. Not anywhere near the end. The last time I saw him he was younger than I am now. I'm older than the memory of my father. Why did he just up and leave us like that?

MARC: Well, if he was the way you say he was . . . . *(Returns to legal pad.)*

WAYNE: I told you. I didn't have a choice.

ROY: Tell me again.

WAYNE: There was no other way. There was no reasoning with your mother . . . and that crazy church. Just like there's no reasoning with you.

ROY: There's no reason.

WAYNE: Things didn't work out. That's all.

ROY: You didn't try.

WAYNE: All I ever did was try.

ROY: I don't believe you.

WAYNE: Is that what her folks told you?

ROY: I got eyes. Nobody needed to tell me anything.

WAYNE: You were a kid. Eyes lie when you're a kid.

ROY: Not mine.

WAYNE: Everybody's.

ROY: I know you.

WAYNE: They poisoned you against me. That whole clan really did a number, monkey. They filled you with their poison and that's why you hate me, the world, and yourself.

ROY: I don't hate myself!

WAYNE: Of course you do. You hate yourself for being queer.

ROY: You don't say that word! I can say that word! But you don't say that word!

WAYNE: Sure, kid. Anything you say. . .but, it don't change the fact that you're one sad and bitter, self-loathing . . . homosexual. You hate yourself, all right.

ROY: Bullshit! I don't hate myself! For being queer or for anything else—I don't hate myself!

MARC: What did you say?

ROY: I said, I don't hate myself.

MARC: Oh, I think you do.

ROY: Really?

MARC: Between the Catholic Church and your father, how could you not? Only, you should be over it by now. You need to get over it, Roy.

ROY: Is that your expert opinion?

MARC: Children who are abused grow up to be abusive adults. I see it in the courts all the time. Fathers abuse their sons and the sons grow up to abuse their sons . . . or spouses. But, the church is the worst abuser of all . . . especially toward homosexuals. The church abuses us with threats of eternal damnation and hatred toward whom it is we really are.

ROY: Good God! Pontificate, why don't you!

MARC: Most homosexuals have turbulent or short-lived relationships, a high rate of suicide and are, most generally, an unhappy minority. Yes, I think you hate yourself.

ROY: Thank you for the analysis.

MARC: Don't mention it. I think religion is the granddaddy of all father figures. And when the father turns against you, you turn against yourself.

ROY: What in hell are you raving about?

MARC: Nothing. I was just thinking out loud . . . about relationships . . . churches and fathers . . . fathers and sons . . . sons and lovers.

WAYNE: This homosexual stuff you're into . . . it's not all about sex, is it?

ROY: Stuff? I'm into?

WAYNE: You know what I mean. It's not all about sex.

ROY: Of course not! It's about relationships.

MARC: Relationships . . . they're so difficult to fathom. Much less, to make work. A trucker alone with himself on the road for weeks on end . . . no wonder he didn't have any friends.

WAYNE: He really loves you, doesn't he?

ROY: Of course he really loves me. But then, that's a concept for which you have no real knowledge, isn't it?

WAYNE: I'm dead. It's over. No hard feelings.

ROY: Oh, there are hard feelings. There are plenty of hard feelings, Wayne.

WAYNE: Since when did you start calling me Wayne?

ROY: What do you expect me to call you? Dad?

WAYNE: You used to. You used to call me Daddy. Remember?

ROY: You used to beat the crap out of me . . . the few times a year you did come around. Remember?

WAYNE: I remember. She had lists. The minute I'd walk in the door, your mother would hand me a list of grievances against you: The monkey did this, the monkey did that . . . and then she'd add them all up and that determined how many licks you'd get. Sometimes, six months worth of grievances. Would she lift a hand to discipline or punish you? Oh, no . . . she made sure that it was me who did it. She had lists.

ROY: You seemed to enjoy every minute of it.

WAYNE: Now that you mention it, I believe I did.

ROY: How can you admit such a thing!?

WAYNE: I'm dead. You want me to lie?

MARC: *(Looking up from his salad.)* No. I suppose not.

ROY: What?

MARC: I said if he was the way he was it's no wonder he didn't have any friends. How awful it must have been for you.

ROY: About as awful as it gets.

WAYNE: Do I hear violins?

ROY: Tied up. Beat up. Locked up. Talk about child abuse!

WAYNE: Me too.

ROY: You?

WAYNE: You think you were the only kid on the block? You don't know what abuse is, my little monkey boy.

MARC: Sex?

ROY: Sex?

MARC: Sexual abuse?

ROY: You mean, did he fuck me? No. No such luck.

WAYNE: Watch your filthy mouth, monkey!

ROY: Just your everyday, generic child abuse.

WAYNE: I don't want to hear this! What kind of disgusting talk is this!?

ROY: He'd come home from after months on the road to God knows where . . . and he'd strut . . . strut around the house like some fabulous bird of paradise, naked. Oh, God!

How I wanted to reach out and touch him.

WAYNE: Have you no respect for me at all?

MARC: Sometimes I'd imagine Jesus and all the apostles in one big, sweaty pile having the orgy of orgies. Now that's a religious experience, I'll tell you that.

ROY: Disgusting. Have you no respect?

MARC: It made me feel close to God. It helped make a lonely childhood less lonely. It made me happy, all right?

ROY: I know I never knew a single day of happiness.

WAYNE: Why? I'm not responsible for your happiness. But if it will make you feel better, neither did I.

ROY: Not my fault.

WAYNE: Mine. All mine. My lack of happiness, my fault.

ROY: And mine. You robbed me of mine.

WAYNE: No. You robbed yourself. I won't take the blame.

MARC: Mother used to put lit cigarettes out on my arm . . . for no reason. She just didn't like any of my answers . . . my attitude . . . my truth. Once, she nearly split my skull with a coke bottle. She asked me if there was anyone else in the world who could possibly love me more than she. I told her that I didn't know, but I said that I hoped there was. And then she nearly killed me. All behind us now. History. Water under the bridge, as they say.

ROY: No. It's here. Now. Staring me in the face.

MARC: Now she runs around in her slip whenever I go over to visit. What does she think she is doing, anyway?

ROY: Some twisted homage to Electra, no doubt.

WAYNE: I was a goddamned kid and I was hurting and I didn't know any better. I would've liked to have lived in the same house for more than six months . . . take Sunday drives in a new forest green Buick. I would have liked a typical family . . . a wife who wasn't a crazy religious fanatic . . . a son who showed me just the slightest amount of affection, of respect. I would have liked it all! But that's not the way it was.

ROY: You knew better and you blew it. You just blew us off and took off in high gear! The long-distance truck driver . . . in love with the road. Or was it just long distance?

WAYNE: The road was my life, goddamnit!

ROY: I needed an example.

WAYNE: Give your old man a break. I didn't do to you nothin' that wasn't done to me. Nothin'! I'm sorry. I've paid. All right?

ROY: Save your breath.

WAYNE: For what? I'm dead.

ROY: I'm glad.

MARC: *(Looking up.)* What?

ROY: I said that I was glad.

MARC: About what?

ROY: Wayne's death.

MARC: Words, Roy. You don't mean that.

ROY: Why didn't he call me? Why didn't he let me know he was dying. He just wanted to hurt me . . . haunt me . . . leave me with guilt.

WAYNE: It wasn't a conspiracy. I thought I was doing the best thing all around.

ROY: Wrong.

WAYNE: You never answered my letters. Finally, I gave up and thought you'd come looking for me when you were ready. I thought maybe then we'd talk.

ROY: Too late. It's just too late.

MARC: Too late for what?

ROY: Some kind of reconciliation with my father.

MARC: Make the reconciliation in your mind. Sometimes that's all one can do. Sometimes that's all there is.

ROY: Yeah, well, what do you know?

MARC: According to you, not much. I'll keep quiet and work on this.

ROY: Do that. What exactly are you scribbling away on?

MARC: The neighbor's deposition. According to her, until she heard him killing his parents, the boy was a model child.

ROY: Right. That's what they all say on the evening news. He was so sweet and well-mannered, the perfect boy next door; that is, until he butchered his parents in the dead of night, right?

MARC: More or less, yes.

ROY: And what chance do you have defending him? He's guilty, for Christ's sake! Why are you even bothering with a trial?

MARC: Because this is America, sweetheart. They kept him locked in the basement for the entire summer. They tortured and starved him . . . made him eat his own excrement.

ROY: Christ! Why?

MARC: To cure him, I suppose. Rid him of evil demons. He told them he was a homosexual and they just couldn't handle it. So, they proceeded to administer their own kind of demented, black medicine. After three months of torture, he broke free one night and murdered them with a large screwdriver . . . sharp enough to penetrate, but blunt enough to be messy.

ROY: Justifiable.

MARC: My point, exactly.

ROY: No wonder you drink so much.

MARC: Look, if I have a little more wine than you feel is socially acceptable, maybe it's because I have a little more on my mind than just myself! Do you understand what I'm telling you?

ROY: Perfectly.

WAYNE: Like father, like son.

ROY: And fuck you, too!

MARC: One day I'd like to go just fifteen minutes without an argument.

ROY: Would you now? And I suppose that you're going to tell me next that it's my fault. I'm the cause of all the ill in the world, right?

MARC: For pity's sake, Roy, why do you do this?

ROY: This?

MARC: Make life miserable for yourself and everybody around you.

WAYNE: Abuse. Listen to yourself, monkey. You treat him like shit. I guess the term "lover" with your kind is a misnomer. Like father, like son.

ROY: Will you stop saying that!

MARC: Saying what, Roy?

ROY: You make me sound like some kind of monster or something!

MARC: Sometimes that's exactly how you behave.

ROY: Then, why do you continue living with me?

MARC: Good question. I find I've been asking myself that same question, lately.

ROY: Really? And what answer do you come up with?

MARC: That maybe I am immune. That maybe all those cigarettes burns . . . the scars . . . the coke bottle to the skull—maybe I've become immune. And the wine . . . that helps, too.

ROY: What in hell do you want from me, huh? What can you possibly expect?

MARC: Reason. I expect you to be reasonable.

ROY: When am I not?

MARC: Sometimes.

WAYNE: Now.

MARC: Just sometimes.

WAYNE: Right now.

MARC: Come on, Roy. Eat something.

WAYNE: He doesn't want to eat. He wants to be unreasonable.

ROY: I'm not unreasonable!

MARC: I said sometimes. Just sometimes. Please. You know how irritable you get when you don't eat. It has something to do with the chemical balance in the brain.

WAYNE: Always making excuses for you, isn't he?

ROY: What are you talking about?

MARC: Nutrition. A balanced diet. Maybe, you're not getting enough iron . . . or, something.

ROY: I get iron! I get iron and zinc and potassium and fucking riboflavin. . . .

MARC: Please . . . the waiter . . . .

ROY: Fuck the waiter!

MARC: I just thought . . . .

ROY: I know what you thought!

MARC: I'm sorry. *(He withdraws to his salad and/or to his writing.)*

WAYNE: What a piece of work you turned out to be. You have so much venom inside you. It can't be all mine.

ROY: Where did you go all those months?

WAYNE: Away. Just away.

ROY: You just left us to starve. You never sent us a penny. What did you do with all your money?

WAYNE: There were women. There was gambling.

ROY: Jesus Christ! Just like that! Without blinking an eyelash you tell me things like that!

WAYNE: I already told you, monkey boy, I'm dead. What's the point of lying now? But, before you go pointing fingers, you better take a good hard look at yourself.

ROY: I've seen myself.

WAYNE: I don't think so.

ROY: I've looked and I've seen and it's a hell of a lot better than anything that you've got to show.

WAYNE: That's it, monkey boy! Take the easy way out.

ROY: Like you did when you walked out on us?

WAYNE: I wanted to end it peacefully, but there was no peace to be had. What with her being Catholic and all.

ROY: And all?

WAYNE: Fanatic. You can blame that priest for that. You always enjoyed his company better than your old man's. What was his name?

ROY: Father John.

WAYNE: Father John, that's right. He sure had your mother fooled, but not me. He never fooled me for a minute.

ROY: He treated me like a son.

WAYNE: He wanted you in his lap! Bouncing up and down! The pervert!

ROY: You don't know what you're talking about!

WAYNE: There's nothing worse than a converted Catholic!

MARC: *(Looking up.)* What religion was your father?

ROY: He didn't have any as far as I know. Mother converted to Catholicism when I was four.

WAYNE: And made a sissy out of you.

ROY: But, he remained an atheist.

WAYNE: She was a fanatic . . . not a Catholic! And for your information, monkey, I've never been an atheist.

ROY: Then, what are you?

WAYNE: I'm your father, goddamnit!

MARC: Same as you, Roy. Somewhere between Earth and Humanistic Christianity, I suppose.

WAYNE: And I believe in God. My god. Not yours. Not your mother's. Not the Pope's. Mine. Get it, monkey?

ROY: I get it all right. I get it. And I am not your monkey!

MARC: What's that?

ROY: Just before he was about to punish me for something or . . .

WAYNE: . . . teach you a lesson you won't soon forget.

ROY: . . . or, "teach me a lesson I won't soon forget," he'd start calling me monkey. Well, he can't touch me now.

WAYNE: *(Rises, crosses behind ROY and puts his hands on ROY's shoulders.)* Can't I?

ROY: *(Shivers.)* He's dead.

MARC: It's all over now. He can't touch you anymore.

ROY: He's dead. My father is dead.

MARC: We'd better be going if we're to make that plane.

ROY: Don't push me, all right?

MARC: I don't mean to push you.

ROY: You push me! You're always pushing me!

MARC: I'm sorry.

ROY: Is that all you can ever say?

MARC: What would you have me say?

ROY: Can't you fight back? You're a lawyer, for God's sake! I've seen you in action. Why are you always such a wimp around me?

MARC: Because I love you . . . and I'm afraid of you.

WAYNE: Like father, like son.

ROY: That's really not what I wanted to hear.

MARC: I'm sure it wasn't.

ROY: Why don't you just leave me alone!

MARC: Is that what you really want?

WAYNE: Is it, monkey?

ROY: I don't know!

WAYNE: Be a man for once in your life, monkey boy.

ROY: Leave me alone.

WAYNE: Take life into your own hands. Feel it pounding in your veins.

ROY: Stop it!

WAYNE: Life's so short. Shorter than you imagine, monkey boy.

ROY: I'm afraid . . . .

MARC: We've discussed this before. If you really think we'd be better off apart . . . let's do it.

WAYNE: You know you don't mean to hurt him.

MARC: I know you don't mean to hurt me.

WAYNE: But, you do.

MARC: But, you do.

WAYNE: Feel your life. Grab it.

MARC: The pain you cause is just too much for me, sometimes.

WAYNE: Touch it. Touch him.

ROY: I'm afraid . . . .

MARC: I know he treated you and your mother like shit.

WAYNE: Touch him. Touch life.

MARC: But, it's over. Finished. For God's sake, Roy, let it go.

WAYNE: Break the pattern, monkey. Break the pattern.

ROY: You set the pattern!

WAYNE: It was set long before me. I never began to do to you what they did to me.

ROY: You expect me to feel sorry?

WAYNE: I expect you to feel life! Don't be responsible for another's tears!

MARC: Break the chains.

WAYNE: You want someone to blame? Here I am . . . your daddy. But, nothing's going to change until you break the cycle.

ROY: Don't you understand? I'm afraid.

WAYNE: Of what?

ROY: Of ending up like you!

WAYNE: There are worse things.

ROY: I'm afraid of ending up old . . . nothing but old . . . and derelict, telling anybody who will listen what I could have been.

MARC: Please, Roy. *Please.*

WAYNE: You're about to commit one of the greatest crimes of all, monkey.

ROY: I could have been . . . happy.

WAYNE: You are about to make another human being cry. Believe me, that's a tough one to forgive. Remember why you called me here? *(Putting pressure on ROY'S shoulders.)*

ROY: You're hurting me.

MARC: I never wanted to hurt you, Roy. But, most of what you feel, you do to yourself.

ROY: I never called you here. I came to your funeral because I'm your son. For Christ's sake! Why didn't you let me know you were dying?

WAYNE: What good would it have done?

ROY: There was so much I wanted to say to you.

WAYNE: *(Crosses back to his table.)* Then, say it. Say it, monkey. Say it. *(He sits.)*

ROY: I can't. You're dead. You're dead.

MARC: Roy, are you going to be all right?

ROY: Yes. No. I don't know.

MARC: I think we'd better leave.

ROY: In a minute.

WAYNE: Say it.

MARC: The plane . . . .

ROY: To who? You're dead, you sonofabitch! You're dead.

MARC: We don't want to miss the plane.

WAYNE: To your lover, monkey boy. Say it.

ROY: I can't.

WAYNE: Cat got your tongue?

ROY: No. We won't miss the plane.

WAYNE: You sure are a tough nut to crack!

ROY: My father is dead.

WAYNE: You're all alone, now. Got no one but yourself . . . and your mate, if you're lucky. How lucky do you feel, boy?

ROY: *(Trying to hold back the tears.)* He's dead. He's really dead.

MARC: I know.

WAYNE: Come on, monkey. Feel it. Feel it, boy. Feel it. It's your life. It's all yours . . . only yours. It's in your own hands, son.

ROY: Marc.

MARC: Yes?

ROY: I . . . I . . . .

WAYNE: Say it!

ROY: Am I really so abusive?

MARC: Is the Pope a heretic?

ROY: I don't mean to be.

MARC: I know that. I'm sure the Pope doesn't, either.

ROY: I just get crazy, you know?

MARC: I know.

ROY: Crazy . . . like my father used to get with my mother and me.

MARC: I know.

ROY: It's like he's inside me sometimes . . . acting out all his hostility.

MARC: He's dead now. Maybe . . . maybe, you can let him go.

ROY: I wanted to tell him I understood him. I wanted to tell him that I've walked in his shoes. I wanted to tell him that I understand. I wanted to tell him so much. Now, he'll never know. Never.

MARC: I'm sure he already knows all you had to tell him, Roy.

WAYNE: I do, son. I do.

ROY: I'll try, Marc. I'll really try. I want us to make it. I don't want to lose you. I really don't want this to end—us to end.

MARC: Nor do I. Ready?

ROY: Yes. I'm ready. Now.

MARC and ROY rise and walk upstage toward exit. They stop for a moment and then ROY turns around and comes back to the table. He reaches into his pocket and takes out a couple dollars and lays them down on the table for a tip.

ROY *(Continues. To WAYNE.)* I'll try.

WAYNE: I know you will. *(ROY turns to leave. After a pause.)* Hey! *(ROY turns back)* That's a good beginning.

ROY: Yes. Yes it is . . . Thank you . . . Dad.

(THEY embrace and kiss fully on the mouth.)

WAYNE: Goodbye . . . Son.

(ROY picks up the hand luggage, turns and crosses to MARC. They EXIT as LIGHTING slowly fades to BLACK OUT.

END—*Leaving Tampa*

ROAD KILL

SYNOPSIS: (1M/1F, Bare Stage) We meet Mary and Joey, a young homeless couple, late teens to late twenties, waiting by the side of the road for Joey's ride to his first day on a new job. In the shopping cart, along with all their belongings, is their infant son. In this tender story of love and sacrifice, optimism abounds next to the road kill they find along the side of the road.

Enter JOEY and MARY, a young married couple. They are pushing a shopping cart filled with their belongings, including their infant child wrapped in a quilt. There is a helium-filled red balloon tied to the cart, rising overhead. A bare stage. Morning. Early autumn. The present. Along the side of a highway. Traffic sounds.

JOEY: *(Dressed in slacks in need of ironing, a white shirt, tie and sweater. He stands back to display himself for MARY'S approval.)* Well?

MARY: You look wonderful, Joey. Just wonderful! I know you'll get it.

JOEY: You think so?

MARY: Certain.

JOEY: He should be here soon.

MARY: He could have picked a spot where there's someplace to sit. Are you sure this is where he wanted you to meet him?

JOEY: Absolutely.

MARY: What kind of a car does he drive, Joey?

JOEY: One that works. What more do you need?

MARY: Very funny. *(A little soft-shoe.)* But seriously, folks. *(Finishes her little dance with her hand extended toward him as if to say, "It's your turn.")*

JOEY: *(He's too serious to dance today.)* Green. Yes, green.

MARY: *(Pointing.)* Is that him?

JOEY: *(Looking down the highway.)* No. Besides, that's not green. That's blue.

MARY: Well, kind of greenish-blue, wouldn't you say?

JOEY: *Yeah,* but his is green-green. Unmistakably green.

MARY: *Oh,* that kind of green. That's too green, if you ask me. I mean, for a car. *(A pause to look down the highway.)* You know what I'd like? I'd like one in silver. Can we get a silver car? I mean, when things get all right again.

JOEY: Maybe.

MARY: Well, I don't want a green one. Least, not too green.

JOEY: *(Looking down highway.)* We'll see.

MARY: I hope you get it, Joey. Maybe, if you get it and they like you—of course, they'll like you—they'll give you overtime. Overtime's good, Joey. And soon, before you know it, we'll have ourselves a silver car. *(To the baby.)* Wouldn't that be nice, sweetheart? Oh, yes. That would be wonderful. And mommy and daddy will take you for nice long rides. Maybe, we'll take a vacation to Yellowstone. *Yes.* You'd love that, wouldn't you? *(She reaches into the cart, adjusts the quilt before removing a loaf of bread. She takes out a slice and hands it to JOEY who proceeds to eat it. She takes a slice for herself and puts the loaf back in the cart.)* I was thinking the baby and I would go to the zoo today.

JOEY: They charge.

MARY: Really?

JOEY: Almost certain.

MARY: But, isn't it like a public park or something?

JOEY: They still charge.

MARY: That's not fair.

JOEY: *(Looking down the highway.)* What is?

MARY: I'm not staying in that bus station all day anymore. They're getting funny about it.

JOEY: Nobody said anything to me.

MARY: Nobody said anything to me either, but they look at us funny.

JOEY: I never noticed.

MARY: That's because you're too busy looking at my ravishingly, beautiful body. *(Does her little soft-shoe.)* But seriously, folks . . . I don't like to be looked at funny. That's why we took a nice long walk when you went to the unemployment office. Saw some awful pretty houses, Joey. Even saw the street where I want us to live.

JOEY: *(Distracted.)* That's nice.

MARY: *(After a pause.)* Are you sure this is where you're supposed to meet him?

JOEY: Yes, Mary. I'm sure.

MARY: Well, where is he? Maybe he was a phony. Maybe he was just saying he'd take you to see his boss. Maybe he was making it all up.

JOEY: Why would somebody do a thing like that, *huh?* If he said he'd be here, he'll be here. All right?

MARY: *Yeah.* But, I hope it's soon. *(After a pause to look down the highway.)* I need some big plastic garbage bags. If you run across any today bring them back with you, okay?

JOEY: 'Kay.

MARY: I'm going to start collecting aluminum cans. Dot and John got a regular business going. There's good money in aluminum cans.

JOEY: Who's Dot and John?

MARY: A couple I met when you were at the unemployment office. They live in their van, only it doesn't run. John's working on it though. Dot says John's a mechanic. There's big money in being a mechanic, isn't there?

JOEY: *(Looking down the highway, distracted.)* I suppose.

MARY: Sure there is. *(Looking down the highway.)* Wouldn't a van be nice, Joey? We could take all kinds of trips then, *huh?*
JOEY: *(Still distracted.)* Uh-huh. That would be nice, Mary. I hope we didn't miss him.

MARY: I don't see how. He'll be here. *(To baby.)* Won't he, sweetheart? He'll be here with bells on. Then, daddy's gonna get a job. Maybe in an office with real wood paneling and a brass lamp with a green glass shade on a great big desk. Then, we could visit daddy in his office. *(To JOEY.)* He's been sleeping an awful lot lately.

JOEY: That's what babies do. Keep him covered good with Mom's quilt

MARY: I do—may she rest in peace. But he never cries. Babies are supposed to cry.

JOEY: *Naah.* When they cry all the time there's something wrong with them. He's a prince. Princes don't cry.

MARY: I hope your right. *(To baby.)* I sure hope your daddy's right. *(To JOEY.)* Did he say what kind of job it was?

JOEY: Keeping count of things. Electronic stuff, I think.

MARY: Electronic stuff? Oh, maybe it's computers. That's the thing nowadays. I hope it's computers. There's a big future in computers, Joey. *(To baby.)* Daddy's gonna be a computer operator like those men at NASA. Won't that be nice? *(To JOEY.)* Are you sure he said today?

JOEY: Eight o'clock.

MARY: Well, it's just about that now. *(Looking down the highway.)* Oh! There he is! There he is! *(BOTH watch the same passing car.)* Nope. I guess that wasn't him. It was green though, wasn't it?

JOEY: Yes. It was green.

MARY: *(After a pause.)* Fart.

JOEY: *What?*

MARY: Pass gas.

JOEY: I don't have to pass gas.

MARY: That's too bad because if you did, he'd come. Every time I'm waiting for someone and I got to pass gas, I hold it in 'cause I'm afraid they're gonna show up and smell it. But, as soon as I let it out, sure enough, there they are! It's one of those laws of nature.

JOEY: I'll remember that. *(After a pause.)* Mary . . . maybe we should find someplace to keep the baby. Until we get ourselves—situated. Not for long. Just a few weeks maybe.

MARY: We are situated. We got each other. You'll get that job and everything will be just fine.

JOEY: But, suppose I don't?

MARY: *Suppose, suppose, suppose.* Suppose you do and you will. How can you talk like that? You scare me when you talk like that.

JOEY: Sorry, but things haven't been turning out the way we thought.

MARY: They will, I promise.

JOEY: It's not yours to promise.

MARY: Everything will turn out just fine. You'll see.

JOEY: Until it does, I think we ought to find someplace for—

MARY: *(Cutting him off. Covering her ears.)* No! I don't want to hear it anymore! You promised! You promised!

JOEY: We've got to face the facts, Mary.

MARY: What facts? Everything's looking up. Everything will be just fine.

JOEY: *(Resigning.)* I hope you're right.

MARY: I am. You'll see. You make me so mad when you talk like that. *(To the baby.)* He makes me so mad.

Doesn't he, sweetie? You won't ever be negative, will you? Oh, no. Negative is a bad thing to be. It sets all kinds of bad things into motion. Doesn't it? Our little prince will be so positive . . . why . . . you might grow up to be the President of the United States of America. *(To JOEY.)* Wouldn't that be nice? I mean, he could be the President, couldn't he? Or, a doctor. I think there's more money in being a doctor.

JOEY: He could be both.

MARY: That's right! A doctor first and then the President. Did we ever have a President who was a doctor?

JOEY: I don't know.

MARY: Then he'll be the first. *Oh,* I'm excited already.

JOEY: Now don't go pushing him. He might want to be something else.

MARY: Like what?

JOEY: I don't know. A mechanic, maybe.

MARY: Of all the things in this world to be, why on Earth would our son want to be a mechanic? *Yuck.*

JOEY: Maybe he won't, but maybe he won't want to be a doctor or the President, either.

MARY: Don't be silly. Who wouldn't want to be the President?

JOEY: I wouldn't.

MARY: *Go on.* You wouldn't want to be the President? Don't tell me. You mean to tell me you wouldn't want to rule the world?

JOEY: The President doesn't rule the world.

MARY: He does our world. He runs the country, doesn't he?

JOEY: Running the country and ruling the world are two different things.

MARY: I suppose. Ruling the world would be more fun, wouldn't it? I mean, the President doesn't really do anything, does he? I mean, who's in charge anyway?

JOEY: We. The people. *Us.*

MARY: *Yeah,* that's right. Kind of makes you feel proud, doesn't it? I mean, this great big country of ours, for good or for bad is run by we, the people. *(Shivers.) Oh, God!* Can't you feel the power? It gives me goose bumps. But how come we're not doing a better job?

JOEY: I don't know. Maybe, we don't know how.

MARY: That's it! We don't know how. Here we are—we, the people—running the best country on earth—America. We don't know how we do it, but we do it. *What a shame.*

JOEY: What's the shame?

MARY: The shame, Joseph Carpenter, is that we don't do it better. If it were run more by the people and more for the people, we the people would be a lot better off.

JOEY: *Humph.* I can't argue with that.

MARY: There's no good reason why you should want to argue with that. *(To the baby.)* Is there, sweetheart? *(To JOEY who is looking down the highway.)* Maybe, he meant eight o'clock tonight.

JOEY: No. In the morning. He said to be here eight in the morning if I wanted a ride.

MARY: Well, this is the morning he meant, isn't it?

JOEY: Yes. This is the morning he meant.

MARY: Just checking.

JOEY: Are you sure I look all right?

MARY: You look wonderful, Joey.

JOEY: It's important to make a good first impression.

MARY: You will. I promise, you will. *(After a pause to search the highway.)* I was thinking. I mean, when things are better. You know, when we get a place to stay. A real place, not like the bus station. Do you think I could get a job?

JOEY: You know how I feel about my wife working.

MARY: I know, but it would be like a kind of insurance. You know, insurance against this happening again. I guess we didn't manage things quite right, *huh?* I'm not complaining. What's done is done. Things could be worse. I just don't like the way they look at me. You know, *funny.*

JOEY: Nobody looks at you funny, Mary.

MARY: They do. Honest, they do.

JOEY: Who? You tell me who looked at you funny and I'll—

MARY: You'll what, big man?

JOEY: *(Making a fist.)* I'll have a word with them. That's what I'll do.

MARY: *(To the baby.)* Listen to your daddy talk. What a funny man. What a big, funny man your daddy is. *(Notices something on the ground, several feet away.)* What's that?

JOEY: What?

MARY: *(Pointing.)* That. That, over there. On the ground. *(Crosses to it.)* Oh, no. *(Sad and angry.)* Oh, no. No, no, no.

JOEY: What? What is it?

MARY: Look.

JOEY: *(Coming over - looks.)* Come on. Get away from it.

MARY: But, somebody should bury it.

JOEY: It's half eaten and decayed already. In another week there won't be a trace of it left.

MARY: It's not right to just leave it there.

JOEY: *(Pulling her back to the cart.)* Come on. That thing carries all kinds of diseases. Think of the baby.

MARY: I am thinking of the baby. *(Rummages through the cart and comes up with a small quilt.)*

JOEY: What are you going to do? That's the Mom's quilt!

MARY: Not it's not. Mom's quilt is covering the baby. This is just an old one they gave me down at the shelter. If it's not going to get buried, it needs to be covered.

JOEY: But, not with that.

MARY: I'm sorry, Joey. But that little animal needs it more than us.

JOEY: It's dead, Mary.

MARY: *(Crossing to the road kill.)* I know. I know. *(Covers it with the quilt.)* There. Nobody deserves to be left out in the open—even if they are dead.

JOEY: *(Reluctantly.)* Yeah . . . sure.

MARY: I found this beautiful street yesterday lined with trees and grass as green as green gets. Greener than that man's car, I bet. *And the houses.* They were so pretty. And somebody was burning leaves. I love the smell of burning leaves. There was this woman in the window of her beautiful house. And she looked at us looking in at her and she grabbed her baby. . . .

JOEY: She had a baby?

MARY: Yes, 'bout the same age as our little prince. She grabbed her baby, held it close to her, then gave us a look. I'll never forget it. *Never.* I saw myself, Joey. Looking out as I was looking in, I saw myself in her eyes. It frightened me.

JOEY: *(Embracing her.)* She wasn't looking at you. She was looking at a stranger on the street. *Not you.* If she was looking at you, Mary—really looking at you—she'd have come to the door and invited you in. *(Kisses her.)*

MARY: *(After a pause.)* What were you thinking of?

JOEY: When?

MARY: Just now. When you kissed me. What were you thinking of?

JOEY: I was thinking . . . well, I was thinking of you.

MARY: No, you weren't. Your eyes looked off to the side. You didn't look at me. You avoided me, Joey.

JOEY: That's not true.

MARY: You avoided me.

JOEY: I'm sorry. I just wish to God he'd hurry up and come, that's all.

MARY: He will. Be patient. *(To the baby.)* Good things come to those who wait. Don't they, sweetheart?

JOEY: There was a man. One of those people who were forced off the church property. He moved in with that bunch living in the parking lot under the bridge. His wife's in the city jail. They picked her up for shoplifting. So, he celebrated by getting drunk. Stinking, dead drunk. This was the day before yesterday. That night, the night before last when that storm hit us—

MARY: That was some storm! *(To the baby.)* Wasn't it, sweetheart?

JOEY: Dead drunk, he crawled into one of those dumpsters near the bridge and passed out. Yesterday morning the truck came to get the garbage—

MARY: *(Picks up the baby wrapped in the quilt and clutches it tightly.)* Oh, no.

JOEY: And they hooked the dumpster to the truck, lifted it and dumped it into the truck. Then they turned on the switch to compress the garbage—

MARY: *Oh, God.*

JOEY: They heard a squeal. Like a sheep, they said.

MARY: Is he . . . dead?

JOEY: No. He lost both his legs, but he's not dead.

MARY: Poor man.

JOEY: *(Seeing his ride coming.)* There he is! Across the street!

MARY: *(Putting the baby back into the cart.)* Oh, hurry, Joey! Don't keep him waiting!

JOEY: *(A quick embrace. Kisses her. Kisses the baby.)* You sure I look okay?

MARY: You look magnificent. Now, hurry up and go before he leaves you here on the side of the highway.

JOEY: *(Hurrying towards exit.)* Wish me luck. Where will you be?

MARY: *(Calling after him.)* Look for the red balloon! *(JOEY exits. To herself.)* Luck. *(To the baby.)* What are we gonna do today, *huh?* What does mommy's little prince want to do? We could go to the park, collect aluminum cans, look at the leaves turning—falling. We could find another nice street with pretty houses on it. Would you like that? There's all kinds of things we could do. *(Pushing the cart, slowly, towards the exit opposite the one taken by JOEY.)* Maybe today somebody will invite us in for tea and cookies. One never knows. Wouldn't that be nice? It's possible. In these United States of America, anything is possible. Isn't it, sweetheart? *(She does her little soft-shoe dance and then abruptly, stops.)* But seriously, folks—*(She exits.)*

LIGHTING fades, leaving a narrow spot on the quilt before fading to BLACK OUT.

END—*Road Kill*

SAMSON AND DELILAH

SYNOPSIS: (1M/1W) A bed and a small vanity with chair. Set in New Orleans, this is the story of two outcasts suffering the consequences of the hustle in the time of hurricane Katrina.

AT RISE: SAMSON is stretched across the bed. He is wearing underwear or nothing at all. DELIAH is brushing her hair at the vanity. She is wearing a slip or a bra and panties or nothing at all. New Orleans. A summer's morning in late August, 2005. SOUND of howling wind and rain.

DELILAH: *(Stops brushing her hair.)* Get yar lazy bone-ass outta bed. *(A pause to see if he moves. Slams down her brush.)* Don't pretend yar still asleep—'cause I knows ya ain't. Ya can hustle da ballers down ta Funky Bo's, but yar ain't gonna hustle Delilah.

SAMSON: Ah been awake all night.

DELIAH: I s'pects ya have. Ya only come home two hour ago, drippin' wet and smelly likes a mongrel. Get up. We got things ta do.

SAMSON: And ah got things ta figure.

DELILAH: *(Rises. Crosses to SAMSON. Playfully.)* Ya don't get outta dat bed, ya'll be lookin' at the meanest piece ya ever laid—

SAMSON: *Fa Shiggety.*

DELILAH: Ain't no other way ta say it. *(She rubs her breasts, runs her hands down along her body, enticing him.)*

SAMSON: *O mama. Fine dinin'.*

DELILAH: Wanna taste?

SAMSON: Too much goin' on fa dat.

DELILAH: When's there ever been too much goin' on fa dat? Ain't never been too much on. *(She straddles his body and goes as far as the traffic will bear.)*

SAMSON: Ah told ya, I got things to figure. *(Pushes her off.)*

DELILAH: *(Getting up. Confused.)* Ya one bad motha fucka. Ya figure. Ya figure, and when yar done figurin' we gonna buy me the finest ruby-red dress ya ever saw.

SAMSON: Sure, babe. Da finest. There's a hurricane. Katrina—

DELILAH: *Katrina, Katrina!* Ya see one ya seen 'em all.

SAMSON: Ain't a good time.

DELILAH: You promised—soon as ya made some bones.

SAMSON: Ah did, did ah?

DELILAH: Wid shiny red beads dat'll blind ya.

SAMSON: What?

DELILAH: On the dress ya gonna buy me.

SAMSON: S'pose ah don't want ta be blinded?

DELILAH: Not ya, just da gawkers and da coon ass. Wear yar sunglasses.

(A flash of LIGHTNING followed by the SOUND of THUNDER.)

SAMSON: *(Alarmed.)* We gotta take da Chevy and—

DELILAH: Well I ain't ridin' in no street car, not in this rain.

SAMSON: Ah know, but—

DELILAH: Ain't no buts. Dinner in da Quarter and jazz all night—like a coupla high ballers. Where's da bones?

SAMSON: Don't ya listen to nothin' I say?

DELILAH: Not when I don't want ta hear it.

SAMSON: Ya got that right. Da Quarter will be boarded up by night. I told ya, there's a wicked storm comin'. Besides—

DELILAH: *Besides, besides.* There's always a besides.

SAMSON: Delilah, there's this deal went down bad—

DELILAH: *(She reaches over and tickles him.)* C'mon now.

SAMSON: Delilah, ah told ya—

DELILAH: Where ya hid dem?

SAMSON: *(Gives in.)* Uner the bed. *(DELILAH reaches under the bed.)* Looka here. Before ya go ta openin' that, ah gotta tell ya somethin'.

DELILAH: *(Retrieving shoe box from under the bed. Removes the lid.)* Hoooly Shit! Dim ain't mudbugs, I can tell ya dat!

SAMSON: That's just what I brung in in ma pockets, dawlin'. That's what ah was fixin' to tell ya.

DELILAH: *(Removing handfuls of money.)* Where'd ya get alla dis?

SAMSON: Playin' boo ray with some coon ass.

DELILAH: Fo True?

SAMSON: 'Cept ah didn't actually win it.

DELILAH: Ain't seen nuthin' so pretty. Nuthin' so pretty—'cept maybe ya. *(She runs her hands along his body, sensuously. She licks his chest and slowly moves toward his crouch.)* Dat sure a lotta money.

SAMSON: *(Pushing her away.)* Ahm down bad, baby.

DELILAH: Ya down good—real good.

SAMSON: Did ya hear me? Ah was playin' boo ray—

DELILAH: Ya musta took alota tricks.

SAMSON: Ah took every one.

DELILAH: God musta dealt dem cards. He sure musta.

SAMSON: Delilah, we gots ta leave fo up north. Somethin' bad's comin'.

(A flash of LIGHTNING followed by the SOUND of THUNDER and the increasing WIND.)

DELILAH: Da fuck?

SAMSON: We gots ta get outta here.

DELILAH: Look at all dis green. What 'bout ma new dress? And some jazz ta dawn? Ya got da bones.

SAMSON: Won't be no jazz tonight.

DELILAH: Course there will.

SAMSON: They boardin' everything up. We got to get in the Chevy and go. Didn't ya hear me?

DELILAH: I heard ya. I heard ya all right, Samson, but I ain't goin' nowheres. I'm goin' down Bourbon in ma ruby-red dress, sparklin' like fireworks and get me some jazz.

SAMSON: Dey wasn't the dumb coon ass ah thought. Dey musta figured it by now. Da cards—

DELILAH: *(Sudden interest.)* What cards?

SAMSON: Ya know—

DELILAH: Ya didn't use *dem* cards, did ya?

SAMSON: Ah told ya. Ah took dem fo coon ass.

DELILAH: Ya used dem cards?

SAMSON: Yeah, but dey never figured it.

DELILAH: Den there ain't no problem. We can go get me dat dress—

SAMSON: Ahm down bad, babe. *Real bad.*

DELILAH: Ya said dey never figured it.

SAMSON: Not whiles we was playin', but—

DELILAH: *But, but?*

SAMSON: Ah left dem there.

DELILAH: *(Cautiously.)* Left what there?

SAMSON: There was all those bones. Biggest pot ah ever saw. Ah been playin' boo ray a long time and ah ain't never seen nuthin' like it. There's mo hidden in da Chevy.

DELILAH: Mo what?

SAMSON: Money.

DELILAH: Mo money?

SAMSON: Mo money than ya ever saw.

DELILAH: We be struttin' down Bourbon.

SAMSON: We gotta get outta Nahlins.

(Howling WIND, LIGHTNING, THUNDER.)

DELILAH: What ya talkin'?

SAMSON: Ah told ya. Ah left dem there.

DELILAH: Tell me. Tell me exactly what ya left there?

SAMSON: Ah told ya. *Da cards.* Ain't ya been listenin'? Did ya hear a word ah said? Ah was in such a hurry to get outta there—ah went and left da cards.

(There is a long fearful SILENCE except for the howling WIND.)

DELILAH: Ya think dey figured it?

SAMSON: Had to.

DELILAH: What about ma dress?

SAMSON: We'll get you dat dress, but not now.

DELILAH: Ya promised.

SAMSON: Ah know ah did, babe.

DELILAH: I told ya dem cards would get ya down bad one day. Get on some clothes.

SAMSON: *(Putting on his trousers.)* Ah gotta get those bones.

DELILAH: *(Digging in her heels.)* Ya might s'well leave dem in da Chevy 'cause I ain't goin' wid ya.

SAMSON: Ya be getting' yar things together, Delilah. Ya ain't stayin' here.

DELILAH: Samson, now *ya* ain't listenin'. Take dem what ya got in da Chevy. I got plenty right here.

SAMSON: But, babe—

DELILAH: You heard me. Get on out.

SAMSON: Ah ain't goin' nowhere widout ya.

DELILAH: Get out ya sonabitch! *(She beats him with closed fists. He stands and lets her hit him.)* Sonabitch! I told ya 'bout those cards. I told ya! I told ya! *(She continues beating him until she can't hold back her tears.)*

(WIND, LIGHTNING, THUNDER.)

SAMSON: Ah know, babe.

DELILAH: Git out! I don't wanna see ya sorry ass ever again.

SAMSON: Ahm sorry, babe. Please come wid me.

DELILAH: Don't babe me, just get da fuck out!

SAMSON: Ya don't mean dat. Ah know ya don't.

DELILAH: *Get!*

SAMSON: Ahm sorry. *(In the SILENCE he dresses, then slowly walks toward the door.)*

DELILAH: *(Breaking the SILENCE.)* And don't ya come back! *Hear?*

SAMSON exits to the SOUND of howling WIND. DELILAH sits on the edge of the bed and begins to count the money. She stops and throws the money across the room and then openly sobs. After awhile, the distinctive SOUND of a single GUNSHOT rips through the bedroom. DELILAH freezes in terror, looking toward the door. Shortly afterward there is the SOUND of two more gunshots in quick succession. DELILAH puts on an old ragged dress. She stands unmoving while staring at the front door, perhaps hoping that SAMSON would soon walk through it. He doesn't. Slowly and tentatively she walks towards the door as the LIGHTING dims to the SOUND of howling WIND.

BLACK OUT.

END—*Samson and Delilah*

SLOW BOAT TO CHINA

SYNOPSIS: 1M/1W, Minimal set. She's working on her memoirs. Her memory is fading as the early symptoms of Alzheimer's begin to take root. He's turned his back on fieldwork and writing to teach anthropology at the local community college. Together, they have shared forty years of marriage. It is their anniversary and the last day of summer as he tries to coax her into a metaphorical walk into the woods. The universality of long term relationships, the abrasive familiarity, the language of a husband and a wife who have become indifferent yet bound by tepid love mixed with the impending consequences of Alzheimer's Decease—all add to an engaging exploration into the long-term intimacy of a marriage.

SETTING: Minimal to abstract. Table, chair.

AT RISE: SHE and HE are at home where sunlight pours through an opened window. SHE is toiling over the loose pages of her handwritten manuscript, while HE moves nervously about.

SHE: *(After some consideration.)* You've no right to accuse me of that.

HE: I have every right. Have you ever considered how what you say affects others?

SHE: Others?

HE: Me.

SHE: *Ah, you.* So, that is what you mean by others.

HE: I accused you of nothing.

SHE: You call indifference *nothing?*

HE: You sit and write and I don't exist.

SHE: I never thought of you as not existing. *You over-exist.*

HE: What does that mean?

SHE: It means I cannot get a sentence completed with you roaming back a forth like a limping something or other. Pick your euphemism.

HE: *(After a pause to ponder what SHE just said.)* They say we're all connected.

SHE: To anyone I know?

HE: I only want what's best.

SHE: Nonsense. If I am indifferent to anything it is to the unfounded accusations of the well-meaning. That I choose to remain inside with my memories and my thoughts on this last dreary day of summer, does not make me a deserving target for your antagonism.

HE: *See?* See what I mean? That's the sort of thing that really ticks me. Now I'm an antagonist. An antagonist to your what? The woman in your memoirs? It's all so unnecessary.

SHE: Then, don't provoke.

HE: It was not my intent. I'm sorry you saw it that way.

SHE: So am I. *(A prolonged silence.)* I have heard it is an angel passing.

HE: *Huh?*

SHE: The awkward silence.

HE: *Ah.* When was that?

SHE: Just now. *(A pause. A blankness.)* What? *Ahh...* what was I saying?

HE: Don't provoke.

SHE: What I? *Oh, yes.* Don't provoke.

HE: I was simply trying to motivate you.

SHE: Simply, yes.

HE: *(Sighs.)* I thought today was special.

SHE: I see nothing special about it and I don't need motivation. I need to be left to my work.

HE: You've stayed locked-up in this house all summer.

SHE: I've been working on my memoirs. I'm trying to remember. Can't you understand that? I am trying to remember.

HE: Sorry.

SHE: You're beginning to get under my skin.

HE: Is that a bad thing?

SHE: Of course.

HE: Summer's come and gone and we haven't so much as taken one walk through the woods.

SHE: I don't like the woods.

HE: Of course you do. You've always liked the woods.

SHE: Only as metaphor.

HE: That wasn't always the case.

SHE: People change. I don't like them anymore.

HE: People? You don't like people?

SHE: That's right—people and woods. Do you have a problem with that?

HE: No. Well...come to think of it, no...but how can anyone stop liking the woods? It's like suddenly not liking the ocean—or magic.

SHE: I never liked the ocean and there is no such thing as magic.

HE: But if you had—if you believed?

SHE: I can't. If I could, I would reserve the right to change my mind. Besides, you know perfectly well that I never learned to swim.

HE: There's nothing to learn. Everybody knows how to swim.

SHE: So you've told me.

HE: Only because you haven't had to. If you had to, you would.

SHE: I wouldn't. This body can't. I tried. It sank.

HE: Knowing you, you'd probably drown just to prove me wrong.

SHE: Tellingly amusing. That is a problem, isn't it?

HE: I'm not asking you to swim. I'm asking you to walk. You can walk, can't you?

SHE: Of course I can walk.

HE: Then walk with me—through the woods.

SHE: I've already told you that I'm working. Don't you have papers to correct—students to fail?

HE: No, summer school finished weeks ago. Don't you remember?

SHE: Remember what?

HE: What I said.

SHE: Stop testing me! I want to work.

HE: Don't let the woods stop you...me stop you. *(A pause to watch her.)* Am I in there?

SHE: In my memoirs? *(HE nods "yes.")* What do you think?

HE: I think, if you could, you'd figure out a way to avoid ever having to mention me by name. I will forever be known as he, him, the husband or, God forbid, *the other.*

SHE: *God forbid?* You've got to be kidding. Go out and play. I wash my hands of you. You've too much time on your hands. Do something to further your cause.

HE: Unlike you I have no cause, no impending destiny with celebrity. I've thrown my dreams for the unobtainable out the window years ago.

SHE: Please don't make fun of me.

HE: And while you're washing your hands of me take a good look at them. Look what all those years of holding onto countless unrealized dreams have done to them. At least I had the good sense to let go.
SHE: Is that what you call it—good sense?

HE: I'm not in pain and suffering while playing beat-the-clock with the grim reaper.

SHE: Not so grim, perhaps.

HE: You don't know that.

SHE: You think giving up is the answer? It's not my answer. Never was. You might have been a great writer —a notable observer of Human culture.

HE: I thought I was.

SHE: Well, you might have been successful at it.

HE: We'll never know, will we?

SHE: That puts you in a win-win situation, doesn't it?

HE: If you say so.

SHE: Can't lose now, can you?

HE: Guess not.

SHE: Am I supposed to feel sorry for you?

HE: You're not supposed to feel anything.

SHE: Good, because I don't.

HE: I know. You can't just feel anything without thinking about it first, can you

SHE: *Stop it.* You don't know anything.

HE: I know you've been at those memoirs a lifetime.

SHE: That's what it takes, a lifetime.

HE: Not much left in this lifetime's tattered grab bag.

SHE: When I finish them—

HE: When you finish them you'll be no further along than you are now. No celebrity for you, either, I fear.

SHE: *Wretched man.*

HE: Not so much as a kewpie doll for all your barren efforts.

SHE: *Barren?*

HE: *Efforts.*

SHE: I see.

HE: Creative endeavors.

SHE: You know perfectly well I couldn't have any!

HE: I don't recall our ever really trying; you ever really trying. You always had an excuse.

SHE: Then there is nothing to talk about. Subject closed.

HE: Stay with me. I was talking about birthing art and literature. I was talking about realizing a sense of worth.

SHE: I realized my worth a long time ago. And that will always be mine no matter what I forget.

HE: Not much to hold onto when all else fails—when the mind addles and memories begin to lie.

SHE: My memories are in my memoirs. *(Clutching a pile of papers.)* Every one of them in here—the details of a Human life. Nobody is going to take them. *Nobody!* I will read them and I will remember.

HE: *(Reaching out for the papers. SHE clutches to them.)* It's okay. Hand them to me.

SHE: *No!* This is my life. My life, goddamnit! My life. *(SHE randomly organizes pages on the desk before slowly lifting both hands to where she can examine them. After a pause and a sigh.)* Oh my God. I don't remember them being so. . .

HE: Old?

SHE: Mature.

HE: The hands of a woman dispel the slightest illusion of youth. They're one of the first things to go.

SHE: How typically cruel.

HE: For this moment, I suppose. But not typically. Did you know that the wrinkles, the liver spots, the veins—

SHE: With a man it is his lips. The corners of his lips are cut with deep creases that tremble with fear and uncertainty.

HE: I've nothing left to fear and I've never been certain of anything. Any tremors that you see are from years of unsolicited criticism—thank you very much.

SHE: You give back in spades.

HE: I've learned.

SHE: Very little. I believe you fear the truth.

HE: What truth? *Your truth?*

SHE: The truth of yourself. You have begun to believe the many lies you have told yourself all these many years.

HE: Not so many.

SHE: Years or lies?

HE: Years. There were never lies.

SHE: Plenty enough.

HE: Never lies.

SHE: Lies you've told yourself! You can no longer afford not to believe them. Not at your age, sir. You are far beyond that point. The pain of others has become your only pleasure. You insulate yourself with the pain of others.

HE: Whose?

SHE: Mine, to begin with. The more you inflict the less you feel of your own.

HE: You've become rather sinister in your decline. Is it deliberate?

SHE: I am still able to think before I speak, if that is what you mean.

HE: I'm not sure. That may be what I mean. Perhaps, that is why you sound like one of your unfinished—though highly quotable—manuscripts.

SHE: It is a sound earned honestly. I may not have published but I have not perished. Unlike you who has taken on the vernacular of his students.

HE: Honestly?

SHE: I am always honest with you. *(As an accusation.)* At least, I try .

HE: Really?

SHE: *Absolutely.*

HE: *(A sly pause.)* But not about the boys.

SHE: The boys?

HE: You had your boys?

SHE: And you your girls.

HE: Sometimes there were boys.

SHE: I always suspected that.

HE: Did you?

SHE: Often. But then, I had a few girls too.

HE: You're kidding?

SHE: No. It was a time when we were all experimenting.

HE: I don't remember a time when we were all experimenting.

SHE: You were busy taking the road most traveled.

HE: It was the path of least resistance.

SHE: You were busy trying to be the next Carlos Castaneda as I recall. Whatever happened?

HE: Memory fails.

SHE: A miscarriage of convenience no doubt.

HE: No doubt. So what about the time you were experimenting and I was busy being the genius.

SHE: I've done much that you are not aware of.

HE: Really? Such as?

SHE: Had I wanted you to know I would have told you long ago. I have my own interior life.

HE: Sometimes, my beloved, you are an evil woman, plainly and simply.

SHE: Some of my memories are certainly evil—most having to do with you. It's all around us, isn't it?

HE: What? Evil or memories?

SHE: Both, I imagine. It is as if we were underwater and memories, some good and some not so good, fly through the liquid ether like fishes. It's all here. It's all there. Every bit of it. Our ideas. Our choices. Our dreams. Our lives. We never really see it—just the momentary flashes.

HE: *Fish.*

SHE: *Fishes.* Fish is plural when they're all the same. I'm talking about more species than you are aware.

HE: So you say.

SHE: Yet I remain, as always, unchanged, *here*—the eternal haven for the spiritually actualized. Now, I am tired of this game.

HE: Not yet. Not so soon.

SHE: Yes, now. You wear me out.

HE: Where am I in your scenario?

SHE: Right here next to me.

HE: Precarious, at best.

SHE: It was your choice. It has always been your choice.

HE: I didn't choose wisely.

SHE: *(A thoughtful silence.)* Few do.

HE: Still, it would be nice to choose with the benefit of foreknowledge.

SHE: That would be a beggar's paradise.

HE: I suppose. But it's not too late.

SHE: For what?

HE: To change, to make another choice, to move on, to reinvent, to be somebody else, somewhere else—

SHE: It's not too late. You're just too frightened by the idea of it.

HE: Am I?

SHE: Exactly. What kind of loss do you think you'd be to me?

HE: Someone to remind you of yourself. Someone to reflect upon. I'd be a great loss. I am your mirror.

SHE: That's the last thing I want to see! Does it never occur to you that I may no longer need reminding—that I may no longer like what I see through you?

HE: Who would you be without me? You have no friends to speak of.

SHE: Neither have you. You've chased them all away.

HE: There are my associates at work.

SHE: They're hardly friends. They're anthropologists.

HE: What does that mean?

SHE: It means they are not your friends—just the people in the anthropology department of a backwater community college who give you the appearance of friendship and deference out of fear for your age.

HE: I see. *Tick, tick, and tick!* And you can't beat the clock.

SHE: I'm talking about the mindset. Anyway, I'm not afraid to find out. There's always the door.

HE: There's always that.

SHE: Which side would you prefer to be on?

HE: I've made my choice.

SHE: Have you? Or have you gone with the flow? Is that what your students say, *"Go with the flow?"* Is that the current vernacular?

HE: I'd say it's a an ancient aphorism.

SHE: Still, certainly applicable. You go with the flow and you imagine yourself divinely dispensed of responsibility. *(Raising her voice.)* I repeat, what side of the door do you choose?

HE: This side, with you. It's where I am, isn't it?

SHE: It is. But, if I were not here?

HE: You want to know where I'd be without you, is that it?

SHE: I want to know *who* you would be without me.

HE: *(After a thoughtful pause.)* I think I would be afraid.

SHE: *(Softening.)* Perhaps, I would find it—difficult. Where will we go?

HE: After here?

SHE: Yes.

HE: I don't know. How could I?

SHE: I want to go with my memory intact.

HE: Does it matter?

SHE: I believe it does. I don't want to go in installments, chapter by chapter—all at once or not at all.

HE: There's no such thing as not at all.

SHE: You don't know that.

HE: *No. (Pause.)* I've thought about ending it.

SHE: *What?*

HE: *(After a pause.)* I've thought about divorce.

SHE: I thought you meant…

HE: I know. I changed the subject. I was referring to our relationship. Our marriage.

SHE: Were you? So the subject is your thinking about divorce? Often?

HE: Often enough.

SHE: So have I.

HE: Has it been all that bad—all these years?

SHE: Does it matter?

HE: Forty years.

SHE: That long?

HE: Does it seem that long?

SHE: *(After a pause.)* I can't remember. What were we talking about?

HE: Our years. There were times of romance.

SHE: There always is. In the beginning.

HE: We enjoy each other's company.

SHE: From time to time.
HE: There were times I wanted to kill you.

SHE: There were times you nearly did. *(Touching her neck.)* The scar hasn't faded very much, has it?

HE: I try not to look at it.

SHE: So do I.

HE: I try not to think of it.

SHE: So do I.

HE: The things one remembers. It was an accident.

SHE: I know. But, like most accidents, it could have been avoided.

HE: I wasn't aiming to hit you.

SHE: I know. You weren't aiming at all. You were reckless. You couldn't control your anger.

HE: I was young.

SHE: I know. We both were.

HE: I'm so sorry.

SHE: I know.

HE: What was it about?

SHE: I don't remember.

HE: I don't remember, either. You'd think one would remember something like that. *(After a pause.)* What do you think causes that?

SHE: *That?*

HE: Causes one to forget?

SHE: I haven't forgotten.

HE: Then, what was the argument about?

SHE: I don't remember.

HE: But you—

SHE: No, I didn't. I said—

HE: You hadn't—

SHE: The incident. The blood. I could never forget the blood.

HE: I thought—

SHE: I know what you thought.

HE: Then you really don't remember how it began?

SHE: No.

HE: Neither do I.

SHE: So you said.

HE: Just the incident . . . the blood . . . the waiting.

SHE: The waiting, yes. Always the waiting.

HE: I might have been a murderer.

SHE: Easily.

HE: But you survived.

SHE: Barely.

HE: I'm so sorry.

SHE: I know.

HE: So you said. *(After a pause.)* There were times I, too, nearly died.

SHE: But, not at my hands.

HE: No, not at your hands.

SHE: There were times we nearly died—together and apart.
HE: Together and apart, yes.

SHE: You're not going away, are you?

HE: You mean from here? Now?

SHE: Yes.

HE: No. I'm not going away. *(Removes Post-It notes from desk, writes on one and attaches it to her.)* "Wife."

SHE: I'm not going to get any work done today, am I?

HE: It's doubtful. *(Writes and sticks a note to his chest.)* "Husband."

SHE: All right. What do you want?

HE: I want us to take a walk in the woods—before the sun sets. Tomorrow the fall begins and you haven't left this house all summer.

SHE: I'm sure that is an exaggeration. We spent three weeks in Europe. Is your memory that short?

HE: That was last summer.

SHE: It was not.

HE: Think about it.

SHE: There's nothing to think about. *(After a pause. Alarmed.)* Oh my God. It was last summer. How could I have forgotten? How did that—

HE: *(Comforting.)* It's okay.

SHE: *(Worried. A bit frantic.)* How did I—

HE: *(Physically soothing her.)* You just got lost in your memoirs.

SHE: Yes. In my memoirs…safe.

HE: Yes. Safe.

SHE: Where I can read about my living.

HE: Yes. Where you can read about your living.

SHE: It's all in there—my life.

HE: Preserved.

SHE: In my memoirs.

HE: Yes.

SHE: *(After a pause.)* I've been thinking—

HE: About?

SHE: That walk in the woods.

HE: Yes?

SHE: Still?

HE: Yes.

SHE: Now?

HE: Yes. But first—

SHE: First?

HE: Dance with me.

SHE: There's no music.

HE: Does it matter?

SHE: I may have forgotten how.

HE: Just like you've forgotten how to swim?

SHE: I told you, I *never* could swim.

HE: Yes, and you don't believe in magic.

SHE: No, never could.

HE: But you could dance.

SHE: I could dance. God, how I could dance!

HE: How *we* could dance. Hold me.

The MUSIC: "Slow Boat to China." SHE slips into his arms. They dance.)
SHE: You've done it. You've got me dancing. Are you happy now?

HE: More than you know. *(A pause, dancing.)* Happy anniversary.

SHE: *(After a pause.)* Is it?

HE: Yes.

SHE: I thought. I don't. Well, then happy anniversary to you, too. How? How many years have we…?

HE: Forty.

SHE: That many?

HE: The world will end soon.

SHE: Ours will.

HE: Are you afraid?

SHE: Would it help?

HE: I don't see how.

SHE: Nor do I.

HE: It's been a life.

SHE: That it has.

HE: *Yes.*

SHE: You'll tell me when it's over?

HE: The music?

SHE: *Yes. The music.* We shouldn't want to dance too long.

HE: I will tell you when it's over.

SHE: Thank you. *(Touching the Post-It note on his chest.)* Husband.

HE: *(With a warm smile, touches her note.) Wife. (After a pause.)* Are we going to be all right…the two of us?

SHE: If I remember.

HE: You'll remember. I'll be here to help you remember.

SHE: Promise.

HE: Promise—right up to the end.

(MUSIC swells.)

The LIGHTING dims to BLACK OUT.

END—*Slow Boat to China*

BY THE AUTHOR

PLAYS (Full Length)
3 Guys in Drag Selling Their Stuff
A Baker's Dozen (short play collection)
Desert Devils
Flowers Out Of Season
In The Venus Arms
Poet's Wake
Streets of Old New York (Musical)
Tales of Darkest Suburbia
The Moon Away
The Proctologist's Daughter
Thor's Day
Wait A Minute!
West Texas Massacre

PLAYS (30 to 60 minutes)
20th Century Sketches
Empire (40-minutes)
Slow Boat to China (30-minutes)
Tough Cookies (60-minutes)

PLAYS (under 30-minutes)
21 Today (monologue)
Civil Unionized
Cornered
Dick and Jane Meet Barry Manilow
Harry the Chair
Leaving Tampa
Missing Baggage
Next
Pedaling to Paradise
Pink Gin for the Blues (monologue)
Road Kill
Samson and Delilah
Sisters of Little Mercy
Slow Boat to China
Vampyre Holiday
Whiskers

COLLECTIONS
A Baker's Dozen
19 One-Acts, Monologs & Short Plays
6 Full-Length Plays, Volume ONE
6 Full-Length Plays, Volume TWO

SCREENPLAY
Road Kill

NOVELS
Queen City
Gnarled Pines

ECW, Denver, Colorado
2020

edwardcrosbywells@yahoo.com

Printed in Great Britain
by Amazon